1977

Web

Torday
The shirt front

The Shirt Front

The Shirt Front

CHARITY BLACKSTOCK,

pseud. of Torday, Ursula

Coward, McCann & Geoghegan, Inc.
New York

First American Edition 1977

First published in Great Britain under the title
I Met Murder On The Way

Copyright © 1977 by Charity Blackstock

SBN: 698-10831-0

Library of Congress Cataloging in Publication Data

    The shirt front.

    I. Title.
PZ3.T6306Sh3   [PR6070.065]   823'.9'12   77-4823

Printed in the United States of America

For André and Judy,
with love

Recruiting for Defence.

Start today of two new reserves.

15,000 men needed. Extensive Air Attacks.

Raid on Madrid. Heavy Fighting in Estremadura.

Lord Swinton. Defence Policy.

Speaking at a Conservative Fete, referred
to the strengthening of the Air Force.
If this country went wrong, he almost thought
the world would give up hope . . . He had not
a thought of war in his mind.

Nuremburg. Nazi Parades. More attacks on Russia.
Herr Hitler's Speeches. Enthusiasm at Nuremburg.

Warsaw. Labour Camps in Poland. Army's Proposal.
Employment and Preparedness.

The first intimation of General Rydz-Smigley,
Inspector General of the Polish forces, for
increasing the country's preparedness for war.

Herr Streicher and the Jews.
"Extirpation the only Solution."

Herr Streicher advanced the view that
extirpation was the only solution of the Jewish
problem . . . Not suggested as a policy for
Germany alone, but as a solution for all the
nations to apply to a "world problem" . . . If
a final solution of the Jewish problem is to
be achieved one must go the bloody way . . . "in
order to secure the safety of the whole world
they must be extirpated".

During the same address Herr Streicher
expressed a desire for an alliance with Great
Britain but regretted that the hand which had
been stretched out towards that country had not
yet been grasped.

Die Fahne hoch! Die Reihen dicht geschlossen.
S.A. marschiert mit ruhig festem Schritt,
Kamraden die Rot-front und Reaktion erschossen,
Marschiern im Geist in unsern Reihen mit.

Horst Wessel Song

£1,450. Lady wishes to sell her country
house. 7 bedrooms,
4 sitting-rooms, servant's bathroom.
2 acres garden.

Parlour-maid, £60 per annum. 2 family.
3 staff. No valeting.

House parlour-maid. £52 - £55 per annum.

September, 1936

Chapter 1

WHEN I WAS very small — I think I was three years old — I made myself a story, which I at once declaimed to my father. It tickled his Attilian fancy, so he wrote it out and it was actually printed in some magazine or other. I am afraid it was on the cute side, but then all children tend to be cute, and it was at least quite genuine. Here is cute little Victoria Katona, spreading her embryo wings. I think they will remain embryo, too. I don't think I'll ever write anything, though my father writes not only in his native Attilian but in English, French and German too. Here is the masterpiece:

> I have a canary. One day the canary gave me a great surprise. It laid an egg. And what do you think came out of the egg? A little parrot! That is the surprise.

Certainly our parrot, called without originality Polly, did not come out of a canary egg. He is grey with scarlet tail feathers, he has a cruel beak and wicked eyes, and he comes from Central Africa. My father picked him up on one of his Congo explorations, and brought him back to England, together with the dog who accompanied him throughout his travels. The dog, who died two years ago, was called Bombosh, after an African chieftain. He was a darling creature, and I cried for weeks after his death. My father also brought with him an enormous number of African artifacts, some of which are in the British Museum, and some that fill his study. They are mostly rather rude, and a friend of mine who once peeped into my father's room and was confronted by an unusually well-equipped statuette, was so shocked that she never spoke to me again. I am so used to them myself that I do not even notice, but my mother insists on their being kept upstairs.

The parrot is rude too. He really is a horrid bird, and I detest him. He lives in the kitchen with Mary and Maggie, and mimicks everyone. Mary adores him, and gives him the best bits of her cooking. It is just as well that someone adores him, because I usually want to wring his scrawny neck. Once, as a small child, I came downstairs with a violent cold. I suppose I sniffled and snuffled, and now that revolting bird snuffles every time I come near him. "He has such a good memory," Mary says. She finds this very funny.

I suppose he has, and my father says parrots have no real brain, so it must be some kind of reflex action. Yet one has to see that he — he did once lay an egg, but I think of him as "he" — seems actuated by deliberate malice: he always remembers the wrong things and says them at the most embarrassing moments. And of course if one wants him to talk, he does not utter a sound except for a displeasing noise produced by cracking his beak together.

His favourite trick is to make the neighbouring children late for school. When the weather is fine, Mary brings the cage out into the area, and the children gather round to watch him as he waddles on his perch, rocking to and fro.

"Hallo, Polly," they say. "Pretty Polly. Talk to us, Poll."

But not one word will he utter until they give it up and walk away. Then he bursts into a volley of conversation. "Get on your perch, you naughty bird, or I'll chop your head off!" he squawks then, "Scratch your poll, scratch your poll."

They come running excitedly back. Immediately he falls silent again, cracking a derisory seed with his beak, knocking at the mirror that dangles on the bars of his cage.

This will be repeated three or four times. My classes do not start until half past nine, so I stop to watch the pantomime. The children never learn. They look imploringly at me, then try again to provoke Polly into speech. Then the church clock strikes a quarter past, and they rush off to school in a panic. They must always be so late, and I cannot help feeling that the teachers must grow tired of hearing that their pupils were held up by a parrot.

"I'll chop your head off," Mary says through the window, shaking her fist, but the parrot knows perfectly well that she does not mean it, and sometimes bursts into triumphant song. Goodness knows where he gets that from. Maggie hums little Scottish songs to herself, and I possess a meek soprano, but neither of these bears the least resemblance to this appalling mad screech that sounds like some manic Melba the worse for drink.

He is singing now as I come back from school. It really is an awful sound. I was so cross with him that I shouted through the area railings. "Beastly bird!" I called him. "Horrid, smelly, beastly bird! I hope you die."

Of course the creature instantly snuffled, then made a noise as if he were blowing his nose. There was no point in going on bawling, and after all I am seventeen, but this made me cross as it always does and, as I came in, I slammed the door.

I saw that my mother was trailing wearily down the stairs. She said, "I wish you wouldn't be so noisy, Victoria. It's surely not too much to ask you to shut the door quietly."

I could see that she was already exhausted. She was doing what in the family we call "jangling", tossing her head, plucking at her collar, pushing in her hairpins and thrusting out her plate with her tongue. She has always hated dinner parties, and I remembered now that there was an important one this evening. I suppose she organises them badly because they simply do not interest her. She has almost no polite conversation, and the Attilians, I sometimes think, have very little else. They are always bowing like actors in a musical comedy, and Count Asztalos will certainly kiss her hand. He kisses mine too, which is nice of him: he must really regard me as a little girl. I enjoy this very much, he is such a handsome man, but I am never quite sure what to do with my hand afterwards. I cannot leave it dangling in mid-air and, if I instantly remove it, it gives the impression that I want to wipe the kiss away. Sometimes I manage very well. Perhaps I should practise up in my room, in front of the mirror.

9

My mother, now down in the hall, opened the dining-room door.

I thought that Maggie had laid the table beautifully. When she first came to us from Scotland she knew nothing about anything. She used to dump our plates in front of us, dropped half the serving dishes and plainly thought us mad because we changed our knives and forks for different courses. She used to giggle too, especially when my father flirted with her, and she was always wiping her hands on her apron. But Mary has trained her, and now she is marvellously efficient, except that when she is serving guests she tends to look as if she were undergoing a mystical experience. This is a little unnerving to strangers who look up at her intense face and wonder if they are being offered the Holy Ghost.

The table looked very nice indeed, with candles and all. There was a mouth-watering smell coming up from the kitchen. Mary is a wonderful cook, though inclined to be temperamental. Once or twice when she is badly upset, our dinner is late, and my father rushes down to find her with her apron up to her eyes, weeping into the soup. But she will be all right tonight. She admits to a partiality for those foreign gentlemen and she is a terrific snob: the fact that the Attilian Minister is coming will really put her on her mettle.

However, from force of habit, I looked carefully down the table. "There's a red wine glass too little," I told my mother. "The one on your right. That'll be Count Asztalos. You certainly can't leave him without the right lot of glasses."

My mother said, "Oh dear," then, "Maggie's growing careless again."

She made no attempt to remedy the omission. I took another glass out of the sideboard, then walked round the table to examine the little cards by each plate.

I said, "We're very posh tonight."

"That's because the Minister's coming," said my mother without enthusiasm. It sounded as if the Lord were descending. Then she said in her most irritating voice, "You'll have to change, Victoria."

"Oh really, Mummy! You don't think I'll come down in my gym tunic, do you?"

"And I want you in bed by ten, dear." My mother

seldom listens to a word I say. "Just slide out. Don't break up the conversation, just go." She added, "No one will notice."

"Thank you very much!" I must have sounded as cross as I felt, but my mother paid no attention. I said, "I'm seventeen after all. I'm not a baby. I don't see why I have to go to bed by ten. Lorna goes to bed much later, and we're the same age."

Lorna is my best friend. My mother does not like her very much. She said vaguely, "Well, it's different for Lorna."

"Why is it different?"

"And there's school tomorrow. You know what you're like in the mornings. What are you going to do about your homework?"

"I've done it. Except for the bit I have to précis. I can read that through on the bus."

My mother looked disapprovingly at me but made no comment. I think sometimes I am as alien to her as my father is. I wonder again, I am always wondering, why they ever married. They both like music, and I suppose they both like me, but I do not find that a sufficient bond. She is terribly bored by politics and as for Africa, which is my father's obsession, she hardly seems to know where it is. I do not think she is in any prejudiced, she is, just uninterested.

Then she suddenly said to me, "I wish I was sitting next to Mr. Gyori."

This made me laugh. Mr. Gyori is such a dull little man, with a face like a bush-baby. He never talks much about anything, and sometimes it baffles me why my father, who prefers clever people, invites him. Perhaps, like my mother, he is the odd one out. At least he doesn't throw names at her of people she has never heard of, and he doesn't make subtle, sophisticated jokes that she never understands. I understand suddenly that my mother is desperately out of place in the whole gathering, which is why she sits there so silent and never laughs. I think she is frightened of laughing in the wrong place, especially as she is a little deaf. I am sometimes frightened too, but then I don't matter, I am just the little daughter, nobody notices me and I hardly ever say a word.

I said, "Put him on your left-hand side. Who have you got there? Mr. Zoltan Halasz. I've no idea who he is. Switch the cards over and put him next to me. I don't want to sit next to little Gyori, and I'm sure he doesn't want to sit next to me."

"Oh I can't do that — Don't be silly, Victoria. You know Daddy thinks a lot of Mr. Gyori."

But my mother is laughing too at the devilment of it, there is a glint of childish mischief in her eye, and this delights me so that I instantly change the cards round. After all, it makes no difference to me. Mr. Halasz will not notice me either, except when I pass him the salt.

"Oh darling, you are naughty! Put that card back at once."

"Oh leave it, Mummy. It doesn't matter. As long as you have Count Asztalos on your right, and Daddy is lumbered with the Countess and Mrs. Bradley. Why are the Bradleys coming? They are awfully dull and they don't speak a word of Attilian. And Miss Jessamy is bound to be shy. I think this party is the most peculiar mixture."

"Everyone speaks perfect English," said my mother. She made no attempt to rearrange the cards. "And I don't like your saying things like that. You know the Bradleys are our oldest friends."

She made no comment on Miss Jessamy, only at this point drifted away, presumably to change. I knew I should be doing this too. In an hour's time they would all be here. But for some reason I still stayed there, swinging my satchel and gazing at the table.

There will be the best dinner service tonight. The wine glasses and the service belonged to my great-grandmother, whose portrait hangs on the far wall. I always think her one of the ugliest women I have ever seen. She is small and dumpy, with a big nose and a fleshy, wide mouth. Even the artist cannot make her handsome. She was four foot ten, and they all say she was brilliantly clever. In her heyday she collected Sheraton furniture, Georgian silver and celebrities: everyone attended her parties from Disraeli to Jenny Lind. It was she who brought the Steinway grand, which Mr. Goldschmidt plays and where I practise my amateur scales. And it was at one of her salons that young Miklos Katona, newly back from the Belgian

Congo where he had discovered an unknown civilisation, met the little granddaughter and persuaded her, probably without much difficulty, to marry him. He was a very handsome young man, though on the small side, and at that time he wore enormous, buccaneering moustaches, which he has long since shaved off. Perhaps my mother was swept off her feet, or perhaps she was sick of living with her autocratic, domineering grandma.

And so she married an Attilian, knowing nothing of Attilia or indeed, as she once confessed to me, of life itself: I suppose they have managed as well as most people. Sometimes they have violent rows. I hear them when I am in bed. My father seldom raises his voice, but my mother easily becomes hysterical and screams. The noise always frightens me. I pull the bedclothes over my head and try not to listen.

I was still gazing at the table. I have seen all this many times before, there is no real novelty in it except that it is all rather grander than usual. But for some reason I could not take my eyes off that long array, with the neatly folded napkins, the silver and the gleaming glasses that Maggie polishes with such care.

And suddenly I felt strange — not ill, not faint, but simply as if what I was watching was no longer real, something remote in a far distant country. This has happened to me before, but never so strongly. I did not like it. It frightened me. It was almost as if I were looking upon a play. And, as I stared, one hand gripping the back of a chair, I saw the guests materialise at the table. Only they had no faces, they were simply white blanks above their spotless, starched shirt fronts. I could even smell the delicate eau-de-cologne they all seemed to use, see the carefully smoothed dark hair above the oval where their faces should have been.

Then it seemed to my blurred gaze that on one of the white shirt-fronts there was a stain, like red wine, spreading slowly outwards.

I was convulsed with terror. I called out, then pelted from the room in search of my father, the one person who could lay these terrifying ghosts. And, as I tore up the stairs, I nearly knocked Maggie flying, Maggie looking distraught and coming down with a can of hot water in her hand.

13

She exclaimed in the lilting Highland accent that she has never lost, "Now what's the matter with you, Miss Victoria? You look as if you've seen a ghost."

"I think I have!"

"Havers," said Maggie briskly, then, "Well, you go and change now, that's what madam says. She says you are to wear the green silk. Miss Victoria, are you listening to me?"

"Oh Maggie, stop nagging at me!" And I threw at her the childish sobriquet that used to make her chase me with a broom. "Naggie Maggie, that's what you are."

"You do what you're told," she said, but the smile was tilting up her mouth.

"All right. But I must have a word with my father first."

Maggie looks at me sternly, the smile vanished. Now that she knows how to wait at table, how to announce guests without giggling, and how to wear a nice, starched apron, she expects everyone else to behave with the same decorum. I sometimes think that if we could change place with the servants, we would have a terrible time: they would demand a behaviour that we would never dream of expecting of them. As far as I am concerned, I think she looks on me as one of her innumerable little sisters. Or perhaps she would like to pin an apron on me too, and have me saying, Yes mum, No mum, turn me into a Victorian kitchen-maid.

She says coldly, "There's not much time, Miss Victoria. The Minister will be arriving any moment now."

"Oh nonsense, Maggie. There's lashings of time."

Maggie says with great emphasis, "The Minister must not be kept waiting."

It is interesting how people adapt themselves. Maggie comes from some small Highland village, I have forgotten where, and was brought up under the auspices of the kirk. The only minister she ever knew was the one who made the Sabbath day a burden to her: certainly she never knew of the existence of the diplomatic service, much less Attilia. But now the names roll off her tongue, and she speaks them with the utmost reverence, though Count Asztalos has never so far been to dinner, she has never even heard of him until today. I wonder if she practises the heathen names in front of the mirror. She always manages them with magnificent aplomb.

We once had an African chieftain to dinner, with a rolling polysyllabic Nigerian name. Maggie spoke it as to the manner born, and did not turn a Highland hair, though he arrived in a wonderful striped toga and was six foot three inches tall. The only thing to signify that this was something of an occasion was her expression of marked austerity.

I did not answer her last remark. In my present mood I do not care if Count Asztalos has to sit down on the front doorstep. I have met him, of course, at Legation parties, where I am now considered old enough to be invited, and I remember him as very good-looking, but I am in no mood for Ministers, and the only Attilian who now concerns me is my own father, who holds no official nationality at all.

I can see that Maggie's face is tight with conventional disapproval. But she is a darling girl, and Mary tells me the milkman has his eye on her. I bet she deafens him with stories of the Attilian nobility.

My mother's room on the first landing is half ajar. I creep past before dashing upstairs to the study. She will be changing, putting on some limp, unsuitable dress, probably black, which does not suit her. She has no dress sense, for herself or for me. If she had her way she would dress me in Liberty's voiles and little frills, which would look as good on my father as on me. Oh poor lady, how she does hate all this. But her jewellery will be beautiful. It is all great grandmother's jewellery, and it belonged to her mother before her. It is magnificent. It is utterly unsuitable for middle-class types like ourselves; it looks absurd plastered on dull dresses. I can picture her wandering about aimlessly, wishing it were all over. She will be sipping at her small and secret glass of sherry. There is no reason for it to be small or secret, and my father would neither object or even notice, but I think she likes to look upon it as a desperate kind of vice: we all know about it but it is never mentioned.

My father, of course, should have been getting ready too, but from the look of him, as I opened the door of his study, he had simply forgotten about the whole evening. He was sitting at his typewriter. He turned his head

15

as I came in, and motioned me to the one dilapidated armchair by the fireplace.

How I love my father's study! The smell of it, books and typewriter and ink and dust. The look of it—It is the archetypal study, such as I have never seen before or since. There are books everywhere, in cases, on shelves, piled on tables, stacked on the floor. The great King Shamba, whose civilisation my father discovered, is in plaster-cast by the window, the original being under Mr. Goldschmidt's care in the British Museum. The various little statues that worry my mother so are everywhere.

"You can't leave them downstairs, Mikki. I mean, it would upset Maggie."

"Maggie," says my father, "does not have to look at them, she only has to dust them."

"Well, I think they're disgusting. I mean, really — It's not *nice*. I would just feel I could never ask anyone to tea. Besides, it's embarrassing for Victoria when she has her friends in. It's silly," says my mother triumphantly, her eyes moving to the statues' salient points then instantly away, "for people to take these things out of Africa. It's all right for the jungle, but it's all wrong for Kensington."

We live in Earl's Court, actually, but I daresay it is not all right for Earl's Court either.

"I suppose," says my father, "you want to put trousers on them."

But he takes them upstairs all the same, and in a way my mother is right: they look fine in the study but would be out of place in the drawing-room, just like the original owners. I am so used to them that I hardly see them, but sometimes when I look closely, I want to blush.

But I look at them now with great affection, for after all my father still lives in the equatorial forest he loved so passionately, and these are his sentinels, his guardians.

The books are three quarters anthropological, Frazer and Stanley — "He was a bastard," my father said once, astonishing me, for he seldom swore except in Attilian — and Rattray and Malinowski and Evans Pritchard and Leakey, many of them personal friends who visited us from time to time. My mother and I hardly saw them for they retreated to the study. There were a great many French books too, in those dilapidated paper covers that

16

all fall off: my father spoke French as fluently as he did English, and had a passion for Anatole France.

There were two rugs in front of the fireplace. One was an okapi skin, rather moth-eaten, and the other a lion with the head still on, the mouth ferociously wide over great false ivory teeth. There had once been whiskers, but these I pulled out as a child, in an abstracted moment.

I did not sit in the chair. I knelt down on the lion-skin, and picked up the nearest book to hand. It was about the Ashanti. My father went on typing. In a moment he would stop, but it was understood that his work came first: I could come in and out as I pleased, but only on condition that I never interrupted. And I was entirely happy with this: some of the best moments in my life have been spent in the study where Maggie despaired of the dust, where my mother deplored the rude statues, and where Africa still encircled us.

My father at last stopped typing. He took the page out of the machine and laid it on the pile beside him. He removed his spectacles and turned to look at me, lighting a cigarette as he did so then, as an afterthought, offering me one out of the tin.

It was a great point of dissension between him and my mother. I think really that my mother was right, but of course I always sided with my father, especially in something that was so much to my advantage. My father, who would not let me use lipstick and who was so Victorian in his moral views, accepted the fact that modern girls drank and smoked. Wine was a normal thing in our household and I, like French children, was used to drinking wine and water from my infancy upward, but cigarettes were less usual. However, my father, though ferocious on the subject of any sexual indulgence, seemed to accept that smoking was permitted: he had provided me with one tin of fifty Gold Flake every week since my fifteenth birthday, on condition that I never exceeded this amount.

"It is not good for her," my mother said. She herself smoked twenty a day, but always glared at me when I lit up.

"She'd probably do it anyway," answered my father, and so the tin of fifty appeared every Monday morning,

17

only exceeded by the odd cigarette that he offered me, himself.

He lit my cigarette. He said, "Well, Victoria? What is your news?"

"We have a dinner party, Daddy."

"What dinner party?" He was fiddling with his papers, his brow furrowed. I thought how good-looking he was. I always admired my father's looks: they were mine too, of course, but somehow feminised and watered-down.

However, this really was a bit much. I said in a firm, rather loud voice, "Daddy, Count Asztalos is coming. And a lot of other people. You ought to get changed. Mummy will get frantic if you don't go soon."

"Who else is coming?"

"Well, let me see. Mr. Gyori—"

"Oh him!"

"Don't you like him?"

"Oh yes. Yes. He's a strange kind of man. What do you think of him, Victoria?"

"I don't care for him particularly. I don't really think about him. He never seems to me to be quite real."

My father looked at me oddly. "Is that how you really feel about him?"

"Well—" I considered this, stroking the lion's head. The lion had killed my father's favourite boy, and my father waited for the murderer by the dismembered corpse, then shot it. He preferred to photograph animals rather than kill them, but this was a case of pure vengeance. "He just doesn't seem to me much of a person. He kind of reflects other people. I just don't know what he's like. He smiles a lot, and he usually agrees with whatever one says. He looks like a bush-baby with his large, round eyes. What does he do in the Legation?"

My father laughed, but he only said, "He's not in the Legation at all."

"Then what's his job?"

"Well, Victoria, that is hard to say. But don't underestimate Mr. Gyori. He's a good deal tougher than he looks. Those big eyes of his take in more than people think. I would say that he is quite a dangerous man."

"Mr. Gyori dangerous!"

"Oh yes. Yes indeed."

18

I wondered then as I was always wondering exactly what connection my father had with the Legation. It was a matter he never discussed. He was, of course, quite famous as an Attilian; he was certainly concerned with politics and often visited the Legation, but what he did there neither I nor my mother knew. However, this did not interest me particularly: like my father I was far more concerned with Africa, and I wished that there was no dinner party so that we could talk about the book and some of the odd ceremonies and customs that existed in the Congo.

My father said, "Who else is coming?"

"You ought to know, Daddy. You invited them."

"Well, I've forgotten. Enlighten your poor absent-minded father."

I looked at him expressively, and he grinned at me. He must have known that my mother was growing frantic. It was after all nearly six o'clock.

"Well?" he said.

"There's Miss Jessamy."

My father made no comment. Though I am sure he was absolutely faithful, he still had an eye for a pretty girl, and poor plain, dowdy Miss Jessamy, who did not even play the cello very well, meant nothing to him, though he was always polite and friendly to her. I think Attilians are rather nasty about women: they do not approve of any feminine independence and simply look on us as sex-objects.

"Then of course," I said, with some malice, "there are the Bradleys."

My father remained silent. I suspect he did not care much for the Bradleys either. We have known them for ages: Mr. Bradley is my mother's solicitor. There is nothing to dislike in either of them, but nothing much to like either. There are three children: the boy will eventually go into the firm, and Prue and Dorothy, both like their mother, are nice, rather dull girls. They live in Hampstead. I quite like Mrs. Bradley, but she has one bad habit, she will quote her husband's more boring remarks as if they are wonderful, profound sayings. Once — it was disgraceful of us — my father and I in a wicked, light-hearted mood, capped each other by remarking. "It's a long lane that has no turning, don't you agree?" and,

19

"One man's meat is another man's poison, that's what Jim always says, right?"

We of course got the giggles, and my mother after listening to us for a few minutes, simply said, "I've no idea what you're talking about," and walked away.

I am sure Mrs. Bradley is very excited about meeting the Attilian Minister. She will always do the right thing, and she has a line in social chatter that will bore Count Asztalos to death, but she will at least ensure that there are no bleak silences. Not that I would ever expect silence at an Attilian gathering: they are great conversationalists, and my father more than makes up for my mother's apprehensive boredom.

When I was younger I used to go to tea with the Bradley children. I quite liked Dorothy, the older one. We played games, which was a novelty for me as an only child, and there was a good tea. But I still could not see why my mother had invited the Bradleys this particular evening, except perhaps that Mrs. Bradley is a homely person who gives her courage.

"And who else?" demanded my father.

I considered in my memory the little cards on the dining-room table. "Well, there's Mr. Palotas. I know you don't like him."

"I can't imagine why you say that," said my father, adding irrelevantly, "He's the Legation attaché. I couldn't leave him out with Count and Countess Asztalos coming."

My father, like many clever people, believes he has an inscrutable countenance. In point of fact, when he dislikes someone, it radiates from him like a vast beam of inimical light. I have a horrid feeling that this is something I have inherited. He has always disliked Mr. Palotas, but nonetheless we have invited him several times. I dislike him myself, because he so plainly has no time for little girls. He is a handsome, dapper man, small and immaculately groomed and I think from something my father once let fall that he is a great one for the ladies. He has odd political views and once remarked that Hitler was a brilliant man. He belongs to some very right-wing society. But he hardly bothers to speak to me, and I only know that whenever politics are mentioned, my father shuts up like a clam, and on this subject he will not speak to me, though once or twice I have tried to find out.

"And there's Mr. Zoltan Halasz. Who's he? I've never heard of him before."

"You've met him," said my father, smiling.

"Daddy, I haven't—"

"You have. Wait till you see him. What do you want me to tell you about him? He works at the Legation. He's in the Press section. He's very well-known as a journalist in Dunavar."

"Is he good-looking?"

My father stared at me in bewilderment as if amazed that such a foolish remark should be uttered by his little daughter. I saw his brows begin to meet. I believe that at that moment he saw that I was no longer a little schoolgirl, but perhaps I flatter myself. I suppose fathers always believe that their children never grow up. He said dryly, "Yes, Victoria, I suppose he is. It is not a matter that interests me particularly, but from what I remember of him, he is even what one might call handsome. Are you proposing to flirt with him?"

"I'm sitting next to him at dinner." Then I said rather crossly, "I'm so tired of being a schoolgirl."

My father said with a sigh, "Well, you won't be one much longer. You'll be going to Oxford next year. What's the matter with you, baby? You'll be sitting next to a very handsome and charming man. Put on your best dress. You are not a bad-looking girl. Perhaps you could do something to your hair—"

All this was so extraordinarily out of character that I could only stare at him. I self-consciously put my hand up to my hair, which made him smile, and then I disgraced myself by giggling. The hair was after all such a give-away and, unless I went to a hairdresser, I could not see what was to be done with it. It was really quite pretty hair, being dark and thick and wavy, but I wore it bobbed with a slide, and I was quite certain that Countess Asztalos, whom I had never met, would be wearing hers in some ultra-fashionable style. But one thing was now obvious: we must both do something about changing. I jumped to my feet only, as I was half-way to the door, I suddenly remembered something I had meant to ask my father.

"What was the matter with Mr. Goldschmidt on Sunday?"

21

"What are you talking about?" My father was putting the cover on his typewriter, and I could not see his face. "He seemed so upset. I've never seen him in such a state. He's always such a calm and orderly sort of man." "He's a German," said my father, then seemed to recollect himself. "He is too calm. His piano playing is technically brilliant, but it is entirely without soul. That is why Miss Jessamy in some ways is the better musician, though as a performer she is sometimes appalling."

It was only when I was running downstairs to my room that I realised how neatly he had managed to avoid my question. I brooded on this for a while. Maggie, no doubt instructed by my mother, had laid the green silk dress out on the bed. It was supposed to be my best dress. I had never liked it. Green was not my colour, and the whole thing was far too little-girly, with puff sleeves and a high, tight waist. I visualised myself in something long and flowing and off the shoulders, with long, dark hair falling over my face. I even looked in my cupboard to see if there were something else I could wear, but everything was made in the same pattern, for my mother always went to the same shop to choose my clothes for me.

I made a face at the green dress, and continued to brood on Mr. Goldschmidt.

He and Miss Jessamy have been coming for as long as I can remember. I have no idea how it started. At least my father and Mr. Goldschmidt know each other through the Museum, but what brought Miss Jessamy into our circle, I simply cannot imagine. She is a brassy-haired, middle-aged dumpy woman, who dresses very untidily. I cannot imagine her being attractive or having a boy-friend. Her hair is always falling down, and usually there is a button missing on her suit or a split under the arm. It is not because she is poor. She works in the Civil Service, and my father once said she had a very good job indeed but, as he never referred to it again, I do not know what it is. Miss Jessamy never mentions it, nor does she gossip about her colleagues. If she were younger and prettier I could have made up a romance between her and Mr. Goldschmidt, but of course this would be ridiculous, and indeed, I have never met two people more incompatible.

Mr. Goldschmidt is much younger than she is, and somehow looks as if he never had a first name. He is really quite good-looking, tall and dark with huge eyes that are almost black, but he seldom smiles and it seems to me that he regards me as if I were a small child to be patted on the head and ignored. He never makes any attempt to talk to me. I cannot believe he has many friends. I wonder occasionally if his immaculately brushed hair is ever ruffled, or if at home he sometimes wanders around in unpressed trousers and an old sweater with holes at the elbow. He is always so correct. You somehow know that he never spills anything and always changes his underclothes on the right day. I get the impression that he does not like anyone very much, but he certainly does not like Miss Jessamy: Sometimes when she plays a wrong note or comes in a bar too soon, I see a flicker of quickly controlled exasperation cross his face. It is the only emotion I have ever seen him display.

The strange thing about Miss Jessamy is that she seems to derive a kind of malicious enjoyment from us all. This goes oddly with the rest of her, but I have watched her when my mother is jangling away and upsetting everything, and my father being temperamental about the tempo. A cat-like smile comes on her face, and every time I see this, I have to wonder if we are not under-estimating her. Whatever she is, she is no fool, but I really do not care for her, and sometimes when I watch her, knees apart, sawing away with her large, capable hands, I wish we could find ourselves another cellist.

Last Sunday it was obvious from the beginning that Mr. Goldschmidt was in a very strange mood. Calm would be the last word to describe him. I saw this the moment he arrived. He nearly tripped over an occasional table that he must have known was there as we never move our furniture around, then, as he sat down at the piano, he took out a handkerchief to wipe his face as if it were sweating. He did not even speak to my mother, to whom he is normally very polite and, when he put his glasses on, his hand was shaking.

It was the "Spring Sonata". We have done it before. Sometimes my father chooses to play without Miss Jessamy, and I think she quite enjoys her respite from two men who play better than she does.

It seemed to go well enough, and it is something we all like very much. But once or twice I could hear that the two were not together, and I saw my father, impatient as usual, shoot a lowering glance at Mr. Goldschmidt. Then we came to the movement that is quite difficult to play: it is syncopated, with the violin just behind the piano. Mr. Goldschmidt always manages this perfectly well, though my mother makes a dreadful mess of it, but on Sunday he seemed quite unable to cope. My father, as is his way, plodded on, but it was plainly hopeless, and suddenly Mr Goldschmidt dropped his hands on the keys in a crashing chord, and stopped.

He said, "I'm sorry, Mr. Katona."

"Well," said my father, concealing his annoyance very poorly, "shall we try it again, Mr. Goldschmidt?"

They always use each other's surnames. Sometimes they sound like cross-talk comedians.

"It would be no use, Mr. Katona."

"What do you mean? Really, Mr. Goldschmidt, I don't know what's the matter with you this afternoon. It's not so difficult. We have played this before. It is not like you to give in so easily. Now let us take it from—"

"I'm telling you, Mr. Katona, it's no good." It was the first time I remember hearing Mr. Goldschmidt speaking with an accent. He stumbled to his feet, kicking the piano stool back. He said, "I am upset. I've had bad news from home."

My father is a single-purposed man. He has the kindest of hearts, but he likes to concentrate on one thing at a time. At that moment the only thing that concerned him was the "Spring Sonata", and Mr. Goldschmidt's domestic problems were to him entirely irrelevant. But before he could say anything, Mr. Goldschmidt rushed on, speaking with a passion that was utterly remote from his normally composed tones.

"You see," he said, "I am a Jew."

I could not quite see what this had to do with anything, but I saw my father's face tighten, then he glanced quickly at me and away. He said in a carefully controlled voice, "Well, perhaps this is the moment for a little break. I think a cup of tea would be good for us all. Will you ring the bell, please, Victoria?"

As Maggie brought in the tray and cakestand, I saw

24

my father clap Mr. Goldschmidt on the shoulder. He said something to him that I did not hear. My mother seemed unaware that anything had happened, and simply poured out the tea, but Miss Jessamy's eyes were alight with curiosity. I don't think she misses much, she always seems to take an eager interest in other people's troubles. Nothing further was said on the matter, and my father and Mr. Goldschmidt fell into some long story about a colleague in the Museum. Men are just as gossipy as women, only more scurrilous. There was no more music, and Mr. Goldschmidt left earlier than usual. My father accompanied him into the hall, and I heard them talking for several minutes before the front door closed.

When he came back into the drawing-room, my father said to me, "Come on, baby. We'll do your favourite minuet."

So we played the Boccherini minuet, and followed this with the Haydn serenade: both are charming and simple and I have played them many times before. I enjoyed myself enough to forget about poor Mr. Goldschmidt, only my mother suddenly said — like all deaf people she hears isolated, unexpected things — "What does he mean by saying he's a Jew? I don't see what that has to do with playing the piano."

My father only said, "He has had very bad news," and presently went up to his study, leaving the three of us there to talk desultorily about nothing in particular. Then Miss Jessamy went home too, carrying her cello-case. I think sometimes she must wish she had taken up the flute. She once told me that people on the bus are always calling out to her, "Play us a tune, love," which is a little embarrassing.

I think of this now, wondering what really happened. It is very late, the guests will be here any moment, and I am still in my gym tunic, with my newly gained prefect's badge above my form-captain's ribbons. We have a different coloured ribbon for each form, and it looks rather pretty, but this is certainly no way in which to beguile a handsome Attilian. All Attilians seem so alarmingly sophisticated, and Mr. Halasz will probably pat me on the head and enquire about my dolls. But I feel disturbed and strange, as I did when I looked round the dining-table and, though I do at last change my clothes and pull that revolting green dress over my head, I cannot concentrate, only sit in front of the dressing-table, my hair all on end and my dress unfastened.

"Victoria! Are you ready?"

"Yes, Mummy. Just coming."

"Well, do hurry up, dear. It's seven o'clock, and the Bradleys are always early."

"All right, Mummy."

Yes, Mummy. All right, Mummy. They all regard me as a child. They never tell me anything that might upset or harm me: I am too young to know. Whatever has happened to Mr. Goldschmidt obviously falls into this category. It is true that I am very wrapped up in school and my own little world, but of course I am aware of the bad things around me. I do not read the newspaper as often as I should because there does not seem to be time. I know this is a wicked thing to say: there is always time, it is simply that I cannot be bothered. But I do know, I have to know, despite my father's silence. We all know. It is there in the background. I have read about the Night of the Long Knives and the Reichstag Fire; I remember that when Hindenberg died two years ago, my father for once did speak. He said, "This is the end." He stayed up in his study all day. He did not even come down for lunch. I did not understand what he meant, but then I was only fifteen.

We never talked about these things at school. There were two Jewish sisters in my class, twins. There is no one at school who could possibly be called anti-semitic, and I do not think it ever entered our heads that there was any difference between us, except that the two girls were always having extra holidays. But I see now that within the past year the sisters have changed. They used to be lively girls, rather cheeky, and very bright in exams, but somehow they have grown quieter, and once I found Judith in tears in the cloakroom. I tried to comfort her, asked her if she would like to tell me what was the matter, but she only shook her head and said I wouldn't understand.

I suppose one really does not bother about things until they affect one personally. I hear about the concentration camps which are such a nightmare that I hardly believe in them. I am more shocked to learn that Einstein and Freud have been thrown out, and that the Germans are destroying pictures by Cezanne, Gauguin and Van Gogh, but then that does concern me a little, that is something I can understand. But the school is always there, and it is somehow of vital importance that Miss Thomas sets a beastly homework, or Mademoiselle loses her temper for the hundredth time. There are exams and the school play, there is gossip and scandal, and we lose our netball match against our greatest enemy. Lorna and I go to see Laurence Olivier in *Hamlet*, in the sixpenny gods, and become silly and excited over a Clark Gable film. Around us is death and cruelty and evil, but our world is full, not of persecuted Jews and occupied Rhinelanders, but of little girls in gym tunics who giggle in corners, who announce they are "off-games" when they have their period, and who are beginning to look sideways at handsome boys who are looking sideways at them.

And there is Michael. Michael is my steady. He takes up most of my spare time.

Perhaps Mr. Goldschmidt's family has been taken away. He comes from Berlin, as he once told us. But that is too horrible, that cannot happen to people one knows. I cannot bear to think of it. He is such an ordinary, rather dull, sort of person, not the sort to whom tragedy happens.

I see crossly that I have not grown up at all. Mr. Halasz will be quite right to see me as an idiotic schoolgirl, and this beastly green dress is all I deserve. I shall sit there as I always do, straight-backed and silent. I shall sip my one glass of wine and make sure that everyone has the salt and pepper. Count Asztalos will kiss my hand and talk charmingly to my mother. Mr. Gyori will smile at me; he always smiles a great deal. My father will hold forth, my mother will be silent, jangling and bored, and Mrs. Bradley will no doubt enlighten the company on her new anti-burglar campaign, while quoting aphorisms from Jim. She is a very nervous woman. She always has a chain on the front door, and has recently had made a peep-hole, which seems to me complete nonsense. I know there have been quite a few burglaries in Hampstead, but now she has even hung a strip of red velvet over the letter-box so that no one can look in. When I go to tea there I always have a terrible urge to lift it up and shout through it.

You see, even now I don't want to think of everything that is happening. I am letting my mind wander to Mrs. Bradley, who doesn't matter at all, and to my silly self, who matters even less.

"Victoria!"

"Oh Mummy, just five minutes — I've got to do my hair."

But this is not good enough. I have gone too far. My mother always nags at me, though half the time I think she really forgets my existence. I suppose she does love me, but she can never concentrate, even on me: this has its advantages. However, now, what with the awfulness of the impending party, and the agitation of having to sit next to the Attilian Minister and make sophisticated conversation, she is furious, venting her nerves and apprehension on me.

She swept in, exclaiming frenziedly at the sight of me sitting there with my hair all over the place and my dress open at the back. She was, as I knew she would be, wearing a black dress a little too large for her — she is very thin — and a magnificent double pearl choker that looked completely out of place. She was jangling like mad. She began to tug at my dress, half choking me, then scowled despairingly at my hair.

"Well," I said, "I only have to comb it. It won't take a minute."

She cried out, "It is just too bad. I can't even depend on you. The Bradleys will be here any minute, Count Asztalos is bound to arrive early, and your father is still shaving — Shaving!"

"Count Asztalos will probably arrive late," I said. "Attilians usually do. Daddy told me once that in the old days it was frightfully bad manners to arrive on time, it had to be two hours later."

This was not very tactful of me, and my mother at once flew into a panic, tearing at me and herself. I then made things worse by adding, "Anyway, no one ever arrives at the specified time."

"Specified time!" wailed my mother, making this sound like some fearful swear-word. "Why do you always talk like that? It sounds so affected. People just think you are showing-off. You never used a one-syllabled word when five will do — Mary will give notice, I know she will."

"Oh Mummy, what are you talking about?" But by now I was as flustered as she was, and I tugged at my hair which, being newly washed, blew into a froth round the comb. The jibe at my vocabulary was of course routine. I don't myself think I talk any differently from anyone else, but I was ill for a year when I was little, as the result of rheumatic fever — I used to read about Beth in *Little Women* and die regularly — and as I had no brothers or sisters and nothing much to do, I read everything I could lay hands on, from the Bible to *The Sheikh*, rather preferring the latter. So I grew accustomed to using long words, and now I have edited the school magazine for the past two years and will eventually be reading English at Oxford. My father encourages this, having the European concept of education, but my mother has always preferred me to speak in monosyllables.

"She's so temperamental," cried my mother, "and the sauce for the fish is so delicate — She'll just give up. She'll sit there, doing nothing. You know how she is. Everything will be ruined, and Mikki will be furious, he'll say it's all my fault."

My father is really not like that at all, but I saw that matters must be taken in hand. What with Mary in tears and my mother in hysterics, the evening had somehow to be rescued. I said in a firm, calm voice, 'I don't suppose Count Asztalos will be late at all. It's only a quarter past seven, you know. I'll be ready in a jiffy, and then I'll go down to Mary to see how things are."

My mother whispered tensely, "Isn't that a taxi?"

"That'll be the Bradleys or Miss Jessamy." Then, as the idea came to me, I said, almost as tense myself, "Mummy!"

She was at the door. She turned her head wildly. Her hair was already coming down. She wears the front over a kind of cushion. It is fine hair. It looks very old-fashioned, and I am always trying to persuade her to change it.

"What?" she said.

"Mummy, let me wear that choker."

Her eyes were almost starting from her head. She said in a gasp, "You're out of your mind."

"Oh please — Please! Just for once."

"Of course not. Don't be ridiculous. It's much too old for you. It's not the kind of thing little girls wear."

"I'm not a little girl any more. I'm seventeen."

I could see that she was half relenting. She said, "And what am I supposed to wear?"

"You've got masses of things. The ruby pendant would look gorgeous. It would go much better with that dress."

We could hear Maggie running to the front door. Maggie always runs, but once the door is opened and she has to usher guests in, it is like the "Dead March" from *Saul*. My mother still hesitated, but a little impish grin was tugging at her mouth. She has, tucked away, a certain sly sense of humour that usually appears at the wrong moment. I could see that she thought it very funny that her little daughter should want to wear something so grand. Then suddenly she unfastened the choker and dumped it down on the dressing-table.

I put it on. My hands were shaking with excitement. Then I stared into the mirror. It was really extraordinary how this glamorous thing, meant to be worn with full evening regalia, transformed my mean little green dress. It somehow obliterated that little Peter Pan collar, distracted the eyes from those puff sleeves. Only the face above it remained a schoolgirl's face, and in a fit of temper I threw my slide to the floor and brushed my hair so that it drooped over one cheek. It might possibly seem odd but at least it was different. Before I left I looked longingly at the lipstick hidden in the top drawer, but I dared not put it on. My father might accept the hair-do, and he probably would not even notice the choker, but lipsticks to him were associated with fallen women, and he would make me wash it off.

I came downstairs. I still felt very strange. It was as if something were going to happen. Maggie calls this the sight, which is nonsense. It was probably because of the choker which lay heavy and cold on my throat, or perhaps the hair falling softly against my cheek. I took my time. I did not want this evening, I would not be happy until it was over. Usually I enjoy our dinner parties, with Mary making marvellous dishes, Maggie behaving as if this were the Ritz, and handsome Attilians teasing me, telling witty anecdotes and turning our house into Dunavar. It is something different, something exciting, and the next morning, when I go to school, I tell Lorna and my friends everything that has happened. This is of course showing-off, but they enjoy it, they say it sounds so grand, they wish they could have been there, nothing like that ever happens in their homes.

It isn't really so grand, but it is true that it is different, it is rather like a comic opera. My father took me once to see *The Marriage of Figaro*, and I sang *Voi che sapete* for weeks afterwards as if ours were an Attilian world, filled with intrigue and witty, pretty people.

Not that anything like that ever happens here. Maggie, for all she is so pretty, is no Susannah, any more than my mother is the Countess. We are extremely respectable and probably rather dull, besides, my father with his violent moral views would never tolerate such amorous goings-on.

But tonight I longed to run upstairs again to my own room, go over the homework I had rattled through, play my records, sit by the fire and read. I felt a little cold, I felt like my mother that everything would go wrong. Maggie would mispronounce the names, Mummy would not hear what was said to her and answer stupidly, while Mrs. Bradley would tell Count Asztalos how much she had enjoyed her trip to Prague, and what nice people the Czechs were.

All Attilians hate the Czechs, as well as the Rumanians, the Serbs, the Poles and the Austrians. It is one of the penalties of living in a many-frontiered country. My father cannot mention any of them without losing his temper, though I daresay if one of them were in trouble and came to him, he would at once offer to help. It is all the Treaty of Tilsit. I am not quite sure what the Treaty of Tilsit was about, but I have in my cupboard a little cardboard map of Attilia produced at the time, with a kind of scissor effect. You press the scissors and the map flies apart, with great portions going to the surrounding countries. Underneath is written in Attilian, "No, no, never", which is a bit silly because it has already happened.

No, no, never, is exactly what I feel. I can hear Mrs

31

Bradley talking, and I can smell my mother's eau-de-cologne. I would love to wear some exotic perfume myself, but it would hardly go with the little puff sleeves. I came into the drawing-room. I was thankful that the other guests had not yet arrived. The Bradleys beamed at me, and I went up to them. "Such a pretty dress," said Mrs. Bradley, then her gaze moved to the choker and a slightly startled look appeared in her eye.

Her remark infuriated me, but then she is very much the puff-sleeve type, and I am sure her daughters will wear this kind of thing until they leave home.

"Your little girl is growing up fast," she said, turning to my mother and speaking as if I were some kind of doll. "One day," she went on, "she will be leaving home, just like my two. But the birds must leave their nest, as Jim always says. Oh, I sometimes feel quite sad at the thought of it, but of course, Victoria, you won't understand that until you have daughters of your own."

This is Mrs. Bradley at her worst. Sometimes she is really very nice, but she is one of those sentimental people who believe that we remain children until we get married, that all mothers and daughters adore each other, and presumably all marriages are made in heaven and remain there. I have no idea if she and Mr. Bradley are happy, but I am quite sure they would never dare to admit the possibility of being otherwise.

There was not much to say to all this, but we kissed and I said rather weakly that I was so glad to see her again, and how were Dorothy and Prue. Only my mother, who always says exactly what is in her mind without for a second considering other people, cried out, "Victoria, you have forgotten to put on your slide."

Of course they all gazed at my hair, and I began to blush. Blushing is a terrible habit. I have always coloured easily, and have no idea how to cure myself. I found myself instinctively pushing my hair aside, but my father suddenly rose to his feet and came to put his arm round my shoulders.

"Oh, leave the girl alone," he said, touching my hair. "It's pretty. It's fashionable. Slides are for schoolchildren, aren't they, Victoria?" Then he said, half to my mother and half to Mrs. Bradley, "Our daughter's not just growing up. She has become a young lady, and very nice too."

"Well, I think it looks untidy," said my mother crossly, but apparently decided to accept this mark of emancipation, for she made no further comment. Her own hair was half down by now, and I could see from the harassed expression on her face that she was worried by the non-appearance of our other guests. She said in a feverish voice, "I think you had better go down to the kitchen, Victoria. I am sure Mary is in one of her states. You usually know how to calm her down. Tell her they'll all be here in a few moments."

"Servants are quite are a problem," said Mrs. Bradley kindly, adding, "But what would life be without its problems? We have to take the rough with the smooth."

As I thankfully went towards the door, she and my mother fell into this topic, while my father and Mr. Bradley stood by the French window that led into the garden, and discussed something more masculine and congenial.

I sometimes think the main function of servants is to fill in conversational gaps. I could see as I closed the door that my mother was looking happy and animated. She is terribly bored by the sophisticated talk of Attilians, but she can discuss Mary and Maggie for hours.

The bell went as I came towards the back stairs. It was Miss Jessamy. It is strange how women nearly always come on time; it is the men who are late. She did not see me because I slid through the door. She looked pleased and a little agitated. I heard Maggie greeting her and announcing her name.

I stepped down into the basement.

Chapter 2

I COULD SMELL lovely cooking smells as I came down the back stairs. It made me feel hungry, and I prayed that Count Asztalos would not be too late. When I saw Mary, I prayed even more fervently. She wore her grand-crisis air. She is a middle-aged woman with a craggy face, and the bones all stood out like rocks. Normally she has a rather wicked sense of humour, but at moments like these she looks as if the end of the world were due in one minute flat. Maggie looked distraught too, almost as if she had been crying. The range was full of pans, all steaming away. I lifted one of the lids, and Mary instantly slapped at my hand, crying out, "Oh leave it alone, do, Miss Victoria. It really is too bad, them being late like this. The dinner will be ruined. I really don't think I can stay here any longer. I'm going to give in my notice."

I was not particularly impressed by this. Mary is always on the point of giving in her notice. Besides, we have something like this every time there is a dinner party, and up till now the dinner has not been ruined. After all, few people are punctual to the minute, and it is a bit ridiculous to expect them to march in as if on an army parade. But I had to admit that this was more of an emergency than usual, so I struggled to be diplomatic.

I am careful not to tell Mary that Attilians are notoriously unpunctual. I say soothingly that everything smells gorgeous, and that the Minister will never in his life have tasted such magnificent English cooking.

This goes down very well, and Mary, being such a snob, is temporarily mollified. But then she remembers something else, and her voice comes out in a stentorian whisper. "And him there!" she says. "What's he doing, that's what I want to know. Gentlemen don't stand about in the area. It's not right, and I don't like strangers looking into my kitchen."

I said, "What are you talking about, Mary?" and Maggie, a little hysterical as she tends to be on these occasions, gave a weak giggle and pointed at the window.

Well, I had to admit that it was a trifle strange. Mr. Gyori was standing there, outside, talking to our parrot. He looked as if he had been there for some time. It was the oddest sight, this dapper little man in full evening dress, scratching Polly's neck and, from what I could see, establishing a great friendship. Most people would have ended by having their fingers nipped, but Polly was positively flirting with him, preening himself, wriggling from side to side and making roupy, affectionate noises. It was really a little ridiculous, and I choked back a laugh. But Mary was looking too furious and catastrophic for me to dare to be funny, so I decided that the best thing was to go out into the area and persuade Mr. Gyori to come upstairs.

I stepped outside. It was a warm night for September, but I still felt Mr. Gyori would be better off indoors. Besides we keep our dustbins in the area, and one of his impeccably creased trouser legs was brushing against them. He was talking to Polly in Attilian, and the parrot was listening intently, his head on one side, his beady eyes flickering. I could see that the school children would soon be more baffled than usual, because he picks things up almost at once if he chooses to do so. It would at least make my father laugh.

"Hallo, Mr. Gyori," I said. "I see you're making a real hit with our parrot."

He turned his head towards me. He was quite unperturbed, as if it were the most natural thing in the world to be standing there, instead of coming upstairs to greet his host and hostess. He smiled. I thought as I always did that he was a peculiar-looking man, chiefly because he was so unmemorable. The only really noticeable thing about him was his eyes. I have said before that he was like a bush-baby, and this is true: the eyes are round and bulbous and very bright. I should imagine he is short-sighted like my mother: myopic eyes always have a misty look. But he does not wear glasses, and he is small and tubby, with a kind of young-old face: I have no idea how old he could be.

He continued to smile at me. "Such an intelligent bird," he said, giving Polly's neck a gentle stroke. "I had to come and make friends with him."

The parrot, on seeing me, inevitably snuffled, and I answered quite angrily that I did not think he was intelligent at all.

"My father says," I told Mr. Gyori, "that he imitates quite automatically. There is no mental process behind it. His brain is as small as a pea."

This is the kind of talk that drives my mother mad and, if she had heard me, she would at once have accused me of showing off. But Mr. Gyori seemed to regard it as the most natural thing in the world.

He said in his beautiful English — Attilians are incredibly gifted in languages, perhaps because their own is so impossible — "I imagine there is more brain than you might imagine. This seems to me a most gifted bird. But then, Miss Katona, I have a great affection for parrots."

I was about to remind him that my parents were expecting him upstairs, and I could see Mary making faces at me through the window, but this deflected me, and I said crossly, "I have no affection for parrots at all. I think they are revolting birds."

Polly at this point emitted a particularly disgusting snuffle, and I wanted to wring his neck. But Mr. Gyori, who could not fortunately understand why the bird was making such noises, said, "Do you really find him revolting? You astonish me. He has such fine colouring. Those bright scarlet tail-feathers against the grey — I myself find it quite beautiful." Then he smiled again. "Do you know, Miss Katona, I think your little Polly must be a member of the Attilian Life Society, though that is hardly a compliment. This is what I have been telling him, and I fear it has pleased him greatly. I think your parrot's politics must definitely be right-wing." He added, making a little joke, "I don't know what he does with his left wing."

I smiled politely, and he added, "I believe your father does not mention such matters to you."

"No, he doesn't. What is the Attilian Life Society?"

I could see out of the corner of my eye that Mary was gesticulating at me as if she were having some kind of fit, but I was beginning to enjoy this conversation and had to wait for Mr. Gyori's answer.

He said pleasantly, "It is, as I have said, extremely right-wing. It is also very anti-semitic. But that of course is the fashion nowadays. The members wear a uniform of grey tunic and trousers, braided with scarlet, which is why I feel your little Polly must be a member. They also wear boots in the Nazi style. They do not carry the swastika, except in purpose, but I remember that a certain amount of amusement has been caused in Dunavar by the little gold statue that is their symbol."

"And what is that?"

Passers-by were peering down into the area, and Mary was plainly having hysterics, but I was far too curious to bother. I was beginning to wish that I had not shifted round the cards. Mr. Gyori was more interesting than I had suspected: he would be quite wasted on my mother who certainly had no time for his particular type of conversation.

"It represents," said Mr. Gyori, removing his caressing finger from Polly's neck, and gazing ahead with the air of a university lecturer delivering his oration, "the golden wounded doe that once, a long time ago, miraculously led my Attilian ancestors to safety."

"Well, what's wrong with that, Mr. Gyori?"

"Nothing, my dear Miss Katona, except for a small, negligible error on the part of the sculptor. The doe, when looked at from a certain angle, has a markedly Jewish profile."

"But surely, that doesn't matter—"

"Oh, not to you or me. But it matters a great deal to the Society's members. It is almost a disaster. It makes them, with their anti-semitic propaganda, look ridiculous, and Attilians, as you must surely know, have an ironic sense of humour and love making fun of the pompous and pretentious. The Society's slogan is after all, 'With God for the Fatherland,' and their purpose — among others, naturally — is to save the Attilian race from the noxious influence of the people of Ahasuerus. You will understand of course that I am quoting. These are by no means my own personal views. But it is a trifle awkward to rail against the Jews with one hand, while in the other bearing as a banner a markedly semitic doe. It causes a great deal of ribaldry. The Society is planning to choose a new emblem. Perhaps a pig. With the snout turned up."

I suppose this was amusing. Mr. Gyori plainly found it so. Only I somehow thought of Mr. Goldschmidt, and I did not want to laugh any more. It seemed to me that the evening was growing chilly. I said, a little nervously, "Mr. Gyori, you must forgive me, but my parents will be wondering what on earth has happened to you. Please come upstairs now. We'll give you a nice glass of sherry. Perhaps," I went on, very much aware of the tension in the kitchen, "you'd better go to the front door, and I'll run ahead to let you in."

"I think," said Mr. Gyori, "that would be quite unnecessary. I will walk through your beautiful kitchen, and then you will conduct me to the drawing-room."

Our kitchen is not particularly beautiful, and I knew Mary would be frenzied, but really, I could not stand there arguing, so I led the way through the back door, after Mr. Gyori had said goodbye to Polly in Attilian. At least I suppose that was what he was doing. The wretched bird seemed to enjoy it: he clacked his beak at him and did his usual old-woman shuffle on the perch.

I hope Mr. Gyori enjoyed our beautiful kitchen. Mary and Maggie watched our progress with what I can only call the eye of the Attilian Life Society confronted with a Jewish moneylender. They are both too well-trained to utter a word except to wish Mr. Gyori a bitter good evening, but I could feel the tension like a taut wire; I was amazed by Mr. Gyori's insensitivity when he smiled at the pair of them and remarked that the dinner smelt delicious.

I rushed him up the back stairs as fast as I decently could. He seemed to have a great affection for all animals and wanted to talk to our cat. But I brutally pushed the cat away. I was terrified that Mary, who is the less controlled of the two, should burst into frantic denunciation. However, fortunately, we heard nothing except the slamming of the area door. I imagine the parrot was being brought inside in case the Minister should follow Mr. Gyori's example and be possessed of a sudden passion to talk to him.

My father greeted us with an air of mild surprise. No one from the Legation had yet arrived, and it was now nearly eight o'clock. For once I entirely sympathised with my mother. I had to feel that the evening was ruined before it started, and that tomorrow Mary would really give notice. Miss Jessamy seemed calm and amused as usual, but the Bradleys were plainly bewildered and growing extremely hungry. I could hear Mrs. Bradley's stomach rumbling, and hastily offered her another glass of sherry. I was sure she would regard this as a social humiliation. I wished passionately that I was allowed to drink sherry myself, but for some inconsistent reason my father, who had always let me drink wine, never permitted this.

My father remarked after some spasmodic conversation — Mr. Gyori, so loquacious with me and the parrot, chose to sit there, silently observing — "Just to fill in the time, Victoria, before Count Asztalos comes—"

"If he is coming at all," said my mother savagely, upset enough to express the feelings of the whole company. She looked quite wild. She was obviously brooding on the domestic situation.

"Of course he's coming, my dear. We Attilians are always late. I've told you so many times before."

"I should have thought," said my mother, forgetting her own frequently voiced rule that one never argues in company, "that he has lived long enough in this country to learn its ways."

The Bradleys looked more embarrassed than ever. I don't suppose this kind of thing ever happens in Hampstead. Poor Mrs. Bradley's tummy gave a kind of trilling moan. She went very pink so I said quickly, "How am I to fill in the time, Daddy?"

My father glanced at my mother, then turned back to me. "Sing for us, Victoria." He added to Mr. Gyori, "My daughter has a charming little voice. Soon no doubt she will learn the proper airs and graces, and then her singing will be no better than anyone else's, but now I find her a delight to listen to. A little Mozart, I think. You have no need to be shy. We are all too hungry to be critical."

I detest singing in public, and it was ridiculous of my father to tell me not to be shy. I was scarlet with em-

39

barrassment before I even opened the piano, and I was convinced that Mr. Gyori was enjoying my humiliation. I think now this was perhaps unfair, but certainly he was a man who derived pleasure from the vagaries of human nature, and the whole situation must be delighting him.

Miss Jessamy came over to turn the pages. There was nothing to turn but this gave me confidence. I tried to comfort myself by thinking that this was hardly a critical audience and the noise would cover up poor Mrs. Bradley's hungry rumbles. I sang the Mozart *Wiegenlied* because my father had handed me the music. I was obviously not a patch on Elisabeth Schumann on my record upstairs, but it is a simple little song that does not go up too high, and I made a fair if slightly quavering job of it. When the front door bell rang just before the end I made no attempt to finish. I stopped immediately in the middle of a bar, whisked the music away and shut the piano.

We all turned with gasping expressions of relief.

I suspect that by now the kitchen was in a state of total war, so I must say for Maggie that she was really splendid, what with the appalling Attilian names and the general emergency. No doubt the delicate sauce was dried-up and ruined, the casserole burnt and the vegetables over-cooked, but the spirit of the Highland reivers was not quenched and her voice rang out like that of a general at the last stand of the Light Brigade. Everyone, it seemed, had arrived at once, presumably in the Legation limousine, and the names pealed impeccably off her tongue.

"Count and Countess Asztalos! Mr. Zoltan Halasz! Mr. Palotas!"

She had forgotten the "Excellency" but apart from that it all sounded like one of Shakespeare's historical plays: all we needed was the trumpets.

I was almost sick with relief. The dinner might be ruined, but at least the guests had arrived. I went to the front door to welcome them, this being our family custom — sometimes I suspect I should have dropped a meek curtsey — and saw as they all trooped in that the door was still open, with a liveried chauffeur standing there. I beckoned everyone in, had my hand kissed by two of the gentlemen — Mr. Palotas obviously regarded me as too young for such an honour — and went a little nervously

40

up to the chauffeur, wondering if I should ask him into the kitchen for a coffee. We do not even have a car, and chauffeurs are quite outside my orbit. But fortunately he was only standing there to see if all was well, and he immediately turned and went down the steps to the car which was enormous and carried the Attilian flag.

I am sure the neighbours must have been madly inquisitive, but I could only think that Mary was probably kicking the pans around, and hoped my father would fill everyone up with wine so that the charred meal would pass unnoticed. As I came back down the hall I saw to my surprise that Miss Jessamy had followed me. Of course she is a very nosy lady, as I discovered long ago, but I thought this was a bit presumptuous of her: after all, she was only a guest.

I had been in such a state of confusion up till now that I had not really looked at her. She is not the kind of person one does look at. She was after all only invited to make up the proper number of females. We do not really know many women. Most of my father's friends, both Attilian and anthropological, are men, and my mother has never been one for gossipy little teas with the old schoolfriend; indeed, she often declares that she does not like women. The only friend she still has from her youth is a plain dull girl who works in an office and whom she bosses outrageously; she occasionally comes to tea, methodically devouring everything within sight and agreeing automatically with what my mother says.

I saw now to my surprise that Miss Jessamy looked quite nice. She had actually had her hair done so that, instead of falling in wisps about her face, it was combed neatly back in a wave. She was wearing a tunic dress with bead embroidery that was quite stylish, and I think she had make-up on her face. I could see for the first time that she might have been almost good-looking as a girl.

She was smiling and peeping out at the open door, just as I was about to close it.

"*Petits pains,*" she said in a roguish fashion, "*Petits pains!*"

I thought for a moment she had gone mad, perhaps with hunger. I said, "I beg your pardon, Miss Jessamy?"

"*Petits pains*, Victoria. Surely you learn French at school?"

There was really no point in going on about *petits pains*, and my mother expects me to hand the sherry round, so I bestowed an irritated smile on her, and came back into the drawing-room. It was only as I closed the door that I suddenly remembered the enormous car. Miss Jessamy was being witty. It had been a Rolls. This on top of everything was almost too much, but my father has always instilled in me a sense of occasion, and this was no moment to behave like a schoolgirl. The dinner might be ruined, but this was all wonderfully dramatic, especially as my father, noting perhaps my flushed, over-wrought face, whispered in my ear, "Try a little sherry, baby. You look as if you need it."

I think there is a lot to be said for sherry. I am not sure if I care for the taste, for my father likes it very dry, but there was no denying the effect as the first swallow descended soothingly inside me. I at once felt much better and for the first time looked round the company, taking them all in, shirt-fronts and all.

Men look good in evening dress. I hope it never becomes unfashionable. And really our guests were an extraordinarily personable lot, with Countess Asztalos, whom I had never met before, looking absolutely gorgeous, making all the other females look like something from an end-of-sales bargain counter. She was small and exquisite, dressed in something unmistakably Parisian, and possessing a soft, sweet-accented voice. She smelt wonderful too, and it was certainly not Boots' eau-de-cologne. Her husband I had of course already met, at a Legation party, and Mr. Palotas was as dapper as usual, as if he had just come off a hanger, and eyeing us with the cynical, disdainful expression of one who was not entirely happy at mixing with the common herd.

I was so startled by the sight of Mr. Zoltan Halasz that I nearly dropped my sherry glass. My father had told me that I had met him before, and I suddenly remembered the occasion, which was not much to my credit, though in my excuse it must be said that I was only fifteen at the time. Apart from that, which was bad enough, he was the most handsome man I had ever seen in my life and this, coupled with the embarrassing memory, made me blush scarlet as he turned to smile at me. I thought, Oh *no*, and I am sitting next to him at dinner, but at this point my mother, who certainly has no sense of occasion at all, cut across the agreeable murmur of conversation. She spoke in what she presumably thought was a stage whisper, but it reverberated across the drawing-room.

"Victoria," she said, "do go and see if everything's all right downstairs."

The conversation naturally snapped in two. My father's brows began to meet, and Miss Jessamy, whom I was beginning to dislike intensely, giggled in a curiously girlish way, quite at variance with her appearance.

But Countess Asztalos, accustomed perhaps to diplomatic incidents, broke in at once. "Oh," she said, "we are so late. I do not know how to apologise. Your cook will be so angry with us, and she will be perfectly right. I warned you, Sandor. In Attilia we have the wicked custom of arriving always an hour late. It is, I think, quite ridiculous, for if one says eight, why should one arrive at nine? Do you know what I think? I think you should go down at once to the kitchens and make your apology to the poor cook."

I saw my mother's mouth drop open. I suppose it was the combination of kitchen in the plural, which presented a magnificent picture of white-capped chefs, scullions dashing madly to and fro, and magnificent copper pans, with perhaps a dog turning the spit, and the extraordinary vision of the Attilian Minister coming down the back stairs and kneeling before Mary, but whatever it was, she looked so horrified that everybody broke into what one might term unofficial laughter. For the first time I saw that the evening was going to be a success. Even Mr. Palotas smiled, and as for Mr. Gyori, he was plainly having a field day.

Count Asztalos was obviously about to obey. He rose to his feet, smiling as if the prospect entertained him, but Mr. Halasz stepped before him and opened the door.

"No," he said, "I will go down. If Miss Victoria will kindly show me the way." He added, "I am very good with cooks. It is indeed my speciality. I will go even further. If the meal is ruined, which I doubt, I will at once prepare another one, for not only am I good with cooks but I am also good with cooking. Do you not

43

remember," he said to the Countess, "the excellent paprika chicken I prepared for you last spring? It was — how shall I put it? — a poetic dream. Now Miss Victoria, lead the way, while singing the Attilian National Anthem. It is a pity we do not have a small flag handy, but we will at least ensure that the Attilian honour is restored."

I was beginning to think that Mr. Zoltan Halasz was a show-off, and I wished I could forget our ignominious first meeting, but we had never before had a dinner-party that was such fun, and what with this and the sherry, I felt happy and elated, though still possessed of the feeling that this was a play and not quite real.

We came out into the hall. Heaven knows what was happening downstairs, but in the drawing-room everyone was talking again and laughing, except for my mother who looked completely baffled. She is a deeply conventional lady. I am sure that her idea of a successful dinner-party is a dull one where nothing out of the ordinary happens, and I could see that Mrs. Bradley shared her views. Whatever this occasion was, it could not be described as dull, but she probably thought it was a complete failure, not noticing for a moment how much we were all enjoying ourselves.

I suspect that my ugly, clever great-grandmother would have enjoyed it too.

I came towards the backstairs and opened the door. There was a deathly silence from below. I somehow saw Mary, crouched like the last survivor of Troy, staring wide-eyed at the blackened pans. What with this and the unease surging within me, I felt almost hysterical.

I said, "I think they must both be packing their things. Do you really think it's safe for you to go down?"

He only replied, "How are you feeling, Miss Victoria?"

"I am very well, thank you."

We were speaking in whispers. It was like being at a funeral. Then suddenly we both began to choke with silent laughter; we stood there, shaking and gasping, yet not making a sound.

Then he recovered himself. He said, "You have grown into a most lovely young lady."

It was hardly an original remark, it was straight out of a bad film, but its effect on me was as if the ceiling had descended on my head. I stared up at him. He was a great deal taller than I am. The lighting was dim: my mother is economical on hall lamps. I did not answer him.

He said, gently touching my shoulder, "I think you must remember our first meeting. I would like to drink champagne with you again."

I only said, almost in a whisper, "I think, Mr. Halasz, you ought to go downstairs."

"Perhaps I should. But my name is Zoltan." And with this he vanished down the kitchen stairs. I nearly followed him, then decided that this was undignified, so I came back into the drawing-room.

Miss Jessamy cried out, "Oh, what has happened? You must tell us, you must!"

"I just don't know, Miss Jessamy. I really don't. Mr. Halasz is in the kitchen. I think Mary must be having a fit."

"I expect," said Countess Asztalos, "that she is greatly enjoying herself. After all, Zoltan is so unnecessarily good-looking. I am sure he will first try to seduce her, then he will make a fresh sauce for her, toss the vegetables in butter and suggest a new flavour for the meat. I am much looking forward to the dinner, and Mrs. Katona—" Here she turned to my poor mother who looked as if Armageddon had come. "—don't worry. It will be superb. I know. I have gypsy blood in me. It will be the most wonderful dinner in the world."

It was too, though I was in no state to appreciate it. Some twenty minutes later Mr. Halasz returned, and almost immediately after Maggie sounded the gong, and we all trooped into the dining-room.

She was beaming. All traces of tears were gone. Perhaps Zoltan had kissed her. I would not be surprised. She is a pretty girl, and Attilians are great on the *droit de seigneur*. This she never mentioned, but she did tell me some time later that the Attilian gentleman had Mary eating out of his hand, that all the difficulties had at once vanished, the sauce was re-made, and he told her that he had never smelt a casserole that was so delicious.

"A real gentleman. He even talked to Polly," she said.

But now, of course, Maggie did not utter a word. She played her role of the perfect parlour-maid, with impeccably clean apron and cap, standing there, waiting to serve the hors d'oeuvres. We all sat down. There was one lady who had not turned up. Perhaps my mother had forgotten to invite her, or perhaps she was ill. I have no idea who she could have been. As I have already said, we did not go in much for females, except for some of my father's students who were all young and earnest, and would be mortally embarrassed by such a social occasion. This is why Mrs. Bradley and Miss Jessamy turn up regularly as feminine stop-gaps. Sometimes I think this is a pity.

Zoltan therefore had Mr. Gyori on his other side, with myself sandwiched between him and Mr. Bradley.

Everything went marvellously. Nothing seemed to be burnt, and the sauce with the fish was delicious and unlike anything I had ever tasted. Only I found I could hardly eat, and most of what was served me went back into the kitchen, where no doubt our cat had a wonderful time. I do not remember now what I said, or what was said to me. I know that Mr. Bradley talked to me: I think he told me how Prue was doing at school, and that Dorothy was determined to take up teaching. Zoltan was holding forth at great length, swapping irreverent anecdotes with Count Asztalos and my father: they were all funny and quite outrageous, as is the way of Attilian stories. I could see Mrs. Bradley blinking, and once she went very red and had to take a great gulp of her wine. I never think she fits very well into this kind of party. But the talk was witty and non-stop, there was a great deal of laughter and not one of those pauses that my mother always dreads and which she is so bad at covering-up. Maggie dropped nothing, served quickly with her vestal-virgin expression, and everyone except myself had second helpings of what was truly a magnificent casserole.

Once or twice Zoltan turned to speak directly to me, and this I managed to avoid by talking to Mr. Bradley, who must have been astonished by my gabbling. Only once I could not dodge him, for Maggie was on my left, and I was compelled to turn my head.

We looked fully at each other. He did not say a word. I do not suppose anyone noticed, though Countess Asztalos had remarkably sharp eyes, but if everyone had fallen silent and pointed a finger at us, I would not have cared. For that moment in time we were entirely alone.

In other words, for the first time in my life, I had fallen head over heels in love. Utterly unprepared, not even realising quite what had happened, I was incapable of the least subterfuge, and Zoltan, who was certainly capable of every kind, especially where women were concerned, could not have missed what was certainly a look of imbecile adoration.

Afterwards I could have killed myself. And after that so much happened that I almost forgot about it. But that was still to come. I only knew that I was engulfed in every sort of emotion: joy, disbelief, an incredulous happiness, a passion of feeling for the whole world.

I think I considered myself rather experienced for my age. If you asked me what experience meant, I would not have known how to answer, but answer I certainly would have done. I would have said that I liked boys, that I had a steady boy-friend, and that Michael and I kissed after parties or dances, held hands in the cinema and went out together at weekends and in the holidays. Sometimes he came to tea, once on my seventeenth birthday my parents took us both out to dinner with a theatre afterwards, and most days he telephoned me. I had a photo of him on my dressing-table. It was the year when he was captain of the school cricket team, and he looked a little absurd in his striped blazer and cap. We had known each other for over a year. I kept the few letters he wrote me, chiefly because I felt it was the thing to do. He did not express himself well and, though he called me darling and signed with love, the letters were hardly emotional keepsakes. I do not think I ever reread them, but there they were, in a neat little bundle: they gave me something to talk about when my schoolfriends came to tea. Mind you, I liked Michael very much, and would have been wild with jealousy if there had been another girl, but it was all proprietary rather than amorous. Never, never in my life had he made me experience half of what I was feeling now and, when we said goodbye with perhaps a furtive kiss if my mother were not there, I frankly forgot about him till the next time.

I read about love, of course, including a great deal of poetry. Donne was my passion, and the Shakespearian sonnets. I was fully aware that love was a great deal more than holding hands and kissing gently on the lips. I also

47

read, with a discreetly curled lip, the books that my mother presented to me, called *Letters from a Widowed Doctor to his Daughter.* It is perfectly true that by no stretch of imagination could I picture my mother telling me the facts of life, but I do feel she could have chosen her proxy better. The first volume, handed to me when I was thirteen, was so veiled that for a long time I could not understand what the silly old man was getting at. It was full of allusions to blossoming womanhood, the threshold of maturity, and delicate suggestions that "you will find that boys regard you with more interest", none of which tied up perceptibly with stomach-ache, messy discomfort and sanitary towels. When I at last discovered what lay beneath the verbiage, I remember that I exclaimed, "Oh *that!*" and hurled the book disgustedly back into the bookcase. The next one, presumably covering my seventeen years, was even more discreet, filled with portentous warnings, but the discretion was so vast that, had not my schoolfriends long ago instructed me without any reserve at all, I would not have had the faintest idea what he was talking about. The only effect on me was to feel a fascinated anticipation about the next book, which must surely concern marriage. The doctor, I thought, will have a field-day on that, and I wondered what his practice could possibly be like for, if a female patient became explicit, he would surely faint with the shock

However, I never discussed any of this with my mother, nor did I ever tell her that once Michael, looking rather self-conscious, let his hand cup my breast as he put his arm around me. I believe I said nothing at all, being very astonished, but my startled, outraged look must have been more than sufficient. The hand was instantly removed. He left at once and did not come near me again for a week. I was more upset by my own stupidity than anything else and, when my father innocently remarked that he had not seen Michael for some time, blushed a frenzied scarlet in my usual ridiculous way.

None of this naturally checked my reading, which was wild, extravagant and omnivorous, with hardly any censorship, but up till now I had never made the most simple of equations: what the poets and novelists write about is neither more nor less than what happens to all human

48

beings under the sun. I read once about an Iron Age couple, buried alive together for the sin of loving. Their skeletons were entwined. They died in each other's arms. I wept for them. Their suffering does not bear thinking of, but perhaps their love sustained them at the end. Only, despite my tears, I never associated them with myself: they were people who died for love, but it was entirely remote from my own personal experience. And so it was with poetry, it was beautiful, moving, exciting, the essence of it was, I am in love, but it was something away on a remote horizon, a beautiful view, a dream.

And now the intellectual innocence is gone. I am one with the Iron Age couple, I am one with the poets. I am in love.

Falling in love comprises an extraordinary and pure happiness. There is for that one point in time neither past nor future, only the uncircumscribed magnificent present. I was ashamed of my self-betrayal, my gaucherie, my youth, yet I was incandescent with happiness: at that moment happiness was simply the fact that the person I knew I loved best in the world, was sitting next to me. I wanted nothing more. I did not think of kissing or endearments or indeed of anything. I simply wished this moment to become eternity, so that I could continue to sit there with Zoltan at my side, occasionally brushing against me as he leaned forward or waved his eloquent, demonstrative hands.

I knew it could not last. I did not want to know. I believe that at that moment I would have been glad to die so that the perfection would become eternal, never be marred or jarred.

My father was speaking to me. His words came strangely through my dreaming, and I jumped, my hand knocking my uneaten roll to the floor. Maggie was pouring out brandy from my great-grandmother's best Georgian decanter. There was a brandy glass in front of me, but it would not be filled, brandy was not permitted.

My father said, "Give her some brandy, Maggie."

Maggie looked positively shocked. She is a very conventional girl, with lots of little brothers and sisters. She always calls me Miss Victoria, but I know she really thinks of me as a child, as one of her family. This was a break in routine. This was not right. She perceptibly hesitated.

"Go on, Maggie," said my father quite sharply, then Zoltan repeated with laughter in his voice, "Go on, Maggie. This time I will let her drink. She is no longer a little girl who does not know the difference between lemonade and champagne."

My father laughed. Everyone was looking at me. Maggie was pouring me out a brandy, with an air of suffering.

He said, "You're dreaming, Victoria. I don't think you heard one word I said."

My mother said sharply, "She's tired. She ought to go to bed. She has to go to school tomorrow."

I wanted to murder her. For the first time in my life I really hated my mother. She once told me in an unusually lively mood that when she was young, she was quite a naughty girl who stayed late at dances and had to climb in through the window. But that was a long time ago: she had forgotten for ever what it was like to be young. I found the tears of shame and anger springing to my eyes, and at the horror of this bent down to pick up my roll. Zoltan did likewise and at precisely the same moment so that we all but knocked our heads together. As we gazed, absurdly eyeball to eyeball, beneath the folds of the tablecloth, he very lightly touched my lips with his.

The tears shot back. The moment of perfect happiness went with them. Now there was a future, though heaven knows what it would be. I was no longer content to sit there. I wanted to be kissed again, I wanted things that I knew nothing about, and in that desperate wanting my childhood departed. The doctor, telling his daughter to beware of too much emotion, to be careful, to be restrained, to ward admiring boys off with delicate gentility, must at this moment have shrivelled to dust in his consulting-room chair.

I sat up, rather flushed, the loose hair falling against my cheek. I did not look at Zoltan, but I am sure that, as he placed the bread once more upon my plate, he appeared calm, amused and entirely self-possessed. Then I grew aware that he was tapping his brandy glass against mine.

"Your health," he said.

"Victoria," said my mother again, with her flair for ignoring everything except the one idea in her mind, "I do think—"

But at this point everyone interrupted her. It seemed that I had suddenly become the focal point for all of them, though they had mostly ignored me throughout the dinner. Now they all turned towards me, and I was wickedly delighted, knew myself in the position of vantage: my mother could hardly send me to bed when everyone there so plainly wanted me to stay.

"No," said Count Asztalos, "I must with all respect forbid it. You will forgive me but I do not see why this enchanting young lady should be dismissed from our company. She is too pretty. I like to look at something pretty. You will leave me with nothing to look at but Zoltan, and he is not pretty at all."

"Excellency," said Zoltan, inclining his head.

"I am not sure," said the Countess, bestowing her most radiant smile on me, "that I should approve of this, but yes, dear Mrs. Katona, let us have the privilege of Victoria's company for a little while longer. She is not after all a child. In Dunavar, where I was born, sixteen is the age when we are considered to be grown-up."

"Besides," said Mr. Gyori, "she is the owner of the most intelligent parrot I have ever met. I should so prefer her to stay. There are many questions I would like to ask her."

Zoltan remarked irrelevantly, "The parrot speaks Attilian."

"No!" said my father.

"Oh yes. And with a remarkably good accent."

Mr. Gyori said nothing to this, but my father, who was plainly enjoying my little moment of fame, remarked, "Well, the opinion seems to be general."

My mother said crossly, "I still think—"

"No. I permit her to stay. When we go back to the drawing-room, then you shall go to bed, Victoria. Now you may drink your brandy and then you will tell us all about the celebrated occasion when Mr. Halasz prevented you from drinking champagne."

My mother, defeated, subsided into sulks. She looked a little like our parrot. But she said nothing more, and indeed, there was little for her to say, with the whole company against her. I do not think the widowed doctor ever foresaw such a contingency. The only possible allies were Mrs. Bradley and Mr. Palotas. Mrs. Bradley would certainly agree that a young girl of seventeen was still a child who should by now be in bed with a glass of hot milk, while Mr. Palotas was as always bored with me, and perhaps wanted to go home. He had spent most of the dinner talking to Miss Jessamy, which was a little surprising for I would not have thought that the two of them had anything in common. But she had become positively animated. I could never describe her as pretty, but the round, dull face had grown interesting in her interest. They made an odd pair. There was almost a generation between them. I wondered what they were talking about.

I answered my father a little shyly, for it was disconcerting to have everyone gazing at me. I said, "Oh Daddy, that was a long time ago." Then I turned to Zoltan. He eyed me gravely, but a faint smile caught at the corner of his lips. "I think Mr. Halasz had better tell you the story. After all, it's his more than mine, and I'm sure he'll do it much better."

This delighted him. He was a great one for talking, at all times, and he contrived to make an immense drama out of what was after all the most trivial of occurrences. And I was content to listen to him, to watch the mobile features, the hands delicately exaggerating every point, and I triumphed in the silence with which the story was received, the laughter that greeted the end of it.

It was really nothing. It was my first Legation party, and I was just fifteen years old. I received, together with my parents, an official invitation. I was wild with excitement. It was a proper grown-up party, starting at seven thirty, and the pleasure of my company was specifically requested. My mother did not want me to go. "She's much too young for parties," she said, "besides, she will be so bored. There won't be anyone for her to talk to. Men don't bother to talk to little girls."

"They'll bother to talk to this one," said my father, laughing. "Why shouldn't she go? She's invited. Besides, she has to start some time. She's pretty and she has nice manners. I think they will all fall in love with her."

My mother said, "Really, Mikki, sometimes you're quite impossible," but she did not argue any more, and actually she took a great deal of trouble over my appearance, even giving me a spray of her best eau-de-cologne, coupled with endless warnings as to what I should or should not do.

I felt very shy at the beginning, and could not bring myself to utter a word, but when a dozen handsome gentlemen clustered round me and began to tease me and make a fuss of me, I enjoyed myself very much. After a little while a tray of drinks was brought round by a splendid waiter in Attilian uniform. I helped myself to a glass and drank it down. I had been eating a great many canapés and delicious things on sticks, and I was very thirsty. The drink looked like lemonade but had a different taste. It was very dry and fizzed down my nose. I had never had anything like it before, and I thought it was lovely: when the waiter came round again I reached out my hand for a second glass.

A gentleman I had not yet met touched my wrist restrainingly, and motioned the waiter away. It was Zoltan, but of course I had no idea of his name, only saw through my confusion that he was handsome and very tall.

He said gently, "That is champagne, Miss Katona. I am not sure if it would be wise to take a second glass. It's a great deal stronger than it may seem."

I said foolishly, angry at being put in my place — for so it seemed to me — "It tastes like lemonade."

"Well, I'm not sure if I should repeat that to the Minister!"

(At this point, two years later, I interrupted to say, "I'm sure I never said it was like lemonade."

"Are you telling the story, or am I?"

"I suggest," said Count Asztalos, "we erase the young lady's last remark, as they say in court. I refuse to believe that my Bollinger could ever be compared to lemonade.")

Well, I am not sure if I really was gauche enough to be so stupid, but it was after all a natural thing to do. It looked like lemonade, and I had never so far seen or tasted champagne. But it all ended quite agreeably. Zoltan had a quiet word with the waiter who a few minutes later brought me a jug of fresh lemonade, which, to be honest, I liked better. I did not speak to him again, though once he smiled at me from the other side of the room. I told my father about it on the way home, and he laughed, saying I obviously had a good head, for it had no effect on me except perhaps to make me less shy.

It was not much of an incident, the little schoolgirl drinking her first champagne by mistake, but Zoltan told it so charmingly that it might have been a story by de Maupassant. And when it was done, we all talked of a variety of things, and it seemed to me that I was no longer seventeen, due to read out my précis tomorrow morning, playing in the school netball match and seeing Michael on Sunday. My dress had a Peter Pan collar, and horrid sleeves, but the pearl choker outshone them so that they no longer mattered. This time I did not remain silent. Everyone was out to flatter and please me, and so I sat there, sipping at the brandy, aware of Zoltan at my side, flirting with Count Asztalos, exchanging jokes with Mr. Gyori, and, oddly enough, very conscious of Miss Jessamy who faced me.

This was strange because, until this evening, I had never thought of Miss Jessamy as much of a person. She was plain and untidy, she did not play the cello very well, and her conversation was dull and devoid of wit. She was the kind of woman who, once she left, was instantly forgotten. Her most noticeable trait was her inquisitiveness, which I did not like. Once I caught her going round the drawing-room, fingering all the little pieces that smothered the tables. My great-grandmother was an obsessive collector, and we had an extraordinary amount of little boxes and trinkets and ornaments. I suppose they were very valuable, but they must have driven Maggie mad. I did not for one moment imagine Miss Jessamy was about to steal anything, but I resented the way she handled every piece, peering at it and holding it close to her eyes. However, a few moments later she was sitting in her usual chair, helping herself to our Sunday sandwiches and cake, making a spasmodic polite conversation with my mother, who was bored by her and made no attempt to hide it.

She did not contribute much to the conversation now. Apparently her intimate talk with Mr. Palotas was ended. I wondered if they had made a date, but it was hard to believe: he was such an elegant, dapper little man, and

54

Miss Jessamy, even when dressed for the occasion, such an old maid.

I felt once again that there was something malicious about her. I knew she was very observant. She could not possibly know that Zoltan had kissed me unless she had peered under the table, but I am sure she was aware of the emotional tension between us. I suspect that it entertained her. Once or twice I caught her looking at me in quite a meaningful way, which made me blush and grow angry.

Just before we left the table, I suddenly thought of something. It was utterly unimportant but it was peculiar, there was no reason for it, and so it intrigued me and in the end disturbed me.

Petits pains. That was what she said, a coy reference to the vast Legation Rolls outside. I suppose she thought she was being witty, or perhaps she was showing off her French. But she could not possibly have seen the car. I only saw it myself because I went to the door to speak to the chauffeur. Miss Jessamy was behind me in the hall, and the car was parked in front of the area where our parrot held his court. She could only have seen it if she had followed me out, and this she definitely did not do for she was leaning against the hall table.

It could not have mattered less except that it proved Miss Jessamy knew the Legation car, had perhaps driven in it. And this I could not understand at all, for how could a dull little woman who worked in the Civil Service have anything to do with Attilian diplomats? I suppose my gaze focused on her, for it made her uneasy: I was aware that she was frowning at me, and I quickly looked aside.

I was to remember this a long time afterwards, but then so many things were to happen, far more important than Miss Jessamy and her *petits pains*, and I forgot all about it until it was to be forced on my memory.

We all pushed our chairs back and rose to our feet. My mother was grimacing at me, indicating that I was at once to go to bed. The table looked as all tables look after a party, an amiable muddle of breadcrumbs, half empty glasses, unfolded napkins. I had enjoyed the end of the dinner more than I had ever enjoyed anything in my life, yet now, despite the fact that Zoltan was behind me, holding my chair, I felt again that strange apprehension, all the stranger because there seemed to be no reason for it.

Zoltan said in my ear, "Did you enjoy the fish sauce?"

Once I would have started, blushed, jerked round to look at him, but I was learning, I did none of these things, only nodded my head.

"I made it!"

"Did you?"

"Was it not delicious? The first poor sauce was ruined. Your cook was in tears. But I am a very domestic man. I took the butter and the flour and the cream, I selected everything I could see around me, and hey presto, the Zoltan sauce, for which princes and popes have died of longing, for once they have tasted it, they are never satisfied with anything again."

My mother interrupted this hymn of praise in her loudest deaf-voice. "My little girl," she said, "must go to bed now. Say goodnight to everyone, Victoria, and go straight to sleep, mind, no reading in bed."

I saw Countess Asztalos smiling at me in a commiserating way, but it could not compensate for this brutal relegation to childhood, in front of someone I longed to impress. My moment of triumph was crushed. I managed to smile as I said goodnight, but what with everything that had happened, the feeling of unease and perhaps the brandy that I was not used to, I was on the verge of tears.

Zoltan, still behind me, said so softly that no one but myself heard him, "I was not quite happy about the Sunlight soap."

I was so startled that I smiled, despite myself, and the tears, perilously near falling, retreated. I recovered my self-control. I behaved now like the good little girl I was supposed to be. Count Asztalos kissed my hand and promised me an invitation to his next party, his wife told me I had such pretty hair, and Miss Jessamy to my surprise, gave me a continental kiss on the cheek. Mrs. Bradley said once again that my dress was so nice, and I must come soon and see Dorothy and Prue. I suppose she enjoyed the dinner, and she looked much happier now that she was fed, but she is so very English, and I still think she must have felt the odd one out.

56

My mother switched out the light, and I paused in the doorway. I felt not so much a schoolgirl as a stranger. Everyone was moving into the drawing-room, and I could hear the laughter and conversation. Only I was not there, I was going to bed, and tomorrow there would be school, and I was seventeen and in love.

Sixteen is the age when we are considered to be grown-up.

I looked once more at the portrait of my formidable great-grandmother. I suppose I was fortunate to have taken my looks from the Attilian side, but I wish I had inherited her brain. The picture was illuminated only by the light from the hall, and the candles on the table that my mother had forgotten to extinguish. I could not see that ugly, clever face clearly any longer, but I knew somehow that she would have been sardonically entertained by everything that had happened: her unhappy granddaughter's dislike of all parties, the confusion about the dinner, and perhaps her great-granddaughter's unprecedented behaviour. As I moved reluctantly out into the hall, to go upstairs, someone brushed against my shoulder. It did not need the hammering of my heart and my hot confusion, to tell me who it was, but I did not turn, only stood there very still.

"Will you drink champagne with me, Victoria, one day soon?" said the soft voice in my ear.

"Yes."

"It will not be lemonade."

It would never be lemonade again, but I did not say anything so silly, indeed I said nothing at all.

"I think we will keep it a secret."

"Yes."

"There is after all no reason for Mummy to know."

"No."

"Shall we put the candles out?"

The echo of a poem — Or a declaration of total war.

"Shall we, Victoria?"

"Yes."

We moved back into the flickering dining-room. I should have prayed that my mother would not come, but I did not do so, I did not think of my mother at all, she might never have existed. Zoltan began to pinch the candles with his fingers, then suddenly swung round and put his arms round me.

Michael and I had kissed. It had not been like this. I heard my voice, my remote voice, saying, "I've wanted this so badly."

He moved away. I could see that he was staring at me. He was not smiling any longer. He said at last in a strange, rough voice, "I will write."

Then he was gone, without even saying goodnight.

Chapter 3

I CAME SLOWLY into the hall. I felt as if I was sleep-walking. I was no longer in my world. Maggie had just come up from the kitchen with a tray in her hand, and she stared at me as I walked up the stairs.

"My, you're late, Miss Victoria," she said, but I did not answer her because I did not really take in what she said, she was nothing just then in my goldfish bowl.

I was just opening my bedroom door when to my surprise I saw Mr. Gyori wandering about the landing, looking vague and lost. This startled me back into some sense and, assuming naturally what his need must be, I said, "If you're looking for the bathroom, Mr. Gyori, it's at the end here, on the right. Actually, we have a little cloakroom downstairs, but nobody ever knows where it is."

I could not see him very clearly. My mother, as I have already said, is economical with landing lights, and sometimes people have been known to walk about for ages, without being able to discover the guest-room, the bathroom or whatever they are looking for. My father occasionally remonstrates with her, but she simply says, "We have to economise." Once Maggie, spurred on by me, put in a more powerful bulb, but from the way my mother carried on, it might have been a lighthouse signal, and it was instantly removed. It is funny how people economise, for my mother often forgets to switch lights off, and they would be on all night if I didn't do it for her. However, I now assumed that Mr. Gyori was another of her victims, wished him goodnight, and was about to close the bedroom door.

He said, "I think you should be careful, Miss Victoria."
I was upset, disconcerted, then furious. As there was

only one thing in my mind, I assumed instantly that he must be warning me against Zoltan. My main reaction was one of rage. I might have known that this horrid little man was spying on me. No doubt he had noticed all my emotion; perhaps he had even watched us in the dining-room. I said haughtily, "I've no idea what you're talking about, and I'm very tired, so—"

He said, "You must listen to me."

"I see no reason why—"

"No, you would not understand. You are too young. I think," said Mr. Gyori who seemed to have a positive obsession on parrots, "I would do better to talk to your Polly."

This really was an absurd conversation to hold on our first-floor landing, and all I wanted to do now was to creep into bed and dream and dream in the lovely solitude of my own room. I said again, "I don't know what you're talking about." And then, so far had I slipped from restraint and good manners, "I think you must have drunk too much wine."

He replied with some energy, "You are a rude, silly little girl, and if you were my daughter, I would spank you."

This was too much to endure, but of course it left me with nothing to say. I rushed into my bedroom, slammed the door, then locked it. I do not know why I locked it, because Mr. Gyori was hardly likely to follow me, but I suppose I was not so much locking him out as locking myself in: my stupid words rang in my ears so that I was scarlet with humiliation. What my father would say if he repeated my impertinence — But I heard him move away, heard the bathroom door open and close, there was nothing I could do about it now except to feel that my beautiful evening was ruined, and entirely through my own stupidity.

But of course it was not ruined at all. The memory of Zoltan's kiss, the prospect of drinking champagne with him, the whole strange dreamlike lunacy of it all, all this obliterated my foolishness. I did not immediately go to bed. I sat for a long time in front of my dressing-table, gazing at myself in the mirror, playing the Mozart *Wiegenlied*. I did not really see myself only in this way painted a picture on my mind, a picture that I would

60

never forget. I was quite safe from discovery. My mother would be playing the hostess, the guests would be relaxing and chatting: no one would come up to disturb the little girl who ought to be in bed, and poor Maggie and Mary would be up to their ears in greasy dishes.

I could not believe that tomorrow I would once more become Victoria Katona, prefect, sixth form, reading out her précis, dressed in gym tunic and white blouse, hair pinned back by a slide. I said aloud, "Victoria Katona, Victoria Katona," while slipping off the hideous green dress and at last falling into bed. But I looked for a long time at the pearl choker. I felt I could not bear to part with it. Perhaps my mother would let me keep it, though even in my dazed state I felt that this was unlikely. I let it slide through my fingers, and at last I put it in one of the drawers, instead of leaving it on top, to be collected next morning. And then in bed I fell instantly asleep: if I dreamed I remembered nothing.

I woke early. Normally I get up at half past seven. Maggie knocks perfunctorily on my door — this is a pure formality — and brings me in a can of hot water. I wash and dress, am down by eight for breakfast with my parents and set off for school at half past. I sleepily examined my watch which told me it was just after seven. I prepared to lie there a little longer, then grew aware of a faint, distant sound that sounded remarkably like screaming. I tried to ignore it but the sound continued; at last I tumbled out of bed, without bothering to put on my dressing-gown.

I came out on to the landing. There was no denying the screaming now. It came from the top floor where Mary and Maggie shared a room opposite my father's study. My parents, exhausted after the evening, must be dead asleep. My mother, in any case, was deaf, and my father was always immersed in his own private thoughts and, if he heard anything at all, would probably tell himself it was something unimportant and outside.

By this time I was terrified. I ran up the stairs. There had never been anything like this before. Mary and Maggie, though they sometimes had what they called words, got on extremely well: their quarrels were usually the silent kind where they did not speak to each other. I had never heard either of them scream. But the screaming continued and, when I arrived at the landing, I saw Maggie, fully dressed, standing there, one hand bunched against her mouth, emitting hysterical cries. There was no sign of Mary: she was presumably in the kitchen, seeing to the breakfast.

I exclaimed in a trembling voice, "Maggie, what on earth's the matter?"

But she only went on screaming in a faint, frantic way, and I tried to remember what one did with hysterics, for this was plainly what it must be, and I had no idea how to cope. There was a girl in my class, an American girl called Maribel, who once fell into a fit of hysteria, and I remembered poor Miss Lamb, our geography teacher, standing in front of her, pale and shaking, with not the faintest idea what to do. She probably remembered that the correct treatment was a slap, but this was not the kind of thing a good teacher should do, so she simply stood there making protesting noises until at last one of us, less inhibited, threw some water over the patient.

I had no water handy, so I caught hold of Maggie's shoulders, crying, "Oh Maggie, do stop, what's the matter, please tell me."

She turned on me a face such as I had never seen. Maggie is such a pretty girl with a lovely delicate complexion; she is, when she is not playing the parlour-maid, cheeky and outspoken. She has always seemed to me the kind of girl whom life cannot do down. I was always fighting with her because she would treat me like one of her younger sisters, but I love her very much, and sometimes I have cried on her shoulder and been most tenderly comforted. Now the beautiful colour was gone, and she looked as she might do in twenty years' time. She could not answer me. She only pointed at my father's study. The door was open and I stepped inside.

Mr. Gyori lay there on the floor. He was plainly dead. There was a hole and a great brown-red patch in the middle of his shirt-front.

It was my horrid dream come to life.

I had never seen death before. When my grandmother died I went to her funeral, but there was nothing to see except a coffin covered with a great black and purple pall, and masses of beautiful flowers. I cried because everyone else was crying, and it was all beautiful and sad, but it meant nothing to me, it was simply a grand drama, it was in no way real.

But this was real, the hole in Mr. Gyori's shirt and the blood, his strange, yellow, sunken face with the mouth open, and the eyes turned up so that all one could see was the whites. It was very ugly, and I felt so sick that for a moment I thought I would actually vomit. I heard myself say in a booming kind of voice that did not seem to be my own, "Go on downstairs, Maggie. There's nothing you can do here. Ask Mary to give you a brandy. I am going to call my father."

As she hardly seemed to hear what I was saying, I caught at her arm and almost dragged her to the staircase. She went totteringly downstairs like an automaton, and then for the first time I felt faint with the shock and horror of it: I had to cling to the banister, then I sat down on the top step until the walls stopped turning.

I managed to reach the first floor. I knocked on my parents' door then, as there was no answer, banged insistently, calling out in a high voice, "Daddy! Oh Daddy, please come, please—"

It was always understood that I never went in without knocking, and even in this crisis I obeyed. When my father at last appeared, with his hair on end, shrugging on his dressing-gown, the unshaven stubble black against his chin, I burst out crying and collapsed into his astonished arms.

He held me tightly. He must have been amazed, for I had never behaved like this since I was a small child, but his arms at once went round me, and he said soothingly, "Baby, baby, what is the matter?"

My mother called out from the bedroom, "What's the matter, Mikki? What does Victoria want?"

He said, "It's all right, Helen. Go back to sleep." Then to me again, "What's happened? Tell me. Oh come on, baby, you're safe now, tell me all about it."

I suppose he thought it was a nightmare, but then so indeed it was. I stammered hysterically through my tears, "Mr. Gyori — Oh Daddy, it's so awful, I can't believe it's happened."

My mother, ignoring his last remark, was now out on the landing too. My father still held me, but I felt his body stiffen. He said quietly, "What are you talking about, Victoria? What's happened to Mr. Gyori?"

"He's dead!"

My mother gave a little gasping shriek. My father for a moment was silent. Then he said, "What do you mean?"

"He's dead. I think someone must have shot him. He's in your study. Maggie found him. She was having hysterics. I heard her. I came upstairs to see what it was all about."

My father did not answer me at all, except to say, as if he were speaking to himself, "So it's happened at last." He released me then, without another word, went upstairs. My mother, looking incredulous and distraught, trailed along behind him. He turned once to look at her. He said, "Helen, I think you'd better stay here."

She wailed at him, "Oh, don't be so silly. After all, it's my house too."

I was to think afterwards that poor Mr. Gyori had committed the final social faux-pas, final in every sense of the word. You should not get yourself murdered in other people's houses, it really is not done. But now I was hardly taking in what was said. I stayed there on the landing; I could not endure again the sight of that pathetic little body with the stain across the starched shirt-front.

After a few minutes my father called down to me. "You'd better go and ring the police, Victoria," he said. "Then ask Mary to make us all a strong cup of tea, and make sure Maggie has one too."

He sounded so detached and practical that he might have been referring to a broken window. But I obeyed him, deriving comfort from his calm tones, and went immediately to the telephone. I had never rung the police in my life, but I read a great many detective stories, being an ardent devotee of Dorothy L. Sayers, and to my shame it must be said that I felt a marked excitement at actually speaking to a policeman on an urgent call.

He asked me what was the matter. When I answered bluntly, "Murder!" there was a perceptible pause.

He repeated, "Murder, miss?"

"Yes. Someone's been shot. Oh please come quickly."

They were there within ten minutes. The neighbours,

what with Rolls Royces and now a police car, must have been having a field-day. The Katona family was providing more excitement in a few hours than our quiet little road had ever seen. We were all in the sittting-room, myself still in pyjamas and dressing-gown, when the police arrived. There were two of them, one, I imagine, an inspector, and they both went out of their way to be kind to me.

My father spoke calmly enough, but he looked dreadful. My mother on the other hand behaved with a surprising dignity with no sign of hysteria, even calming down Maggie, who was still crying, and she had even during the ten minutes before the police came, managed to dress and do her hair.

I do not remember very clearly what happened at the beginning, but I do remember the interview. We were all interviewed separately in the dining-room, with my great-grandmother looking down at us. When my turn came, I felt remote and exhausted. I could not stop shaking, though the tea (laced, I think, with brandy) was comforting, but I managed to answer the questions, and if my answers were not all accurate, that was nothing to do with fright or shock.

The main interest centred on Mr. Gyori's looking for the bathroom.

"If you would tell us, Miss Katona, exactly what was said."

I did not tell them exactly what was said. It was very wrong of me, indeed, in the circumstances, it was criminally wrong, but though I did not realise the full implications of Mr. Gyori's warning, I was only concerned with my own childish stupidity: nothing in the world would have dragged my appalling words out of me.

"You say he was looking for the bathroom?"

"Yes."

"Did he say so?"

"Well, no, but when you see someone wandering about—"

"There is no toilet on the ground floor?"

"Yes, there is. It's at the back of a little cloakroom where people leave their things. But nobody ever knows where it is."

"So it is quite usual for guests to come upstairs?"

65

"Oh yes."

"You directed him?"

"Yes."

"And you heard him go there? You heard him close the door?" "Yes."

"Did you not hear him come out?"

"No. I was playing my gramophone."

"At that hour of night?"

"Yes. It was very soft."

I could see that the Inspector suspected that I was concealing something. He remained gentle and polite, but I saw him eyeing me very closely. He said, "You say you directed him to the bathroom. What did he say to you? I would like you if possible to repeat the exact words."

I blushed, of course. But it is shocking how well one lies when wishing to cover up a personal humiliation. I do not know what the Inspector thought of my scarlet cheeks: he made no comment. I could only pray that he thought I was modest about lavatories. As the major part of the preliminary inquiry was concerned with our guests using the cloakroom downstairs, this would perhaps account for my embarrassment, though I am seventeen, I have not been brought up to that particular form of gentility, and the word "toilet" offends me far more than the usual term.

Lorna sometimes talks of the little girls' room. I cannot imagine where she gets this from, she is in no way a genteel person. And Mrs. Bradley talks of "hospitality" — "Do you want to use our hospitality?" When she first said this, I did not know what she meant.

But the Inspector might think that a young girl would be shy. I was thankful that my father, who is acutely observant and who knows me very well, was not present at the interview.

I said, "I really did the talking. I was just going to bed. When I saw Mr. Gyori wandering about, looking rather lost, I said that if he was looking for the bathroom, it was at the end of the corridor. Oh, and I told him there was a cloakroom downstairs."

"And what did he say to that?"

"He — he just thanked me and said goodnight."

I suppose it did not require much astuteness to see that I was lying. The Inspector said nothing for a while, only scribbled in his notebook, which made me very nervous. I imagine that is why he did it. He said, without raising his head, "Can you think of any reason why Mr. Gyori should go into your father's study which is after all another floor up?"

I was so relieved at the change of subject that I answered too eagerly, saying that no, I hadn't the faintest idea. The Inspector looked at me and said, "You are quite certain, Miss Katona, that Mr. Gyori really said nothing else? Please think before you answer. This might be very important."

I nearly told him. I think a lot of things might have been different if I had done so. It would after all have been quite easy. I did not need to repeat that humiliating threat to spank me. I could just have said that he told me to be careful. But the Inspector would never have left it at that. *What was he talking about, what did he mean, there must have been some reason.* And then I would either have to lie directly, say I had no idea, or tell him about Zoltan. I do not know why I was so certain that I was being warned against Zoltan. He could have been talking of a dozen things, drinking brandy, staying up too late, or, oh goodness, some two-headed maniac patrolling our street—

But of course it was Zoltan. I knew it was Zoltan, and my frightened mind, already recoiling from the implications, prompted me to answer with positive vehemence.

'No, sir, he said nothing else."

"You are absolutely sure?"

"Absolutely." And, because I knew he did not believe me, I stared at him quite boldly, even permitting myself a little smile. I suspect this gave me away more than anything else, for up till then I had been so transparently nervous, stammering and looking down at my own tightly clasped hands.

But he only said, "If you remember anything, anything at all, however insignificant it may seem to you, will you ring me immediately? This is my name and telephone number."

"Yes, of course."

He did not want to let me go. I fancy that like Mr. Gyori, he wanted to spank me. And nobody deserved it more than I did, for I was shamelessly lying, so concerned with my own private emotions that I had none to spare for the violent death of a harmless little man.

I sometimes think that half the lies people tell are for the silliest of reasons: shame at being found picking your nose, talking to yourself or stealing something from the larder.

However, this was the end of my interview, and presently when the finger-print men and the doctor and the police were gone, we all assembled in the dining-room and, however disgraceful it may sound, ate a ravenous breakfast. Maggie had by now quite recovered herself. I could see that she was enjoying the drama. I think Mary must have filled her up with brandy, for my father, as she gaily slopped the milk on to the table cloth, said, "Girl, you are quite tipsy," at which she fell into a fit of the giggles and ran out of the room. I am sure that all the tradesmen who called on us during the week were regaled with a story that grew more and more lurid as the days went by.

My mother too looked better than I had seen her for a long time. I believe that her real trouble was that she was bored. She was not interested in African anthropologists or Attilian diplomats, she hated formal entertaining, my father seldom spoke to her of anything but trivialities, and she had no hobbies of any kind except perhaps music. She was now very lively, positively smiling, though we all fell silent when we heard the body being carried downstairs.

It was quite unmistakable. My father instantly tried to cover it up by making some over-loud comment on the newspaper headlines, and creating a great fuss over the fishcakes that Mary had sent up to us. I suppose they were the left-overs from last night's dinner, perhaps garnished with Zoltan's Sunlight soap sauce.

But we could not ignore the slow, thudding sound of two men coming downstairs, carrying a heavy stretcher. We all somehow saw it, and we looked away from each other, unable to eat or speak until we heard the front door close and the ambulance driving off. I thought I could never go near my father's study again, and it was quite a while before we all started to talk at once, much more animatedly than was our custom at breakfast, which was usually a taciturn meal, with myself rushing off to school, my father reading the paper, and my mother drinking endless cups of tea.

We began inevitably to compare notes about our interviews. My father still looked dreadful, though he had now dressed and shaved. He seemed for the first time an old man, though he was only in his early fifties, his face was grey with shock and horror, and the moment he finished his meal he started chain-smoking, continuing to do so throughout the morning.

The police were, of course, still concerned with the guests' visits to the cloakroom, which overlooked our garden. Not unnaturally after a meal with a quantity of wine and brandy, everyone at some point left the drawing-room. Also, because it was a mild evening, my father had opened the French windows to let the smoke out, and stepped on to the verandah, once with Zoltan and once with Countess Asztalos, so that he had no idea who was in the room behind him: some of the guests might even have gone into the garden by the door behind the cloakroom.

"After all," he said, lighting up his third cigarette, "one doesn't follow one's guests around, nor does one make a note when they leave the room to relieve themselves."

"Really, Mikki," said my mother automatically. She hates any reference to the natural functions and used, when I was a small child, to ask me if I had *been* today, frantically embarrassed by even this euphemism.

"But Daddy," I said, having shamelessly eaten my third fishcake, and now embarked on toast and marmalade, "did Mr. Gyori ever come back into the drawing-room?"

"No. The police hammered away at that. We never saw him again." My father, as if realising the ugliness of these last words, swallowed then went on. "They seemed to think that very odd. We all thought it odd when we realised he was not there. Only the room was filled with people, and it was quite a time before we grew aware that he seemed to have vanished. I know it sounds bad, but when everyone is talking and moving around—"

"He is not the sort of man you notice," said my mother unexpectedly.

My father looked at her in surprise. He is always astonished when my mother says something intelligent, or

69

perhaps he is simply astonished if she says anything at all.

"Yes," he said, "that is true. Nobody really noticed and when we did realise he was not there, we all assumed he had gone home. Helen no doubt thought he had said goodbye to me, and I certainly thought he had said goodbye to Helen. Certainly someone wished to give us that impression, for there was no coat or scarf in the cloakroom. The police were very interested in that. I do know, because I looked in when they had all gone, to see if anything had been left behind. Women always forget their gloves and I remember once someone left a tie in the wash-basin, which I found extraordinary. I never discovered who it was."

"Perhaps he didn't have a coat or scarf," I said. "After all, he came by car."

"It's unlikely he wouldn't even have a scarf," said my mother, "and anyway, what was he doing in your study, Mikki? I think that's the oddest part of it."

"He was a spy," said my father.

He said this as if it were the most natural thing in the world. Both my mother and I stared at him. He went on calmly, "On the right side, of course, so he would hardly be spying on me. But it was the kind of ending he expected. It might even be my ending, the way things are going."

"Daddy!"

"Oh, I don't suppose it will ever happen. But though it's appalling that he's been killed, I can't pretend I am altogether astonished. I told all this to the police. I think they knew. Of course this is an awkward business for them, diplomatic immunity and all that. The fact that Count Asztalos is involved makes it very tricky. I don't envy them their job." Then he said suddenly, "You said no one noticed him, Helen. It was his stock in trade. But he noticed. I'm afraid he noticed more than he should have done."

"It might have been a burglar," said my mother. She seemed to have lost interest in the whole affair. "Victoria, you really should get dressed — Oh I don't know, Mikki. I understand your study window was open. Perhaps poor Mr. Gyori heard a noise and rushed upstairs, and then the burglar panicked."

My father said patiently, "Is that what you told the police?"

"No," said my mother. "It has only just struck me. But I think it's quite possible, and then they needn't bother poor Count Asztalos at all."

My father and I glanced surreptitiously at each other, but he said nothing. Whoever the murderer was, he could not have been a burglar. Burglars do not usually carry guns, and anyone who swarmed up to the third floor window would have to be as agile as a monkey. I was longing to ask more about the spying, but I had to see that my mother was perfectly right: I could not sit around all day in a dressing-gown, even though she had rung my school and explained why I would not be there.

I went upstairs. I felt very tired. I still could not quite believe any of this had happened. I went into my bedroom and, instead of dressing, sat down on the bed and lit one of my rationed cigarettes. At that moment I could not even think of Zoltan. It was as if a barrier had come down between myself and the whole of that evening. When, a few minutes later, my father, looking ill and exhausted, came in, I felt that we must somehow comfort each other, and I got up and came towards him.

My father never gives the impression of being an emotional man. I know he loves me, and sometimes he likes to fondle me, make a fuss of me, tease me, but he has never been very demonstrative. Now he gave me rather a grim smile then, sitting down in my one armchair, held out his arms to me, then pulled me on to his knee as if I were a child again. It was lovely; it was just what I needed, and I buried my face in his shoulder. This was home and family and security. My own things surrounded me, the books, my precious gramophone with the *Wiegenlied* still on the turntable, the photos on the mantelpiece, the huge Victorian tallboy that held all my childish possessions.

We were both silent for a while, my father's hand stroking my hair. The he tipped me off his knee, saying, "Enough of that. I'm sick to death of this whole business. It's ruined my work. How am I expected to get on with my book, with my study stinking of death and the chalk marks still on the floor?"

Even to me this seemed a little heartless, and he must

have seen the expression on my face. He laughed and offered me another cigarette. "I didn't want this," he said. "I knew something like this might happen, but I didn't want it, I imagined that by not thinking of it, I could push it away."

I thought that Mr. Gyori could not have wanted it either, but I knew somehow that my father was not only talking of the murder. I said nothing, though I was longing to ask questions, especially about the business of being a spy: before I could say any of this, my father asked to my astonishment, "Have you rung Michael?"

"No! How could I? All this happening and — No. I suppose he'll see it in the papers. It will be in the papers, won't it?"

"Not if the police could prevent it. But of course they can't. I daresay it will reach the headlines. Attilian counts are good news value. I think you should ring Michael. Do you love him?"

I flushed scarlet at this. Apart from the fact that this was unprecedented, it brought back to me everything that had happened yesterday, everything that had been briefly blurred by the violence of Mr. Gyori's death. I said at last, sounding as I perfectly well knew, very stupid, "I don't know."

"Of course you know. Don't be silly."

"I don't think I do know. I mean, I like him very much. But for goodness' sake, Daddy, we are both very young—"

"It's interesting," said my father in his normal voice, "how you emphasise your youth when it suits you. When your mother and I point out how young you are, you are up in arms immediately. I thought you were keen on him. Isn't that the phrase you use nowadays?"

I did not answer this. I could hardly say that Michael at that moment was irrelevant, but so he was, he seemed like someone I had known a long time ago and not seen for years. It was almost as if I could not put a face on him. Besides, the phrase my father had just employed, went out of fashion a long time ago. I looked down at the floor, and wished he would stop asking me such personal questions.

I think my silence disconcerted him. He said again, almost surlily, "Well, I think you should ring him."

"He'll probably ring me."

"Playing hard to get, are you, baby?" He was silent for a moment then he said, "What did you think of them all yesterday?"

I could not miss the sudden sharpness in his voice. I am sure he had not the faintest idea what had happened to me, but he knew that something had happened, he was aware of the change in me. I suppose he thought that if he ferreted around, I would in the end give myself away.

I said, "They were all very nice."

"Nice! Nice! Why do you use that abominable word? I wish you'd speak English properly." Then he met my eye and laughed. "All right, baby, all right. I'm upset too. I don't like murder any more than you do, and this is only the beginning."

"What do you mean, only the beginning? You don't really mean there'll be more murders, do you?"

But he did not answer this, only repeated, derisively, "Nice!"

He has always hated that word. He has odd ideas about our language. I suppose it is because he had to learn it. He likes to pronounce "cinema" with a "k"; he says it is the original Greek word, and he gets furious if I say something is awful. My mother and I pay no attention to him.

He said unexpectedly, "You want to go to Attilia, don't you?"

"Oh yes, yes, more than anything."

"I see. To meet all the charming, Attilians, drink apricot brandy, eat cream cakes and listen to gypsies playing their hearts out on the banks of the Danube. I see you have a yearning for gracious living."

"What a horrid phrase!"

"But what a nice — you notice, I said it — state to be in. It's a pity it's always at the expense of someone else. Only it's not quite like that, you know. It wasn't quite like that last night, as our Mr. Gyori, presumably now on the left hand of the Almighty, could bear witness."

I wished he would not talk of Mr. Gyori like that, but then my father has an unconventional sense of humour. Sometimes he shocks my mother terribly, but then she is the most conventional person in the world.

73

He went on, "I know exactly how you saw them. Charming and handsome and clean, the shirts so starched and white. Have you ever thought what lies behind those shirts? Behind one of them at least there was murder. I would make a guess that there was a great deal else. Ambition and jealousy, hate and cruelty — The Nazis wear shirt-fronts too. I daresay they look well in them. If Buchenwald and Belsen pop out with the studs occasionally, why should we worry?"

"You're not pretending that any of them are Nazis!"

"No, I'm not pretending. But I suppose I mustn't destroy your illusions. Forget what I've said. Think of them as all charm and *servus* and kissing your little hand, out to flatter the daughter of the house, to charm the cook, not an unkind thought among them, only a lot of money and a devil of a lot of ambition, enough to start a war. They were delighted with you, Victoria. They whispered to me that you are much prettier than Miss Jessamy."

I had the sense not to say that this might not be too difficult. But my father was bewildering me, and I was too tired to take it all in. I said, "Daddy, I don't understand what you are talking about."

He went on as if I had not spoken. He was following his own train of thought. He said, "I have not been home for nearly twenty years. My mother still lives in Dunavar. She is nearly eighty. She will not be there much longer. I never see any of my family. I shall never go home again. At least one of the charming gentlemen with the immaculate shirt-fronts would make sure that I ended up in prison, perhaps see that I followed Mr. Gyori."

"But why? You haven't done anything."

"It's a slow kind of nibbling," said my father, still paying no attention to me, "easy as eating a German sausage. Only in a way the sausage is eating us, first the Rhineland, now Spain, and no doubt Czechoslovakia next on the shopping list. With England as the final bonne bouche. Of course Attilia will be swallowed too, but then Attilians never think of such things, they are too conceited, they like no one but themselves. They say the Czechs are puffed-up frogs, the Rumanians pimps and cocottes, and the Slovaks good Attilians misled, but the Attilians come straight from God, they are the chosen people — only of course such a phrase refers to the Jews so it must never be used. I once attended a meeting, Victoria, of a society — Why do you look like that? What do you know about Attilian societies?"

"Mr. Gyori told me about the Attilian Life Society. He said our parrot must be a member because their uniform is scarlet and grey."

My father stared at me. "What else did he say about it? He seems to have been very communicative. It looks as if someone overheard him."

"He didn't say very much." It seemed such a long time ago. It was yesterday. I could not believe it. Yesterday! I tried to remember what he had said. It had seemed amusing at the time. "He said it was very right-wing and against the Jews. There was something about a golden doe that he thought was funny. The doe had a Jewish nose. That's what he said."

My father looked angry, incredulous and bewildered. "Who would have thought it? Was he perhaps drunk?"

This made me flush, but he was too absorbed to notice. I said quickly, "Oh no, of course not. I don't think Mr. Gyori would ever be — have been — drunk."

"And what else did he tell you?"

"Nothing much. Perhaps he told it to Polly. He spoke to him in Attilian."

"Then I will tell you about it. I think you should know. After all, you are half Attilian. It is a race-protecting society, divided into tribes, clans and families. There is an initiation ceremony like that among my African people, a great deal of presumably mysterious ritual, and disciplinary courts which have the power to inflict the death sentence. No Jews are of course admitted, and one of the tenets of the society, though in my day it was not worded quite so crudely, is the proposed extermination of the Jewish race. They said then that nobody intends to rid the world entirely of the Jews, but simply to save the Attilian race from their noxious influence. I remember the phrase."

"But how did you come to be there?"

"Ah. That, I suppose, is the crux of the matter. I had no business to be there at all. Like the Klu-Klux-Klan — have you heard of them? — they mask themselves at meetings. They found me out, but fortunately, it was too late. They were not so powerful then. Now they are. So I am stateless, Victoria. Do you not remember our little holiday in France last year?"

I did, of course. I sailed through the British customs with no trouble at all, while my parents, with their stateless papers, were held up for nearly an hour.

"And so I shall remain," said my father. He fell silent for a while. Then he said, "They are dangerous people, and now they have a dangerous and powerful backing. There is a clan here in London. I have known about it for a long time, but I have never been able to discover who belongs to it, neither have the police. I know now that Mr. Gyori had that knowledge. But I'll tell you one thing, Victoria. At least two of the people who dined with us last night are members of that clan."

"You know that and you asked them!"

"Oh yes. Why not? I am on very friendly terms with the Legation, after all. Besides, not all the members are Attilian, by any means. They are affiliated with the Fascist party here. There are a great many English clansmen, all presumably with the purest Nordic connections."

For some ridiculous reason the thought of the Bradleys flitted through my exhausted mind. I could not really see either Mr. or Mrs. Bradley as members of the Attilian Life Society, dressed in scarlet and grey, and wearing masks and boots, but I suppose stranger things have happened.

I said, "Do you know which they were?"

"I think," said my father, "I should prefer not to answer that question."

"There's no danger for you, is there?"

He shrugged and did not answer.

I said, "Not Count Asztalos anyway. It couldn't be Count Asztalos."

"You only say that because he is handsome and charming and kisses your hand. But I daresay you are right. He is a Legitimist. He wants the monarchy restored. Whether Attilia under the Hapsburgs would be much better than Attilia under Hitler, I do not know. But I cannot see him as a member of such a society. He is a great snob and title-worshipper. He would hardly soil his elegant hands with such crudities. But one can never be sure. Only—" His voice suddenly deepened,

76

and he rose to his feet, scattering ash everywhere. My mother would have been furious with him. She herself scatters ash like snow, but she cannot bear to see anyone else doing it. "Only, baby, you are to be careful. Keep out of all this. It is nothing to do with you. It is not the kind of thing that little girls should interfere with. If I catch you meddling in any way with what does not concern you, I shall be very angry indeed. You don't want to end up like Mr. Gyori, with a bullet in your heart, do you?"

"No, Daddy," I said, and something in my voice must have jarred him, for he looked at me very searchingly.

But I was truly too exhausted to be impertinent, and he said at last, "I must get on with my work. I need the civilisation of Africa. Do you know, if you asked me where I'd like to be, I could tell you. By the shores of Lake Tanganyika. They say that once you've drunk the lake's waters, you spend the rest of your life wanting to drink them again. Bilharzia and all — Bilharzia, liver flukes, crocodiles and all. But there's no reason in longing. There never has been."

I said with difficulty, "You don't really like living here, do you?"

He said, very wearily, "What is there to like?" It was as if he were talking to himself. "It's a rotten, stinking world."

Until yesterday it had seemed to me a splendid God's-in-his-heaven-all's right-with-the-world. Why should it not seem so? I was young, I was strong, I enjoyed my school. I was going up to Oxford next year. I had good friends, and there was Michael, very faithful, very devoted, perhaps a bit of a bore, but I would have been lost without him. I had a good home, parents I loved, there was no shortage of money: within reason I could do what I liked. I knew I was quite pretty. I would have been silly not to know it. Even now the gentlemen by no means ignored me, and next year I would be properly grown-up, go to dances and parties, wear clothes that did not shame me. The sun shone, the stars were out, and up till now such things as wicked societies and murder had not touched me.

I cried out angrily, "Is it so rotten? I like people. I liked the ones who came to dinner yesterday."

"One of whom is a murderer."

"Yes, I know. It's horrible. But there had always been murderers. Because this one touches us personally, it doesn't make the whole world evil."

"Read your papers," said my father. His eyes moved away from me. I think he was already half back by Lake Tanganyika.

"I do. Mostly. But look, Daddy," I said, fighting as it were for my own personal rose-coloured spectacles, "be reasonable. I know awful things are happening. I am not stupid. I do know about Hitler and the concentration camps and that ghastly war in Abyssinia. But you can't expect me to live in constant mourning. I have my own life and I enjoy it. You don't want me surely to mope around and get no fun out of anything. I know one should think about other people, but if I wore sackcloth and refused to go out with anyone and lamented all day long, it wouldn't do them any good. Would it? I can't see that the world would be any better for me crying all the time and — and beating on my chest."

"It would add a little variety to it," said my father dryly. He was now standing by the door. He looked at me as if he were not quite sure that he knew me. And it was true that I had never talked to him like this in my life for, though I loved him most dearly, I was always a little afraid of him. Perhaps he sensed this. He said more gently, "I'm sorry, baby. You're quite right. You must enjoy life your own way. Only don't be too taken in by exteriors. You thought it was a—" He paused, then emphasised the word. "—a *nice* dinner party. Perhaps it was. No one expected it to end in such a way. But what I am trying to say is this. They are good people. I think in some ways they really are. Enjoy them, be friendly with them. Appreciate their charm. Why not? They are charming. I know that. But don't let it blind you to reality. We are more civilised nowadays, or so they tell us. In the old days we beat people to death, we tortured them on the rack, we burnt them alive, we cut them down still living from the gallows and burnt their entrails before them—"

"Daddy!"

"And we made no secret of it. People paid to come and see. Now it's different. We beat them to death, we torture and burn them, we hang them on piano wire, cutting them down to hang them again. But we make a secret of it. We wash properly, we dress prettily, we talk charmingly of flowers and flirts and the plays we have seen. We use the right knives and forks, we pay compliments and we kiss pretty ladies' hands. But underneath it is always the same: death and cruelty and ambition — ambition, Victoria, the most deadly thing of all. Don't be taken in, baby, for God's sake, don't be taken in. There is a war coming. Even you must know that. All the charm and fine clothes and pretty manners will be blown to blazes; the gentleman who kisses your hand will smash your face in. And be the same gentleman. I do not believe we will ever change. But you won't see that. You don't want to see that. The next generation will look back on ours and think how lovely it must have been to lead such a pleasant, civilised, sophisticated life." Then he said, "I'm boring you, aren't I?"

You cannot tell your father he is boring you, but yes, it was true, he was, and I did not really believe him. I said without meaning to, "I think you should leave us and go back to Africa. Was that so civilised, Daddy?"

"No." He laughed. "Oh no. Of course not. But it was straight. If that's the right word. You knew where you were. You don't understand what I mean, do you?"

"No, I don't think I do."

"I'll tell you. When I'd been out in the Congo for six months, I vanished. At least, that's what my friends thought. There were after all very few communications. There was no word of me. Someone at last wrote to a friend of mine, 'I suppose you've heard that poor Miklos Katona has been killed and eaten by Congo cannibals. I hope you are quite well, yours sincerely—' Well, I don't suppose it was as bald as all that. These things tend to become more dramatic as the years pass by. But it is what what I mean by the basic approach. I disappeared. Very well, I had been eaten. Maybe a few people cried for me, and I suppose your mother was a little upset, but it was really quite simple, Katona had disappeared into a black belly, and that was the end of him."

I said, "I don't think I find that very funny."

"God bless you," said my father. I thought he was in the strangest mood. I had never heard him talk like this before. I was beginning to think I had never heard him talk at all though, like most of the Katonas, he loved words and used them freely. We all talk a lot, even my mother, when she gets going. He gave me again that grim smile that frightened me. "Nowadays," he said, "we disappear only too frequently, but it is no longer quite so simple. We disappear into a concentration camp or a prison — or we simply disappear. And we are never heard of again. Only what happens in that disappearance is a great deal more complicated than a simple grinding of teeth, more prolonged and considerably more painful. That is what I mean. That is our civilisation." He looked at me. His expression changed. He was once again the father I knew, only not quite, he would never be so again. He said gently, "I'm sorry, baby. I didn't mean to frighten you. I didn't want you to know these things. Only now you have to know, and I want to make sure you're careful. Don't interfere. Whatever happens, don't interfere. Is that understood?"

"Yes. All right, Daddy."

He was opening the door. He said, "I wish I didn't feel—" He swung round. His face grew once again menacing. "Is there something you're not telling me?"

"No. Why on earth should there be?" My voice was calm and natural. I did not know I could act like that. Inside I was shaking.

"I don't know. I just — Are you sure?"

"Yes. I don't understand. What do you mean?"

"I suppose it doesn't matter."

But he knew it mattered. We had always been very close. I was never close to my mother. She had odd, startling moments of intuition, but she was not really interested enough to bother about me. I was never much of a liar, even as a small child, but I could never lie to my father at all: he always knew, he would never say how, but a certain look would come in his eye and I would at once blush and stammer, sometimes end by bursting into tears. With my mother it was different but then, as I have said, she did not really care, besides, the things she asked me were so unimportant. Have you *been* today, did you clean your teeth, have you changed your vest — And I would automatically say yes, because it was the simplest way out, and then she would wander away and forget all about it.

My father suddenly changed his mind. He came back into the room and put his hands on my shoulders. There was no affection in that grasp, there was a threat. He said, "You are sure, aren't you, Victoria?"

"Yes, Daddy, of course I'm sure."

"You're a meddling little madam sometimes. This is something you must not so much as touch. I think you don't believe me, but this is not a game, it's something deadly serious. If you know anything about it, if you've overheard something or perhaps feel some misguided sense of loyalty, you are to tell me now, and that's an order. That's an order, baby."

"There's nothing to tell. Honestly."

He said reluctantly, "It's not that I believe you would do anything wrong. But you are so young. It is so easy for the young to be misled."

It was strange but this last word nearly finished me. I almost burst out with the whole story. My father speaks virtually perfect English, with only the faintest intonation to betray his Attilian ancestry, but there are a handful of words he always mispronounces, and "misled" is one of them: he speaks it as if the verb were "misle". Yet even now I managed to say nothing, and he released me. His eyes moved over me, and I met that searching, doubting gaze with perfect calm. His mouth mumbled over the cigarette it was holding, as if he were trying to say something and could not bring it out. Then he went again to the open door.

I said, "Are you going back to Africa?"

He nodded.

"What are you on now?"

"Cannibalism! And Buya."

Buya was the little son of a Mujanzi chief who followed my father devotedly. He was eight years old and an avowed cannibal, boasting of the feasts he had certainly never eaten to innocent Africans from another tribe, who were horrified by him. I laughed at this, but my father said nothing more.

I heard him going upstairs. Once I might have followed him. Now I could not. The room was contaminated, and so was I. I had lied to the police. I had lied to my father. The first was certainly the worst, but it was the last that seemed so to me. Yet I was aware not so much of guilt as of apprehension that I might be found out. It was Zoltan who filled my thoughts. Would he ring me, would he write to me, would he perhaps call? Or would he forget all about me, a silly little schoolgirl whom he had kissed once, twice, who wore a childish frock, whose hair was not set, who had to go to bed early, to be ready for school the next day. He must know so many other women, all much more sophisticated than me, like Countess Asztalos, for whom he had made a paprika chicken — why was he making paprika chicken for her anyway? — and then I was consumed with frantic jealousy, sat down on my bed and cried, longing, wildly happy, afraid.

I did not think of the Life Society, or of grey and scarlet uniforms, except to find that an odd thought flitted through my confused mind, concerning, of all people, Miss Jessamy.

I realised of course that it was ridiculous to think of Miss Jessamy as a murderess. I had never up till now thought much of her at all. She came most Sundays for our musical afternoons, and I suppose I simply felt that this day must be for her the highlight of the week. She did not play the cello very well, but she was not too bad, and she never seemed to mind when my father, at his most dictatorial on these occasions, insisted on going over and over again a difficult passage. Mr. Goldschmidt listened to these tirades with perfect calm, but Miss Jessamy occasionally went pink and dropped her music. But it was all quite pleasant, and afterwards we would have our nice Sunday tea with the silver teapot, Crown Derby cups, little sandwiches and one of Mary's cakes. She makes beautiful cakes: I have never tasted anything like them. Then Miss Jessamy would go home to her bed-sitting-room in, I think, Putney, and I would forget all about her, only reflecting occasionally on the sad life she must lead, and feeling thankful that I had such a good time.

Now, however, I had seen Miss Jessamy in a different light. Whatever she had been last night, it was certainly not dull. she had even looked quite presentable, and had apparently made a great impression on Mr. Palotas who would, I thought, have despised this middle-aged woman. And there had been that strange malice about her that I had vaguely noticed before, but which this time could not be missed.

And, of course, that remark about *petits pains.*

Perhaps Miss Jessamy — how strange that after all this time I did not know her first name — belonged to what my father called a clan. Perhaps — it was inconceivable but then so was everything else — Mr. Gyori had discovered this, and she had murdered him. However, this really was absurd, and no doubt next Sunday we would be playing some trio and all would be as usual: Mr. Goldschmidt would be impeccably right, Miss Jessamy flustered, and my father shouting and brandishing his bow.

Then I forgot about Miss Jessamy. I lay down on the bed and dreamed of Zoltan, dreamed wild, crazy, disgraceful dreams that were lovely and shocking, that made me shake and glow. I did not think of poor little Mr. Gyori, now presumably in a mortuary, nor did I brood on the other shirt-fronted gentlemen who were no doubt being fiercely questioned by the police, if diplomatic immunity permitted this. But then I knew nothing of diplomatic immunity and cared less. As for Mrs. Bradley she would be having the time of her life, telling the tale to friends and neighbours. The police would be hard-pressed to get away from her, she would be so panting to recount everything over and over again.

Zoltan. I pulled the eiderdown over my head and spun myself stories. I heard him say, I could not keep away from you, I love you, Victoria, come away with me, I want to hold you in my arms for ever and ever—

"Victoria!"

Oh no, oh *damn!*

"Victoria! Michael on the phone for you."

Michael — What does he want? I don't want to talk to Michael. I have nothing to say to Michael. I don't want to see Michael ever again.

"Victoria!"

"Oh all right, Mummy, I'm coming."

And downstairs I stumble, hair on end — "Do you mean to tell me you're not dressed yet?" — tying my dressing-gown cord as I go, and tripping over a loose stair-rod that I know perfectly well is there but which I have forgotten.

"Victoria?"

"Hallo, Michael. Sorry to keep you waiting."

"I say, what a thing. Are you all right?"

83

"Of course I'm all right, don't be silly."

"I just couldn't believe it. I saw it in the paper this morning."

"I suppose you did. I suppose everyone did."

"You sound a bit funny. Are you really all right? You – you didn't see the body, did you?"

"I found it."

"Crikey! Have you had the doctor or anything?"

"What on earth would I want a doctor for? I'm all right. I've just told you."

A pause. I knew I was being horrid. I hated the sound of my own shrewish, nasty voice. I used to think occasionally that if Michael were a bit firmer with me, we would get on better, but then it was not in his character, he was a gentle boy. I even wondered sometimes if he was weak, but I do not think he was; we Katonas are a violent lot, really, and the Grant family is much more civilised, they never make scenes and I have never heard them shouting at each other. I began to grow ashamed of myself. It was after all nice of Michael to ring me, and natural too. I said at last into the silence, "I'm sorry, Mike. I'm awfully tired. It has been quite a day. I didn't mean to bite your head off."

He answered amiably enough, "Of course. I quite understand. I expect you'd rather not see anyone just now, but I could look in after school —"

"Oh thank you, but I think I'd rather not. I'll probably go to bed and try to relax a little. This has rather knocked me."

"Well, what about the weekend? There's rather a decent film on at the Roxy. It's got Claudette Colbert in it, and I know you like her. It's won a lot of awards too."

"I'm afraid I'm booked this weekend."

"Oh." I could hear that he was disappointed and hurt. We usually went out at weekends together. I said quickly, "But we could go next week. The parents don't care much for me going out after school, but I think I could persuade them, especially if I've done all my homework."

He cheered up at this, and we arranged our meeting. Only he said a little wistfully, "You're sure you wouldn't like me to come round? I wouldn't stay long, honestly."

I said crossly, "You just want to see the scene of the murder," and then to my surprise he rang off, without so much as a goodbye. I was very taken aback. I felt as if I had been slapped. It served me right, of course. I nearly rang him back to tell him to come if he wanted to, but then my mother, who had been hovering in the background, appeared behind me to say, "For pity's sake get some clothes on. It's nearly lunch time. Suppose the police came back or someone called — Will you please get dressed, Victoria. If you're feeling so ill you can't make the effort, you'd better go back to bed and I'll call the doctor."

"Oh Mummy, don't nag, I'm perfectly all right."

"Then get dressed!"

I wondered if Michael would ring again. He did not do so. I was both relieved and resentful. It was unusual for him to take offence. Perhaps some deep, inner instinct told him that I was no longer interested in him, that my mind was taken up with someone else. And I am afraid I then forgot about him. I dressed, thinking of Zoltan, I came down to lunch, thinking of Zoltan and, when at last I went to bed, dreamed the night away, blinking surlily at the morning light that broke my dreams.

But of course I could not prevent myself from looking forward to seeing my friends at school. There was such a lot to tell them. The police came back in the afternoon, but did not seem to be interested in me. They had a long talk with Mary and Maggie and, so Maggie told me later, seemed fascinated by our parrot who, in his usual obstructive way, chose at that moment to burst into Attilian.

"What's he saying?" the sergeant asked Mary, but she only said, "Oh, it's just a lot of gibberish. Be quiet, you silly old bird," then told him for the dozenth time how the poor, funny little gentleman took such a liking to Polly, and how the other handsome gentleman came down and made a new sauce for the fish.

I said to Maggie, "Did he kiss you?"

She went a bright pink. She told me not to be so cheeky, then was so convulsed in giggles that I began to suspect that Zoltan really had done so. I could see that life with such a man would have its complications, but I could hardly be jealous of Maggie, so I told her she was a naughty flirt and left her still giggling, the beautiful colour bright in her cheeks.

Chapter 4

I WAS GROWING strongly aware that there was something I must ask my father. After dinner I went up to see him, leaving my mother on the phone with Mrs. Bradley who was wild with curiosity as to what was happening now.

I did not want to enter the study. When at last I did, feeling a little sick and shaky, it all seemed the same as it had always been, only my father had moved the furniture round so that the place where the body had lain was covered up.

He did not greet me. He went on typing. I sat in the armchair and watched him. I loved the click-clack of the machine. I always found it a soothing sound. The books hemmed me in. The books were my fortress. I have never seen a room so overflowing with books. The shelves bulged with them, they were stacked in piles on the floor, and any space that was not so occupied was filled with weapons, photographs and the statues that so upset my mother.

I studied one of these. I suppose it was according to our standards rude: I could not see such a thing in the Grant household, and what Mrs. Bradley would say to it, I could not imagine. But somehow, compared with everything that had happened, it was decent, civilised and comforting: I said, the words coming out involuntarily, "That won't alter. It's — honest."

My father turned his head to look at me, over the big, horn-rimmed glasses that he wore when working. He said, "We should make a bonfire of them, and throw in the books on top. They are nothing after all, these things of mine. The source of the Nile. The discoveries of Benin. The Bushongo civilisation. Hottentots, the Trobrianders. People have wanted to find out. People have travelled for thousands of sweaty miles to explore, to see something new, to understand. That's all these books and statues represent. A small record of a vast effort, that in a few years' time will mean nothing, for the whole world will have changed and no one will care. I'm sentimental too, baby. The first person I met in Africa was a dying man in Boma, and all he said to me was, 'Go home'. Why not? There was nothing there but swamp and fever, disease, dirt and death. Yet I stayed. We all stayed, the Stanleys, the Burtons, the Spekes, the Livingstones. Don't ask me why. There was nothing, no place to sleep, nothing much to eat, no other white people to talk to. The only whites in Africa, apart from the missionaries, were the remittance men who were so in trouble everywhere that they could not go home. I remember Schumann. He was wanted in the French Congo, Angola and the Kamerun. For supplying native mutineers with British ammunition. And there was the chap we called Dirty Jim. But he was killed by his servant. It was a miracle he survived so long. Apart from that — Ah, it doesn't matter. You should go to bed, Victoria. You look pale. Leave me to my swamps, my fevers and my remittance men. They are all I need." Then he said, not speaking to me at all. "I wish I didn't always remember. I wish I could stop thinking of the stillness of the forest, the singing of my porters, the sight of the Kasai — It is like a superimposed film."

I said, "Daddy, please, I am just going to bed, but there's something I want to ask you."

"What? What?" His face changed. It was as if he had been dragged back from a long way off. He said, his voice thick with a kind of resentful despair, "Oh, what is it now? You're always wanting something. Are you out of pocket-money again?"

I said, as angry as he was, "That's not fair. I always manage my money very well. And it's an allowance. It's not pocket-money."

"All right. All right, baby. Calm down. Have a cigarette. What do you want to say to me?"

I was too tired to check myself. Indeed, everything that had happened, including the things my father did not know, had somehow unhinged me so that the words fell from me. I said, "You don't want to make a bonfire of your books. They are the only things that hold you here. Why do you go on talking like this about Africa? It's a quarter of a century ago. You are with us now, but you're not interested, are you? All these swamps and fevers and — and things. They're not even romantic. Oh Daddy, please don't talk like this any more. It frightens me. I'm so frightened already, I—"

Then I broke off for, goodness knows, I did not mean to talk like this, and what I really came to say was simple and unemotional.

He said in a calm, cold voice, "Why are you frightened?"

Why am I frightened? It is not just Mr. Gyori's murder. It is more than that. It is something that turns inside me like a piece of cold steel, I do not know why, I do not know—

"I don't know."

"Is there perhaps something you haven't told me?"

"No! It's nothing to do with that at all."

"Nothing to do with what?"

"Oh please don't nag at me. I'm so tired, I don't feel very well, I—" Then I went over to him and put my arms round him. He did not respond, only patted my shoulder.

Then he said, "I suppose I should never have left. It would have been better to die there. Only then I wouldn't have had you, would I? But I daresay you're right. Well, Victoria? Here I am in London, a stateless old man who's writing a book, who resents being disturbed by murder and who is making his daughter cry. What are you crying for? You're too old to cry. Here's my handkerchief. Blow your nose, stop lecturing me, and tell me what all this is about."

I obediently blew my nose. I thought, perhaps I should leave it, this is too much for him, this is taking him back not so much to Africa as to his home and childhood. But I had to speak now, so I said, "The police heard Polly speaking in Attilian."

This made him laugh, and he looked his old self again. "An erudite bird! I wish I could pick up languages so easily."

"Well, I think you ought to listen to what he says. It might be important. After all, the police can't be expected to understand."

"It'll just be nonsense. Probably the Attilian version of, Get on your perch."

"But it mightn't be. It might really mean something."

"If I know Polly," said my father dryly, "he'll speak in every language in the world except the one we want. But I'll try. And go to bed, baby, you look as if you need it, and I want to go on working."

I suspected he would never bother, but at least I had said it, got it off my conscience. And it was plain in the morning, when I went at last to school, that our parrot was acting true to form. Not one word of Attilian passed his beak. He gave a disgusting snuffle when he saw me, then as I went down the road, squawked out, "Scratch your poll, scratch your poll!"

"I'll take a hammer to your poll," I told him, and left him sniffing as I made my way to the bus-stop.

I knew now as I had known from the beginning that what had happened the day before yesterday would change our lives as irrevocably as the war that my father prophesied. My father, knowing this too, was escaping back to the one place where he had been happy. He talked of Africa often enough but never before like this. I believe he loved me as much as he could love anyone in a country where he was not at home, but I understood now for the first time that my mother's life must be impossible. It was not her fault that she wandered about jangling, half-ignoring us, trading on the deafness that pushed her more and more into her own world where we could not disturb her. There was nothing to tether her here, with a husband who was not there in spirit and a daughter — I had to face this — entirely concerned with her own affairs. I suppose they loved each other at the beginning, though it is hard to imagine one's parents in love; it seems somehow indecent. She had after all walked out of a wealthy home to marry a penniless anthropologist, and he — he was so handsome when young — must have known plenty of girls who would have been delighted to marry him. *You are with us now, but you are not interested.* That is what I told him. It was cruel of me, I had no right to speak like that, but it was true, it is true. He is afraid of us, afraid of what has happened: he needs warmth and security and happiness, but not from us, he will not permit us to encroach upon him.

And I found the water coming back into my eyes, and had to blow my nose in the bus, trying to look as if I had a cold.

When I arrived at my school, I saw at once that the staff had decided to ignore the whole sordid affair. Murder was not nice, murder was not the kind of thing young girls should discuss. I remember that once there was a terrible accident in the swimming-baths, where a very beautiful and talented girl was drowned, owing to a foolish, practical joke. It was dreadful, we were all completely shocked, and for a week nobody talked of anything else. Not one teacher, however, referred to the matter, though the effect on us was so violent that one or two girls were actually taken ill. It is as if adults believe that something that is not mentioned no longer exists. We were left, therefore, to whisper in corners, with the horror of it becoming magnified out of all proportion: our work suffered, we became jumpy and nervous, and it was not until after the funeral, to which we all sent flowers, that we began to recover.

I could see from Miss Thomas's expression that I was not to consider myself interesting or important, simply because I was involved in a murder. She made a point of greeting me when we passed each other in the corridor.

She said in a cool, level voice, "I hope you are feeling better, Victoria."

"Yes, thank you, Miss Thomas."

"We have had quite a few of you away. There seems to be some kind of tummy bug around. I'm glad you're all right now."

This really was a bit much, and I longed to say something like, There's a lot of murder around too, but of course I did not. Miss Thomas teaches history. She lives with Miss Hudson, the maths teacher, who is rather horrid and very masculine: we all think we know what this means but are too inhibited to put it into words. Lorna once insisted on lending me *The Well of Loneliness*, which I found dreary and boring: she did not make the actual comparison, but whenever I saw Miss Thomas and Miss Hudson together for a little while afterwards, I felt quite self-conscious. It is a pity because Miss Thomas is rather nice, she makes history very interesting and there is a curious, lost, unfulfilled air to her that makes people leave flowers on her desk, and prevents them from being rude to her.

However, this time I thought she was simply being stupid, especially as the moment I appeared, all my friends rushed towards me.

"Oh Victoria, how awful! Did you actually see the body? Have the police been interviewing you? What happened?"

Well, I am human and just as frightful as everybody else, so of course I gave my friends a slightly guarded account of what had happened, and indeed, we talked of nothing else, between classes and during break. Yet somehow it sounded unreal, even with Lorna. How can you really describe murder? How can you explain that when something so violent and sudden cuts across your life, the whole world changes about you? Perhaps it was Zoltan as much as the murder, but even while I was talking, telling everyone the same thing over and over again, I felt more and more remote as if somehow I was no longer Victoria Katona, who was in the Sixth, who would at the end of next year be going up to college, who was a prefect, who was usually top in exams.

It was Lorna who said, "Are you all right, honey?"

"Of course I'm all right. Oh, it was a terrible shock, I mean, nobody thinks this kind of thing really happens, but it's over and done with now, there's nothing anyone can do about it."

"You seem kind of different. Was it a good dinner-party? Until all this happened, of course."

"It was a marvellous dinner-party."

Lorna said wistfully, "It all sounds so grand. I've never met any Attilians. I suppose one of them did it."

"I don't know. Nobody knows." Then I burst out with something that I never intended to say. "Oh Lorna, I don't know how I'm going to stay on here. I feel I just can't bear it."

She was genuinely astonished. I have known Lorna for three years. she is a doctor's daughter and a pretty blonde. She proposes to go on the stage. I do not know how much talent she has, but she is very ambitious, she occasionally gets the odd job in a children's show, and sometimes I hear her lines. We have always got on since the day she was found powdering her nose. My school does not approve of such immoral goings-on, and there was a fearful row. It seemed absurd to me, even at the age of fourteen, and after that we took to walking round the playground together, arm in arm; we sat next to each other at school functions, and nowadays we sometimes go out to theatres and cinemas with our respective boy-friends. Lorna has a great many boy-friends and is far more sophisticated than I am. It is not a matter we discuss in detail, but sometimes she looks sideways at me as if to gauge how much I really know, and how much she dares tell me. My father likes her very much, chiefly because she is pretty and flirts with him: my mother thinks she is fast. But we tell each other almost everything, and this was an unexpected rift between us.

She said at last, "But what's happened, honey? I just don't understand. I know it must have been awful for you, but what's it got to do with school? You've always liked it here much more than I do. And you've only got another year. You'll probably be head girl. I heard Miss Mandeville saying that you were the obvious choice. Why are you laughing? What's the matter with you?"

What's the matter with me? Murder is the matter with me. Zoltan is the matter with me. The world is the matter with me. Head girl! The good girl of the school, telling people to stop talking, get into line, coping with crushes, wearing a nice new little badge — oh no, no, no!

"I don't know, Lorna. I just feel at the moment I can't bear it. I don't think I even want to go up to Oxford. Yes, I know I've always liked school. I've found it fun. I am not much good at sport, but I adore the work, and I enjoy so much being top in exams. But now since all this has happened — it's as if I feel I don't belong here any longer."

Lorna ruffled her fair, curly hair. She wore it in a bubble-cut. We all thought this rather daring, with our neat bobs, fringes and slides. She said "I expect it's still the result of the shock. It must have been awful. You'll get over it in a few days."

"I'm not sure if I'll ever get over it."

Lorna is too egotistic to bother about analysing other people, but she is very perceptive and she has known me for some time. She gave me a long, intense look. "Are you sure this is just the murder?" she said.

Of course I went scarlet, and at this she gave me another look, then moved a little away.

I said furiously, "Of course it's the murder. Surely that's enough. What else do you imagine it could be?"

"What else indeed?" said Lorna in her most refined R.A.D.A. accent. She did not pursue the matter, but I knew her well enough to see that this was by no means the end of it. She is a persistent girl, and extremely inquisitive. However, we began to talk of other things, her new boy-friend, the possibility of a pantomime at Christmas with Lorna playing a fairy, and a wonderful new lipstick she had just discovered — "it really is kiss-proof, I know." We talked no more of murder. We did the French Revolution with Miss Thomas, we read *As You Like It* with Miss Mandeville, with Lorna doing a spirited rendering of Rosalind, and we had a riotous lesson with Mademoiselle who is so much the stage mademoiselle that I can never quite believe in her. I think she must be a kind of special French export. And at half past four I came out of school to find Michael waiting for me: Lorna tactfully disappeared, and we stood there facing each other.

He looked different, but then the whole world was looking different. He is one year older than I am, but he looks very young, with a round face and a fresh complexion that any girl would envy; he is secretly ashamed of this as if pink cheeks are effeminate. He is intelligent, he has an unexpected sense of humour, and his present obsession is cricket. He proposes to read law like his father, who is a solicitor.

I greeted him a little stiffly, because I was embarrassed and a little ashamed of myself.

He said, "Shall we have a coffee? I thought you might need something. It must have been quite a day."

This was considerate of him when I had been so rude, but then Michael is always considerate. He has a very nice mother. You can always tell when boys have nice mothers. And it was in no way his fault that he was Michael Grant, not Zoltan Halasz. It was in no way his fault that I did not want a schoolboy, however charming, that all I wanted was a six-foot Attilian, far too old for me, and probably far too experienced. I did not think I would hear from Zoltan for a long time, I even suspected that I might not hear from him at all. But nonetheless I dashed into the hall every time the postman came, flushed in anticipation when the phone rang. Of course there was nothing. Of course. The letter was from some dull friend, the phone call was not for me at all. And I said to Michael that I would love a cup of coffee, and we went to a little teashop called Peg's Parlour, run by two old ladies in flowery overalls, and had our coffee and cakes. It was on my way home. We went there quite often, and the old ladies greeted us pleasantly, and the cat who always sat in the window, jumped on my knee.

I said at last, "I'm sorry I was so abrupt."

"Abrupt?"

"On the phone. I didn't mean to be. I don't really think you just wanted to see the scene of the murder."

"Well," he said consideringly, putting three lumps of sugar into his coffee, "I wouldn't, would I? I mean, it's not my thing." He raised his eyes to mine. He had beautiful eyes, a clear dark blue with long lashes. I suppose he is ashamed of this too, but all the girls at school think they are gorgeous. He inherits them from his mother, together with the peach complexion. "After all," he said, "we get enough court cases at home, what with Dad and one thing and another." Then, "You don't look very well."

I said huffily, "I suppose that means I'm looking a fright."

"Not at all. You've just got dark circles under your eyes. I suppose you didn't sleep much after all that's been happening, police and so on. It is perfectly understandable," said Michael. He talks in this pompous way when he is uneasy and embarrassed. Then he said, beckoning one of the old ladies for the bill, "I think you really ought to do a flick. It might take your mind off things." Then suddenly he laughed, looking very young again. "I say, which one of them did it? You must have some idea. Dad thinks it's all rather sinister and political."

"I don't really know. I rather fancy Miss Jessamy."

And I told him all about Miss Jessamy and the *petits pains*, and somehow this made things better. We gossiped

94

and giggled, just like old times, and discussed the films we wanted to see.

He saw me home. He is very punctilious in such matters. He is the kind of boy who always walks on the road side of the pavement, takes your arm at crossings and, though we usually go dutch on our outings, always does the actual paying. He sometimes brings my mother flowers and, once when she was ill, wrote to her. Both my parents approve of him: sometimes I think they are astonished that I have chosen someone so presentable. There is, however, an ironic streak in him that they know nothing about, and which would surprise them. Perhaps this is inherited from his solicitor father. He once remarked that my mother's deafness was a highly personal thing: she seemed to switch her hearing on and off as if it were a deaf-aid, and always heard what she was not meant to hear, even if it were a whisper. And even now as we walked home, to save the bus fare — my monthly allowance was nearly finished — I was conscious that he was closely observing me.

He said, as we came up to the house, "It's peculiar that things like this should happen to one's friends. It's the sort of thing you read about in the papers, and then of course one doesn't take it seriously. To have a murder in your own home must be the most frightful shock. I expect you won't get over it for a long time."

"What on earth do you mean?"

The parrot, put out in the area to enjoy the last rays of the evening sun, suddenly burst into a prolonged squawk of what was plainly Attilian. I do not speak Attilian at all, except to say yes and no and count to ten, but I instinctively recognise it. I said furiously, "Oh, that abominable bird! Sometimes I think he's responsible for the whole beastly affair."

"Oh, I shouldn't think so," said Michael. He is a literal kind of person, and at this minute it made me want to scream. He looked down into the area. "You have got your knife into that poor bird, haven't you? What's he saying?"

"Oh, I don't know. It's Attilian. I haven't got my knife into him at all, I just loathe him. Why do you say I won't get over it? I've got over it already. I'm very resilient. You ought to know that."

95

"You've changed," said Michael, looking away from me and down at the pavement. One of our neighbours passed us and looked at us curiously; I wished her good evening, and she scurried by as if she felt she were intruding. He went on, "I think something like this must be so violent and unexpected that it cuts right into you. I don't suppose I'm putting this very well, but I just don't see how you can forget it in a few days. You don't know how you've changed, but I do. You're completely different."

"Oh don't be so silly. Of course I'm not different."

"You don't see yourself," said Michael.

There was a curious, withdrawn expression on his face that made him look older. It made me blush, for it was almost as if he were seeing Zoltan's shadow behind me.

He said, "Let's make it the weekend after all. I'll call for you on Saturday. It'll be my treat."

"Oh no — That's not fair."

"It'll be my treat. Are you having your musical do on Sunday?"

Michael of course knows all about our trios, but he does not like classical music so I never ask him. His present passion is Maurice Chevalier.

I said truthfully that I had not even thought about it. "I suppose so. There's no reason why we shouldn't. The police will hardly come at the weekend, and I think they're concentrating on the Legation. Daddy spends a great deal of time there. They've done all the finger-print stuff and interviewing and so on. I don't suppose we'll see them again."

"Did they interview you?"

"Of course."

"And did you tell them the truth?"

Then I lost my temper. I felt as if I were being cross-examined. I shouted at him in the true Katona scream, "I just don't know what's the matter with you to-day. How dare you interrogate me like this? Of course I told the truth. Do you suppose I'd lie to the police?"

"Most people do," said Michael. "My father would tell you that. I just wondered."

"Well, you can stop wondering. And I'm not going out

96

with you on Saturday. I'm never going out with you again. We're finished. You – you bore me."

He went quite pale. He must have seen that the tears were already springing to my eyes, but I think he was too angry to care. We sometimes had an argument, but we had never really quarrelled before. I turned away from him, stumbling up the steps because I could no longer see clearly, and his voice, muted and sulky, came to me.

"If that's how you feel," he said, "I don't think I want to see you again either. I don't know what's happened to you. I suppose you've fallen for one of those ghastly Attilian types you have to dinner. Personally I couldn't care less. If you change your mind, you'll have to ring me. I certainly won't get in touch with you."

Then he was gone, leaving me in tears.

"What's all that about?" asked my mother, who was in the hall and who, inevitably, had heard the end of this exchange.

I almost shouted at her, "Oh nothing! He's just being idiotic. I'm going to get myself a new boy-friend."

"What are you crying for?" said my mother.

"I'm not crying!"

"Well, it looks like it to me. There's a letter for you. I don't know who it's from. It's typewritten. "

I snatched it from her. She stood there waiting for me to open it, but I simply shoved it into my blazer pocket and made for the stairs.

"Who's it from?"

"How should I know? It doesn't look particularly interesting. Oh Mummy, do leave me alone. I'm tired, and I've got masses of homework to do."

My mother watched me as I went upstairs. I dared not rush. I looked down at her when I reached the half-landing. I saw that she had changed too. She wore the air of one enormously enjoying herself. I believe that for the first time she was her old self again, delighting in all the drama and notoriety. Neighbours who hardly ever spoke to her, now came running, ostensibly to exchange the time of day. Shops gave her priority, and people nudged each other when she came down the street. I suppose life with my father was boring, exasperating and occasionally frightening: the scenes she made were probably to cheer herself up. The only thing they really had in common was me, and my mother, as she once confessed, always wanted a son, so I was a disappointment too. Africa meant nothing to her at all, and the social side of our life terrified her, except for the musical afternoons which must have been faintly reminiscent of life with her grandmother, though of course not nearly so grand. Her main interest was the household accounts, which she did very badly, but over which she spent hours. She was always talking of economising, and used to rate Mary for spending an extra penny on the weekend joint, and then she would dash out to buy some smoked salmon because, as she said, she fancied it. I sometimes thought that if Mary and Maggie had not been so honest, they could have made a fortune out of us, for my mother was so concerned with the actual figures that she never considered money at all.

Mostly she slopped round the house, jangling, reading, playing the piano, and from time to time knitting me sweaters that were always three sizes too large, and which, of course, I never wore. She never noticed: she forgot about them the moment they were finished. When we went on holiday which we did every year in the summer, she slept most of the day, ate greedily between siestas and drank a great deal of wine. I have never seen her tipsy, but I think that in different circumstances she might have drunk her life away.

Now she looked almost young again, like the girl who loved dancing, and who crept back through her window late at night. There was colour in her cheeks, a smile on her lips. She must have been a very pretty girl when she met my father. The police might not come to us any more, but we were still news, and she would run to greet my father when he came back from the Attilian Legation. She even invited the dreary girl-friend to tea so as to boast of all the excitement, and I am sure that at intervals she shook her head knowingly, indicating that there was a great deal she was not allowed to discuss.

She should never have married my father. She should have found herself a nice businessman who left the house at nine and came back at six: there would have been a pretty suburban house with no rude statues, and the neighbours would call in regularly for gossip and tea.

She called up to me now, "I expect all your friends were very interested in your news."

I answered untruthfully, "Oh, there was too much work to do. We really hadn't time to talk about it."

I saw her mouth droop disappointedly. I felt very mean. She would so have loved to hear that everyone at school rushed to question me. It would have made her feel important by proxy, and we would have been friendly and chatty together as mother and daughter should be. But I could not bear it, I knew the letter in my pocket was from Zoltan, and all I wanted was to reach my room and lock the door so that I could read it in peace.

I sat on the bed and tore the envelope open. I was shaking and shivering as if I had a fever. I looked down at the letter through eyes blurred with excitement. I had not expected him to type it, but then he was a journalist, he probably never thought of writing by hand. Only the signature was his, large, sprawling and dramatic, written with a very thick nib.

"Dear English Miss Victoria," he wrote, a strange affected way of addressing me which in anyone else would have infuriated me, but which now seemed to me the most beautiful thing in the world—

Dear English Miss Victoria,

I wish to take you out to tea. Do you think you could steal out this Saturday afternoon and meet me outside the underground station at Earl's Court? We will make this a secret rendez-vous, we will be very wicked, we will not tell father and mother. If I do not hear from you, I will expect you. I will be waiting for you.

And then simply his name, flamboyantly scrawled across the page.

It did not at first enter my bemused head to query why I should not tell my parents. I was after all seventeen, I was not a little girl, and there was nothing very wicked about meeting an Attilian journalist for tea. It was not even as if he had asked me to his rooms, though I would have gone without a murmur if he had done so. My parents would be entertained. My father would stare at me in surprise for, though he now referred to me as grown-up, he still in his heart thought of me as a little girl. My mother would be greatly amused. If she had to be lumbered with a daughter instead of the son she wanted, she might as well have one who provided drama and excitement.

Then I suddenly knew that my parents would not be amused at all. There had been a murder in my home. Zoltan had been one of the guests when the murder was committed. Neither my father nor my mother would think it right for me to go out with a man twice my age who, however charming, was still a suspect.

None of this naturally had the least effect on me. I was in a daze of excitement and ecstasy. I sat there, reading and rereading the note, thinking mainly of what I could wear, how I would do my hair. I pictured our meeting, and the very thought of it choked me with joy. This was like nothing that had ever happened to me, and the letter like nothing I had ever received. When Michael wrote to me, it was either "Darling", or, "Hallo, old thing", and it was usually signed, "Yours till hell freezes", which seemed amusing at the time but which was really kid's stuff and in no way romantic. We had had our moments, especially at the beginning, but not like this, not like this—

I spent the rest of the week in a daze. My father did not notice, for indeed he was hardly with us, he was back by Lake Tanganyika, desperately digging his heels in so as not to be dragged back to a world he feared and hated. My mother did notice, but put it down to reaction from shock. I do not imagine she ever thought of me in connection with love or passion. When I said, lying with a desperate audacity, that I was going out to tea on Saturday, she simply said, "Oh you've made it up then. I thought you would. I never thought you'd hold out for long."

I dared not pretend that I was going out with Michael, for it was possible that he might telephone. I said we had not made it up at all, it was definitely all over. I was going out to tea with Lorna, and I might not be in for supper. This happened often enough, and my mother accepted it without question, only saying as she always did that I was not to be too late.

I told Lorna next day that I was using her as an alibi. She gave me a wise, wicked look. She has after all made use of me in her time, though her parents are more tolerant than mine and permit her far more liberty.

"I suppose," she said little wistfully, "I mustn't ask. It's not that Michael anyway."

"No. It's not Michael."

"Well, I expect he's a bit dull. He's got dishy eyes, though. All right, honey. Don't do anything I wouldn't do."

"Lorna," I said, hesitated, then stopped.

She looked at me, and I managed to stammer out, "Could you possibly lend me a smart blouse? I've got quite a decent skirt, but Mummy always buys me such babyish things, and I do want to look — well, sort of sophisticated."

This was entirely up Lorna's street. Her face lit up with excitement. I saw that if I were not careful, I would end dolled up like a demi-mondaine. Lorna's taste is for the flamboyant, and she wears the sort of bra that makes her bosom stick out in two points. It looks a little strange under a gym tunic. Our sports mistress, who has no bosom at all, has commented on this several times: she thinks it is positively indecent. When Lorna, who always says what she thinks, exclaimed, "You don't want me all pendulous like a pregnant monkey, do you?" she was sent to the headmistress's study for rudeness and insolence. I do not think she meant to be either rude or insolent: it is just her way of speaking.

She now eyed me up and down in a considering fashion. She said, "I'll bring a couple for you to choose from. You'll have to do something with your hair, honey."

I do not know where she gets this "honey" stuff from. Probably it comes from one of the shows she has been in. It is somehow part of her. In anyone else it would seem affected, but from her it sounds perfectly natural. I let her push my hair back, pull it up on top, drape it over my cheeks. Her face was rapt with concentration; she might have been preparing me for some grand theatrical role. In the end I began to giggle, and she tapped my cheek disapprovingly. "None of that girly stuff, please," she said. "I gather your gentleman's one of the sophisticated kind. In fact I suspect he's an Attilian—"

101

She saw my face change, and giggled herself. "Ah," she said, "I thought so. You dark horse, you. But I can tell you this, he won't care for giggling schoolgirls. You can be demure and shy, if you want to, you can even gaze at him with goo-goo eyes, but no giggling, honey, whatever happens."

In the end when, stiff with nerves, I left my house on Saturday afternoon, I was barely capable of smiling, much less giggling. I had to creep out without my mother seeing me. If she hears what no one wants her to hear, she also sees what no one wants her to see. She would see the forbidden lipstick, and she would know at once that my hair, carefully brushed into a Veronica Lake droop, and the black and white check blouse with its big bow, were not for Lorna. I suppose that what I wore was not really striking. I had turned down a satin blouse and a chiffon one with lace, and I flatly refused to wear one of Lorna's bras, though she brought it to school and scandalised a junior teacher by waving it seductively in front of me.

She wailed at me, "But honey it will give you such a lovely shape. And you've got such nice bubbies—"

"Lorna!"

"Oh, don't be so prissy. You flatten them down as if they're ironed. There's nothing immoral about them, hon. We've all got 'em, you don't have to hide them as if you're back in the twenties. I'm sure—"

"Lorna, no! And do put it away. Mademoiselle will be here at any moment."

"I didn't think you were such a prig," said Lorna quite crossly, but she tucked the bra — an extraordinary affair with blue bows on it — into her briefcase, where it must have cohabited strangely with the textbooks. She sighed resignedly as I chose the quietest blouse, gave me some last words of advice on how to get my man, then settled down to the French lesson, for which as usual she had done no work whatsoever. I have never known anyone who did less work than Lorna, her marks were a disgrace and her exam results a disaster, but everyone liked her for she disarmed reproaches with a quite devastating charm.

It was a pure coincidence that the day before I was to meet Zoltan, when I had the check blouse and a pair of ear-rings carefully tucked into a carrier bag, I should be summoned to Miss Carter's study.

We all like Miss Carter. The headmistress before her was an old devil, cordially hated by staff and pupils alike. She would have done well in Dotheboys Hall. If she had been permitted to use the cane, she would have delighted in beating us. But Miss Carter is young and charming, and normally I would have enjoyed the prospect of talking to her, for, as far as I knew, I had done nothing wrong, this could not be a telling-off. But I was longing to get home, to dream and brood: I slouched into the study looking so depressed that Miss Carter burst out laughing.

"What's the matter with you, Victoria?" she said. "You look as if you're about to meet your doom. Sit down, my dear. I may be able to cheer you up. I've got good news for you. At least I hope you will think it good news."

It seemed that the general decision was that next term I would be head girl. Our present one, a nice, sporty creature, splendid at netball and swimming, and passionately adored by the junior school, was leaving to take up a teaching post in the north.

"We all thought," said Miss Carter, eyeing me thoughtfully as if somehow she were seeing through the carrier bag to the wanton blouse, "that you would be the ideal person to follow her. You have a very good record, Victoria. Your work is extremely good. I know you're a little shy, but I feel the extra responsibility is just what you need. You are a conscientious girl, and the juniors respect you."

I could only think that this had happened at the worst possible moment. I do not feel that I am a very strong person, but I suppose I do my best, in my own way, and this was after all quite an honour, it would probably make a difference to me when I left college and had to apply for a job. And now it simply seemed to me absurd. Here I was, about to meet in a clandestine fashion the great love of my life, prepared to lie myself to hell for him, deceiving my parents, and about to put on a borrowed blouse from Paris — Lorna told me this, but I do not believe it — and my headmistress proposed to make me head girl. I would have a little shield to wear on the bosom that Lorna so condemned. I would have to make speeches at prize-givings, receive guests and quell insubordinate juniors who were talking in the library. It was not only absurd, it was ironic. I felt I just could not bear it. I did not know what to say.

My silence and downcast appearance must have been disconcerting, but Miss Carter, astute as she was, fortunately misinterpreted it.

She said gently, "I know you've been having a bad time these last few days. I didn't speak to you about it because I thought you'd rather not, but I really am sorry, Victoria. It must have been quite dreadful. You're a very sensitive person so it probably hit you harder than most. But I understand that the matter now really concerns the Attilian Legation, so I hope you will perhaps be able to forget about it." She gave me a half-smile. "You see, I'm as inquisitive as the next. I read my papers. How are you feeling? Are you getting over the shock?"

This was so kind that, what with my emotional state and the astonishment of being created head girl, I nearly burst into tears. Miss Carter must have noticed this as she noticed most things, and to my complete surprise produced a packet of cigarettes from her desk drawer and offered me one.

"I know you smoke," she said with the half-smile again. "I once saw you stubbing out a cigarette in the cloakroom. You do see that that must never happen again, don't you? But I think I hardly need to tell you that. You can regard this as your farewell school cigarette. I suppose I've no business to offer you one. What do your parents have to say about it?"

"My father buys me a weekly tin of fifty!"

"Then there's nothing more to say. Besides, I smoke myself." We both puffed away for a moment, then she said, "Is there anything wrong? Apart from this horrible murder, I mean." She added, almost timidly, "If I could help—"

"Oh no, thank you. There's nothing wrong. And I — I would be very happy to be head girl. Thank you for offering it to me. I only hope I'll be all right and not disgrace you."

I had the horrid feeling while I was speaking that "Zoltan" was written in large letters across my forehead, and the word "love" emblazoned on my tunic. Miss Carter, unlike some of the other members of the staff, looks as if she knows what love means. Lorna once said that she was sure she was living in sin with some gorgeous man saddled with a wife who would not divorce him. From Lorna this is an enormous compliment: to her most middle-aged women are one of three things — frustrated spinsters, maniacs or lesbians. I cannot really believe that Miss Carter lives in sin: I doubt if she would have the time, but she certainly is neither frustrated nor lesbian. However, from the way she was looking at me, I could see that she suspected my emotional state was not entirely due to the murder.

She said briskly, "I don't suppose you'll disgrace us. I wouldn't have proposed you if I thought you'd be no good. Put that cigarette out before you go, won't you?"

I forgot about this on the way home. I managed to dodge Lorna who would still be bursting with good advice; she would no doubt go on about the bra which she was quite capable of waving about in the middle of the road. It is true that I was a little tempted, but it would make me look as if I were trying to impress, besides it would be like wearing a pin-cushion and I would be constantly glancing down at myself.

The evening was impossible. I was so excited that I simply could not keep still; I could not eat either and at this — I normally have an enormous appetite — my mother grew suspicious.

"You're sickening for something," she said, then with that odd, cunning perception that is so inconsistent with the rest of her character, she demanded suddenly, "Why did you quarrel with Michael?"

But I merely said that I was perfectly well, that Michael bored me, and continued on my way, to sort out my nicest underclothes and my best silk stockings, the ones with the embroidered clock at the sides.

However, before I went to bed, I looked in at my father's study. He had been almost silent throughout dinner. He looked very pale. The moment the meal was over he went upstairs, while my mother jangled and grimaced, muttering, "And what am I supposed to do with myself? It's a fine household with you working like a slave and Victoria developing a chill or something."

105

He paid her no attention which indeed was his habit, but he did look very strange, and I felt I must find out what was the matter. I had washed my hair and wrapped a scarf round it: it would take a good hour to dry, and a chat with my father would while away the time and perhaps calm me down.

He sat at his desk as always, but he was not typing. He had not even taken the cover off the machine. He was chain-smoking. The ashtray was full of stubs. He looked at me as if he did not know who I was. The smoke and despair surrounded him.

I said, "Hallo, Daddy." Then, "Are you all right? You're not getting another attack of malaria, are you?"

For malaria was still a concrete link with Africa; from time to time he had a violent attack that left him shaking with fever and swallowing down quinine like sugar lumps.

He said, "No. Why have you got that thing round your head?"

"I've just washed my hair. Isn't it malaria? You don't look very well."

He said, "I'm all right." Then, "No, I'm not all right."

"What's the matter? Please tell me."

He did not answer me directly. I am not sure if he was answering me at all. It was like a record on the turn-table. "When the war comes," he said, "we Attilians will be on the wrong side. You know that, don't you? We were on the wrong side last time, but we never learn, we never learn. The Nazis will take over Attilia, and men like Palotas will be in power. He's a good henchman. He's fine at licking feet when it suits him. It's a good thing for poor Goldschmidt that he lives here, though I don't know if it will do him much good in the end. There won't be many Jews left in the world when it's all over. There won't be much left anywhere. It would have been better to have no children. This will be no world for anyone."

"Daddy—" But I did not know what to say. I was to be head girl, I was in love, and tomorrow I was meeting Zoltan. My father's remarks held no substance for me. I was young and happy and alive, and he was talking of war and death and apparently wishing I had never been born.

He said as he had said once before. "I should never have left. And now it is all vanishing. I cannot even remember. A lake. A forest. And the men singing — I

106

don't know any longer what they sang. I cannot hear the forest silence. I can't see the Kasai any more. Once I could retreat there, but now even the retreat is gone. I shall never find it again. I can only think of war and murder. You don't remember the last war—"

"Daddy, I was only born just after the armistice!"

"So you were, so you were. You were a victory baby. I wanted to call you Bettina after my mother, but Helen insisted on Victoria. You were a funny baby. The doctor said your mother would die if you were big, and along you came, eight and a half pounds, with no trouble at all." And though the words were light, he looked at me as if he thought it would better for all of us to die.

I said, "Why are you so upset? Has anything awful happened? What is going on about the murder? Have they found out who did it?"

"How should I know? They wouldn't tell me. I'm not important enough. But they've dug up a number of things, baby. Things I knew about all along, but never mentioned. They are hunting for the headquarters of the Attilian Life clan, where everyone is waiting for the Nazis."

"But the Nazis will never get here!" Then I said in desperation because, dreadful as it sounds, he was exasperating me: I could not bring myself to feel sorry for him, sitting there full of doom and gloom and self-pity, "Would you like a drink, Daddy? I could fetch you something."

He stared at me. I think he was seeing me properly for the first time. He did not answer the suggestion of a drink. He never drank much. My mother really is the drinker in our family. He said sharply, "There's something the matter with you. You look quite different. What is it? I want you to tell me."

"There's nothing the matter with me." But that beastly tell-tale colour was flooding my cheeks. I could feel the heat of it engulfing me.

"What are you doing tomorrow?"

"I'm going to tea with Lorna."

"Lorna? Oh yes." He was, thank goodness, away again; his eyes moved from me. "Pretty little girl. I expect she has a great many boy-friends."

'Oh yes. Dozens of them."

He said with an unexpected ferocity, "You be careful, Victoria. I don't want to make you conceited, but you are pretty too. Don't let it give you ideas. If you ever behave badly, it will be the worse for you. I do not permit any wanton behaviour. We are far too indulgent about sex these days. I will not have any daughter of mine disgracing herself. I'll tell you this. If you ever do anything wrong, you can expect no leniency from me. This is a wicked enough world without indecency and immorality being encouraged."

I was so taken aback that I stammered out without thinking, "What do you mean? Do you think I'm going to have a baby or something?"

He jumped to his feet, shooting his chair back. He came to stand over me. I thought he was going to hit me. I was incredulous and terrified.

He shouted at me, "Don't you ever say anything like that again. Do you hear me? It may be the kind of filthy talk you indulge in with your friends, but never speak like that to me. Go to bed. Go to bed at once. I'm ashamed of you. I never thought a daughter of mine could say such a thing."

I was angry enough not to obey immediately. I stood there looking defiance at him. He had never spoken to me in such a way before. He was a kind man. He was a great one for lame dogs. He always talked to children in the street. Once when we were on a bus he spent all the journey soothing a grizzling baby with his hunter watch, getting the child to blow on it, then pressing the spring to open it. He never mentioned the innumerable people he helped. My mother who tends to be tight with money whenever she bothers to think about it, always suspected that his friends borrowed from him indiscriminately, and sometimes rated him for being so silly and extravagant. I think he has no sense of money whatsoever. As for me, he was always gentle with me, interested in what I was doing and delighted in any small success. When I really wanted to please him, I used to ask him to help with my homework, especially mathematics at which I am particularly bad. It is true that, though the results were correct, the methods were extraordinary, and Miss Hudson, bad-tempered at the best of times, used to be very sarcastic about it, but he was so delighted with himself that I simply did not care. And now he was shouting at me, as if I really were having a baby: if this happened I began to think that he would behave like the parent in a Victorian melodrama and throw me out into the snow.

I was bitterly hurt and very afraid. I knew that in a moment I would begin to cry. I turned away from him and went to the door.

He said as if nothing had happened, "Goodnight, baby. Sleep well."

But I could not answer him. As I shut the door, which I just managed not to slam, I heard him give a deep sigh. On my way down I heard him begin typing.

I cried for a little while, mostly through temper. Then I recovered, mopped myself up, gazing anxiously at my eyes lest they were swollen, and began to sort out what I was going to wear tomorrow. I dared not put out Lorna's blouse in case my mother should come in, but it looked so pretty wrapped in tissue paper in my drawer that I gloated over it for several minutes. And now my excitement was enough to take my breath away, and thoughts were stirring within me that I had never suspected existed, provoked largely by my father's tirade.

I hope I remember this when I have children of my own: parents, when they forbid you to do something, simply put ideas in your head.

There was the little matter of Pepys' *Diary*. I was always allowed to read what I liked, and roamed freely about a house crammed with books, but my father once took it into his head to forbid the *Diary*, of which we had a rare, unexpurgated edition, gorgeously bound in red tooled leather. I simply cannot imagine why he did this. I was ten at the time, not of the age to be remotely interested in seventeenth-century diaries in twelve volumes, but, of course, after this the one thing in the world I longed to read was Samuel Pepys, of whom I had never so far heard. I waited until a day when my parents were out to lunch, then I crept to the glass-fronted bookcase where the forbidden works lay, and took out the first volume.

I will never forget my feelings of terror and guilt as I opened it. I half expected a snake to slide out at me. And I was of course bored to death. I did not understand the language which was, I suppose, my father's reason for the veto, and the only impression I received was of a silly, vain little man who was always carrying on with his wife's servant girls, and whose more private manners seemed to me utterly disgusting. I remember that I looked up the word "piss" afterwards and blushed scarlet at the enormity of it. The main result was to put me against poor Pepys for years: it was only much later when I read an illustrated, expurgated edition that I realised what an interesting man he really was.

Now as I carefully combed out my hair and put fresh pins in so that it would look good in the morning, I found myself thinking of what it would be like to have Zoltan's baby. Poor Zoltan! How horrified he would be if he could look into my mind! We were after all only going to have tea together. But I could not get the idea out of my mind. I continued to brood over it in bed. It was a strange, almost immaculate conception, with the preliminaries not so much blurred as completely ignored: I knew my physical facts but perhaps they frightened me, I chose to push them away.

My father's words were intended as a dreadful warning: they were instead an incitement. I believe that in a way I now began to grow up: boy-friends had simply been people to go out with, to kiss, to flirt with, and now I saw that there was a relationship involved, a progress, even though it might end in my being thrown out of the house.

Chapter 5

I ARRIVED AT the station twenty minutes early. I had just enough sense left in my whirling mind not to stand there waiting. "Never seem too eager," Lorna said. "Always be a few minutes late." She was always full of such maxims. I do not suppose she put them into practice any more than any other female. But I knew it would not be right for Zoltan to find me leaning against the wall, so I walked round and round the station, studying the advertisements with an absurdly meticulous attention, and all the time peering sideways to see if Zoltan had arrived.

He was five minutes late, and we nearly ran each other down, for he was coming from one direction and I from the other. He greeted me with a cool friendliness, kissed me on the cheek and, as he did so, waved his hand at an approaching taxi. I saw his eyes move briefly to the check blouse and then to the newly-washed hair which really did look nice, but he made no comment, and we sat side by side in the taxi, with a decent six inches between us.

Then he seemed to relax. He said with a smiling sigh, "Oh, this is good, this is very good. Have you told your parents of our assignation, or are you a bad girl, Miss Victoria?"

"I am a bad girl," I said, and could not prevent myself from smiling back.

"That is even better. We are going to Gunter's, and I shall feed you up on beautiful cream cakes." Then he said suddenly, "Do you think your father would really mind you coming out with me?"

"Yes, I think he would very much."

"Why?" There was a wary note in his voice that surprised me, but I answered truthfully because I could think of nothing else to say.

"It would be the murder. You were after all at the dinner party, and Dad — my father probably doesn't

111

want me mixed up in the business. Besides, I don't think he would like me going out with someone older than myself. He is a very puritan sort of man, and he has these old-fashioned ideas."

We were by now in Gunter's, and I had in front of me a plate of the most magnificent cakes I had ever seen, together with a tray of little sandwiches cut in triangles with the crust removed. We always have sandwiches at home for Sunday tea, but even Maggie, who prepares them with great care, had never achieved anything like this. I could not help thinking that it must take the cook hours to cut up all this bread, then I met Zoltan's eyes as he faced me across the little round table, and all thoughts of sandwiches, together with my appetite, vanished.

He had strange eyes. I thought they were very beautiful, though I suppose one does not say this of a man. They were a light grey, with long, dark lashes that would have had Lorna swooning, and they seemed to me to reveal no expression, though they were fixed on me.

He said after a pause, "How old do you think I am?"

"Oh, I've no idea—"

"Come now. I'm not a vain old lady clinging to her youth. Make a guess. I promise not to be offended."

I genuinely had no idea at all. I am not very good with ages, though Lorna says it is easy with women: you look at their necks and their hands. I knew he was much older than I was, but then I am only seventeen, and when you are very young, anyone over twenty seems positively decrepit. I was terrified of offending him, despite his promise. Then I saw that he was silently laughing at me, and this made me cross enough to regain my courage.

"I should think," I said, "you're about thirty."

He said, "Bravo! But I'm not, you know. I am even older. Miss Victoria, I hereby confess that I am an old, old man of thirty-four. Your father is quite right. I have no business to be taking you out to tea. Of course you could look upon me as an uncle. That would make it very correct."

Somehow this emboldened me. Suddenly I did not feel like a schoolgirl at all, and I sensed too that he did not regard me as a schoolgirl. Something in the way he looked at me, even in the way he laughed at me, made me know that he found me pretty — and Lorna's blouse really was lovely, it was a pity after all that I had not accepted the bra, I should have liked him to see that I had nice breasts.

I said, helping myself to a little sandwich, "Of course, if you want me to. How do I address you then? As Mr. Halasz or as Uncle Zoltan?"

I think this took him aback. It was of course pure cheek, but then he had invited it. He burst out laughing and reached out for my hand which he patted, then released.

"I think," he said, "I deserve that. But I did not mean to patronise you. I couldn't. You are too pretty. You are the prettiest girl I have ever taken out to tea."

"Do you make a habit of it then, Uncle Zoltan?"

I suppose that in our own way, in my completely in-experienced way, we were already making love. It did not yet enter my head that we might be kissing, it certainly did not enter it that we might be doing a great deal more, but the atmosphere between us now was as electric as a thunderstorm, and my impudence came out like a declaration of war.

He gave me a long look. I do not know what he saw. He said dryly, without a smile, "It is just as well for you that we are in a most respectable tea-shop, Miss Victoria." Then he laughed again. "Shall we call it pax? Is that not what you say in this country? You will call me Zoltan, as if I were a boy again, and I will drop the 'Miss'. Why are you not eating your cream cakes? You cannot be afraid for your figure. I don't think a dozen cakes would harm it. And that is a very attractive blouse you are wearing. It makes you look older. Almost eighteen."

"It comes from Paris," I said.

I daresay he knew it did nothing of the kind. He was the sort of man who is knowledgeable about ladies' clothes. But he only said, "You are an extravagant young lady. That is how it should be. Are you engaged, Victoria? Do you not have a boy-friend? I think you must have a legion of them. In Dunavar we would not let you out alone."

I thought briefly and meanly of Michael. Poor Michael. He was nothing, he was a little boy. I felt I never wanted to see him again. But I only smiled as if I were Helen of Troy with an army of lovers to destroy the world for

113

me, and of course this amused him, I could see it did. Perhaps it touched him too. I do not know. But I met his eyes and then I was afraid, I became a schoolgirl again, a schoolgirl out of her depth. Once when I was learning how to swim I jumped into the deep end by mistake. I was panic-stricken. There were of course a dozen people to haul me out, but in my fright I nearly drowned. I felt like this now. I could not swallow the cream cake on my plate. The fencing between us, the silly words, meant nothing, but the way he was looking at me, the way I felt, terrified me because it was so violent, so strong. I was thankful that the table was between us.

He said, "I wanted to ring you. I felt I should not. I suppose I shouldn't have invited you out. Will you come out with me again?"

"Yes."

"Do you mean that?"

"Yes."

"Even if we do not tell your parents?"

"Yes."

"Yes, yes, yes! You sound such a good little girl, but your eyes are not so virtuous, Victoria. You have the most beautiful eyes I have ever seen, but I daresay your lovers have already told you so. What would happen if your father found out?"

"I think — I think he would be absolutely furious, I am not sure if he would ever forgive me."

"Oh, I can't believe it. Such a kind man and with such a beautiful daughter."

"You don't know my father." As I said this I remembered last night's conversation, and I suddenly shivered.

He said in a rough voice, "No. I am beginning to see I do not. But if ever he frightens you, you are to come straight to me. Is that understood? Here — This is my address." He scribbled something down, pushed the slip of paper across to me, then went on, "It doesn't matter if it's the middle of the night."

I said almost inaudibly, "I think he would shoot you."

The light grey eyes dilated a little. But he only said, "Would he now! We seem to be leading dangerous lives, you and I."

Then I had to laugh too, though I was nearer crying,

114

for here we sat at a little round table with a spotlessly white cloth, sandwiches and cream cakes between us, sipping our tea, and we were talking of a dangerous life. I had not meant to mention shooting. I stopped laughing. The words burst from me before I could check them. "Who do you think did it?"

He understood what I meant well enough. It was as if he were entangled with my secret thoughts. He said, "I don't think this is a very suitable subject to discuss just now." Then, quite savagely, "You found the body, didn't you?"

"Yes. Yes, I did."

"That shouldn't have happened to you. I'll take care that it never happens again. How dare he die for you to see him!"

"But that's a horrid thing to say. Poor Mr. Gyori, it wasn't his fault."

"How do you know it wasn't his fault?"

"He seemed such a nice little man. My father says he was a spy. But I don't think he was killed because he was spying." And out came an idea that so far I had not mentioned to anyone. "I'm sure he wasn't spying on my father. I think he heard someone in the study and came up to see who it was, and then the person shot him—"

I really had not intended to say this. I looked up at Zoltan who was silent. His face was expressionless, his eyes fixed on mine. I wished that I knew what he was thinking. I was frightened again, though there was no reason. I too fell silent, and then he said, "Did you tell the police this?"

"No. I didn't tell them anything. There wasn't much to tell. And I only thought of this afterwards. He was a spy, wasn't he?"

"He was."

"Then you knew too?"

"I know a great many things," said Zoltan. I saw that he was eating nothing and offered him the plate of cakes, but he shook his head.

I said, "Do you know about the Attilian Life Society?"

He jerked his head up. The wary look that I had noticed before came back into his eyes. He said softly, "And what do you know about the Attilian Life Society?"

It was as if all the tenderness between us had gone and

115

I was speaking to an enemy. But I had to go on now that I had started, so I said, stammering a little, "Mr. Gyori told me about it, and so did my father. I am sure it had something to do with the murder. It's apparently a Nazi sort of society that will be terribly dangerous if there is a war. You don't think there's going to be a war, do you?"

He looked down and apparently decided to eat after all. He examined very closely the little sandwiches, then heaped a pile of them on to his plate. He began to devour them in a mouthful each. He said at last, "Of course there will be a war. But you needn't be afraid, Victoria. I'll take you away out of danger. You shall be safe from bombs and annihilation, that I can promise you."

"Will it really be so awful?" I still could not take it seriously, but the grim urgency in his voice was disturbing. This was not Abyssinia or Spain, surely: even if it had to happen, it must be a long way off. I looked out of the window as I spoke. London, on this pleasant autumn day, was so serene, with passers-by going about their business. It was not possible to believe that bombs might be falling, that we would all be running for shelter like frightened rabbits, that the strong, tall buildings facing me could be brought to the ground in crashing dust.

And even as I thought this, I suddenly knew what it would be like. I heard the sound of an air-raid warning, the noise of bombs falling, the cries of people buried beneath the rubble. I saw the falling buildings, the craters, the great toothless gaps, the demolition of a city. The pretty little tea-shop about me had vanished. The life I was accustomed to, that I had been brought up in, would be finished for ever. There would be no more dinner parties with everyone in evening dress, no more big houses, no more Maggie and Mary to look after us.

Perhaps we would revert to savagery, like my primitive ancestors, roaming the streets without warmth or shelter, hunting for our food, fighting for our very existence.

Zoltan's voice came out to me. "What's the matter, Victoria? Are you all right?"

The ugly vision faded. The pleasant little tea-shop world was back again. There we were, cosy, comfortable, cosseted: it was absurd to think that this nice little country could ever be blotted out.

116

I said, "I'm fine. I was just thinking. I don't suppose it will really be so bad. I mean, even if there is a war, we'll probably win it. We always do."

"You cannot win," he said. There was a strange note in his voice. He reached out his hands and took mine in his.

"Anyway I'm sure there won't be a war at all. Why should there be? Nobody will dare attack us. After all, we have the Navy."

"You little chauvinist!"

It was a new word to me. I would look it up when I got home, in the big dictionary my father had given me for Christmas three years ago. I said, "I don't know what that means. But I am sure we will be all right. You're as bad as my father. He's always talking of it. He's full of gloom these days. I don't know why. He used to be so happy writing about Africa. I didn't expect you to be gloomy too. Why—"

Then I stopped dead. I wrenched my hands free. There was a big, gilt-edged mirror opposite me. In it I could see the entrance to the tea-shop, and there, coming in and looking very untidy, was Miss Jessamy.

It was the most appalling bad luck. Of all people to be here, she was the very last I would have expected. I know it sounds terribly snobbish, but I would have thought that Gunter's was out of her class, especially as her hair was coming down under a dowdy hat, and her jacket had a button missing so that it gapped in the middle. I began to feel quite sick with fright. I was sure that she would run to tell my parents that she had seen me taking tea with Zoltan. I began, in an almost hysterical way, to compose a story that would cover up my lies — how I had met him on my way to Lorna's, and how he had persuaded me to come out with him.

I knew I could not possibly stay. Miss Jessamy did not come up to me, but I knew she had seen me, indeed, she could hardly avoid it, for the tea-shop was not crowded. She walked towards a table at the far end, but when she sat down, I saw her taking a powder compact out of her bag, and knew from the way she was holding it that she was observing me.

Zoltan followed the nervous jerk of my head, and saw her too. His expression changed to one of savage anger. No doubt he had already summed up Miss Jessamy well enough, and knew how inquisitive she was.

He said roughly, "We'll go," then muttered something to himself in Attilian, which was certainly a swear-word. He paid the bill, which was enormous: I had no business to see this but my eye lighted instinctively on the total. Then he took my arm, and we walked away quickly in complete silence.

After a few minutes we stopped and turned to look at each other. We both burst out laughing. Indeed, we behaved like a couple of silly schoolchildren, for once we had started we could not stop. We positively rolled about the street, then Zoltan flung his arms round me and kissed me on the mouth, in front of several startled and dis- approving passers-by, who certainly thought we were drunk.

I did not care. I did not mind what they thought. When Zoltan kissed me again, I kissed him back enthusiastic- ally, catching at the lapels of his jacket. Then we both became serious again and walked on, gazing coldly ahead as if it was inconceivable that we could behave so badly.

I said at last, "Do you think she'll tell my parents?"

"I can't see," said Zoltan cheerfully, "why she should bother. She isn't to know what a bad girl you are. There's no reason why you and I shouldn't be having tea to- gether. When are you seeing her again?"

"Tomorrow, I think. She comes to play the cello with us."

This nearly sent Zoltan off again. I am so used to Miss Jessamy playing the cello that I simply take it for granted, but I could see that from his point of view it might be comic: the cello is an ungainly instrument, and Miss Jessamy is an ungainly person.

However, he recovered himself. He said gently, slip- ping his arm round my shoulders, "Don't be frightened, little Victoria. I'll see to it that she doesn't harm you."

"But she's bound to say something. Like, 'Did you enjoy your tea yesterday?' It would be quite enough. My father would soon have the whole story out of her. You see," I said in a slightly shaking voice, "I've told such lies."

"Have you now! What lies did you tell?"

"Well, to begin with I told them I was going out to see my best friend. She's called Lorna. And,—" (I do not know why this came out, but somehow it had to) — "I borrowed this blouse from her. It's not mine at all. I

118

don't have anything so glamorous. My mother always looks on me as a child and makes me wear silly, babyish clothes."

"We'll have to change all that, won't we?" said Zoltan. He spoke very gravely. He did not sound as if he were laughing at me. He said, "You are not a child at all. I am becoming very much aware of it. I think with all deference that your mother is a foolish woman."

"I suppose she is. I think she means well. But it's not my mother I'm bothered about. It's my father. I only hope he doesn't see me when I come back, before I have time to change. He'll know perfectly well that I don't dress up like this for Lorna. And if Miss Jessamy does tell him she saw me—"

"Leave that to me," said Zoltan calmly.

"But what can you do? You can't stop her. And you just don't know Miss Jessamy at all. You only met her at the dinner-party."

"You really are frightened, aren't you?" said Zoltan. "You're trembling. Stop it. Stop it at once. That's an order. Have you no faith in me? I can move mountains as well as I can make fish sauce. If your Miss Jessamy says one word out of turn, I'll break her cello in two and wrap it round her neck."

I still could not see how he could possibly prevent her talking, but this ridiculous picture made me laugh, and I felt a little better. We had by now walked quite a long way. We were in a side street off Piccadilly. It was after six. I was possessed of the feeling that everything was irretrievably out of control. At that moment Miss Jessamy no longer mattered. We stopped by a book-shop. The shop was closed, but at least I could pretend to examine the volumes in the window.

I said in a trembling voice, without looking round, "May I see you again?"

I think Lorna would have wanted to kill me, but I could not stop myself. I turned at last. I stared up at Zoltan.

He was a tall man, and at that moment he looked to me like a mountain. He said calmly, "Do you imagine you could prevent it?"

I could not answer this. I could only stare at him with love and longing.

119

He went on, "It wouldn't matter even if you didn't want to see me. You have got to see me, and to hell with your father and everyone else. I think I am falling in love with you. You'd better run away. Why don't you run away? Not that it would do you any good. I'd find you wherever you were. Your father's quite right. I'm bad for you. You're only a baby lamb after all. But I don't care, I don't care—"

Then he swung round, away from me. He said, "Go home. Don't be afraid. It will be all right, I promise you. I'll ring you—"

"No! You can't do that."

"All right. I'll write to you. I'll sing you a serenade under your window, the whole night through. Only please go away. You must go." Then he shouted at me, "Do what you're told and go home. And I tell you, you'll be all right."

Then he was striding down the street, leaving me to stare after him through blurred eyes.

My original plan — prompted naturally by Lorna who adored all intrigue and would lie herself to pieces for anything to do with love — was to call in at her house on my way home, change my blouse to a spare school one, then come back in the normal way. But now I could not endure the thought of that cosy little talk. Lorna would insist on hearing every detail, and somehow this had gone well beyond the schoolgirl confidence. I simply walked home. I was in a dazed dream. It was a long walk, and took me nearly an hour, but somehow I needed both the exercise and the air: I was almost sorry when I at last arrived at the house.

It was half-past seven. I could see through the slit of the dining-room curtains that my parents were having their dinner. I could smell the food. It seemed to be roast beef. I knew that my mother, when she heard me turn my key in the front door, would come out into the hall. I dared not risk this: at that moment the innocent check blouse seemed to flame around me.

I crept down the area steps, and tapped at the back door.

Mary opened it. She looked at me with suspicion and surprise. I told her I had forgotten my key, I was late and my mother would be cross with me.

120

She let me in, but I could see from her expression that she did not believe me. Maggie, who had joined her, looked fixedly at the blouse: she collects all my laundry and knows perfectly well what clothes I wear. Neither of them said anything, but I have no doubt they spent the rest of the evening discussing it. They are far less easily taken in than my parents, especially Maggie with all her little sisters. But they never tell tales on me, so I simply pushed by them and came up the back stairs, with the parrot snuffling behind me.

Once in the hall I took off my shoes then fled up to my own room, where I took off Lorna's blouse, pulled on one of my own, and fastened my hair clumsily back with its slide.

Then I came down and went into the dining-room.

My parents greeted me amiably enough. I think they were glad to see me. I had the impression that they had been quarrelling. My father looked pale and exhausted, and my mother was jangling: as she turned towards me she sent a spoon flying to the floor.

"I didn't hear you come in," she said.

"No. I forgot my key. Mary let me in downstairs."

She accepted this. There was after all no reason except for my own feeling of guilt why she should not. She asked me quite effusively if I had enjoyed myself, how Lorna was, what I had had for tea, then my father interrupted her to say, "You'd better ring the bell. Mary will have your dinner waiting in the oven."

"I don't want any dinner, Daddy. I had an enormous tea."

"You should eat your regular meals," said my mother.

"I just couldn't. I'm really not hungry. I might go down for a snack later."

My father said suddenly, "You've got scent on."

I had forgotten about the perfume. I had changed the blouse, and removed the ear-rings, but short of having a bath I could do nothing about the Coty scent which I had bought at Christmas for a party, and which was very strong. I blushed, but managed to say calmly enough, "It's Lorna's. I thought I'd try a little of it. Don't you like it?"

"It's vulgar," said my father. "You know perfectly well I don't approve of it. Don't use it again, please. You're

121

too young. The next thing is you'll be putting on lipstick."

All traces of the lipstick were fortunately gone: they had been kissed away. What my father would have said if he had known this, I cannot begin to imagine. I did not answer this, only said, "I suppose I'd better get on with my homework." Then I could not stop myself from asking, "Are we making music again tomorrow?"

"I imagine so," said my father. He was regarding me in a way that I did not like. It had been an angry day and plainly still was, but as always he seemed to sense things that I did not want him to know. I could see that he suspected something, though he had no idea what it was.

My guilt, and my terror at the thought of meeting Miss Jessamy tomorrow, made me feel quite dizzy. I was beginning to understand the appalling difficulties that lay ahead. Lorna would be delighted by all the excitement, but I was simply afraid: everything for her was so different. Her parents seldom enquired where she was or what she was doing; they often went away for weekends, leaving her alone in the house. She could not understand how supervised I was, the watch that was kept on me. My father still insisted on knowing where I was and, if I went to a party and were not back by the appointed time, would always telephone. Michael he now accepted, though even Michael was not allowed to bring me back too late, but the other boys I went out with were regarded with suspicion, and even sometimes interrogated.

I knew he could know nothing, how could he, but his eyes were moving over me, trying to analyse where the problem lay. Any minute now he would start asking me questions. I could not bear it. I seemed to be becoming a good liar, but I could never stand out against my father. I said the first thing that came into my mind. "I forgot to tell you my news," I said. "I am being made head girl next year."

I could not have said anything better. Both my parents were delighted, especially my father. His face, which had been so pale and forbidding, now glowed with pride. This exactly fitted the image he had made of me. It kept me as the schoolgirl he longed for me to remain, but a schoolgirl who did him credit, who had achieved the kind of distinction he wanted for me.

122

He said, as he always did when I came top in exams, "Splendid, baby. Absolutely splendid. But I suppose I mustn't talk to such an important person as baby!"

My mother said, "Will you have a special uniform?"

"Oh Mummy, don't be silly! Of course I won't. What do you imagine? But I will have a badge. A bronze shield. I'm really rather scared of the responsibility."

"I'm proud of you," said my father.

I could hardly bear it. I thought, Proud of me? Proud of your daughter, your baby, who must not use perfume or lipstick, who has lied and lied to you, and has just come back from kissing her lover in the middle of Piccadilly — You should be ashamed of me, not proud.

Then, what with Zoltan and kisses and perfume and deceptions, it was all too much. I burst into floods of tears, and found myself sobbing on my father's shoulder, thankful that at last my burning face should be hidden from him.

"She's overwrought," said my mother. "Do you think we ought to call the doctor?"

"It's just excitement," said my father, over my bowed head. This was right too, and he caressed my hair, making soothing noises. This was his beloved little daughter who was highly strung, who needed Daddy's protection. Then he insisted on giving me a small glass of sherry, and watched with pride and pleasure as I at last left the room to go upstairs.

That pride and pleasure nearly made me cry again, I was so ashamed. I hesitated on the landing. I do not know what I thought I would do. I certainly had no intention of confessing. But as I stood there I heard them begin to quarrel again. My mother has a very piercing voice when she is angry.

"It's quite ridiculous," she said. "You don't let her use scent, which all girls like, but you give her sherry which is not good for her."

My father's answer came clearly to me. He said, "I'm not having any daughter of mine behaving like a whore."

It was like the time when he forbade me to read Pepys. I cuddled the word to myself and found it beautiful. *Whore*, and my own word, *lover*. Wonderful, wonderful words, and I was the whore, I was the head-whore and Zoltan would be my lover—

I did no homework at all. I played my gramophone. Only this time it was not the *Wiegenlied*. I only had half a dozen records, and one of them was Peter Dawson singing *Don Juan's Serenade:* this played non-stop until I heard my parents coming up to bed.

However, by the next afternoon, the dreaming was done, and I was in a state of cold panic. I nearly did not come down. I could hear Miss Jessamy saying brightly, "Did you enjoy your nice tea yesterday?" My father would ask, "What tea is that, Miss Jessamy?" And she would answer, "Oh, didn't Victoria tell you? We met in Gunter's. You know Gunter's. I was so surprised when I came in to see her there with that nice, handsome man who was at your party, what's his name now, oh, Mr. Halasz, Mr. Zoltan Halasz."

Oh God! I prayed shamelessly that she would have an accident, not a serious one, of course, just ricking her ankle or dropping her cello, just enough to keep her at home. But she arrived and she looked much the same as usual, untidy, not quite clean, with her hair back in its normal, straggling state.

I was so choked with apprehension by this time that I could hardly greet her. And she did not refer to Gunter's at all. I was sure she looked at me rather mockingly when we met, but then Miss Jessamy often looks like that, it is almost her normal expression. She only said, "And what are we playing today, Mr. Katona? I hope it isn't something too difficult."

Mr. Goldschmidt was a little late. I thought he still looked disturbed, but I was so disturbed myself that perhaps I was pushing my own emotion on to him. I still could not believe in my good fortune, and was only too thankful when the playing started: every time Miss Jessamy opened her mouth I went cold and sick with terror.

Her hope that it would not be something difficult was not to be fulfilled. We started attacking one of the Mendelssohn trios, which are very difficult and really beyond our talents. Attacking is the only word I can use, for my father was in his most aggressive mood, and at no point did it seem to me that the three of them were together.

He cried out, waving his bow, "From the third bar — And it goes tumpty-tumpty-*tum*, not tumpty-*tum*-tum—"

Mr. Goldschmidt, plainly in no mood to compromise,

answered coldly, "Excuse me, Mr. Katona, but I don't think you quite have the rhythm."

"Of course I have the rhythm, Mr. Goldschmidt? Do you take me for a fool? It's tumpty-tumpty-*tum*—"

"I beg your pardon, Mr. Katona, but it definitely goes like this—"

During all this, Miss Jessamy, as was her way, simply plodded on. The result was quite awful, and at last my father gave it up, and we played a Schubert trio instead: this went rather better.

My mother and I listened. Occasionally we glanced hopelessly at each other, but it was no good saying anything, and at least the Schubert had the three of them more or less in tempo. It was not one of our successful afternoons.

Then we all had our tea, and my father afterwards suddenly said, "Come on, Helen. You play the piano for a change."

My mother was not very pleased by this, but agreed rather sullenly, while Mr. Goldschmidt, who must have been relieved, walked out through the French windows on to the verandah. I decided to follow him out. I saw my mother, who resents being shouted at, drop all her music: in picking it up she nearly knocked herself out on the piano lid. I could see that any moment there would be a family scene, so I was glad to be in the fresh air, and shut the window behind me.

The garden looked magnificent. My father likes to stroll round the garden and admire the flowers, but I have never known him do a hand's turn. My mother too is one who puts on a large straw hat, enormous gardening gloves and arms herself with secateurs, but always she falls into one of her jangling dreams. I have seen her many times crouching by a flower-bed, aimlessly chopping at whatever comes to hand, while caterpillars rear up to sneer at her, and greenfly doze contentedly away. I myself am as inadequate as both of them, though I encourage the little herb plot at the back because it pleases me and smells so delicious. It is Mary who does the garden for us, completely uninvited: it is she too who cuts flowers for the rooms and arranges them beautifully. Every spare moment of her time takes her to the flower-beds: she is always pruning and spraying and cutting back and transplanting. The result is entirely beautiful: I sometimes feel we should be photographed for one of the country magazines.

Mr. Goldschmidt and I leaned against the railing and gazed out from the verandah. The scent of the late September roses came sweetly up to us: Mary is exceptionally good at roses and once admitted to a secret ambition to create a new variety of her own. It was very lovely and very peaceful, but nothing could calm the emotion thundering within me, and presently I grew aware that Mr. Goldschmidt was equally disturbed.

He said suddenly, "I cannot play today."

I said that I was finding it difficult to listen too: there were days when it was impossible to concentrate.

Despite the closed windows, we could hear enough from the drawing-room to know that war had been declared. My father was shouting, "No, no, no! I tell you it is like this," and as I could not hear the piano at all, I assumed that my mother had given up altogether. Miss Jessamy however was plodding on so that she was virtually playing a solo. It was all entirely comic and would have brought the audience down in the halls, but neither Mr. Goldschmidt nor I so much as smiled.

He spoke again. He said, "Such news — I don't know how to bear it. I cannot bear it."

I did not realise what he was talking about, but the raw pain in his voice was such that I instinctively put my hand on his.

He snatched it away. He said, "I think my parents are already dead."

"Oh no!" I said. What else could I say? What can one say to such a pronouncement?

I think it would not have mattered if I had said nothing. He pushed his face close to mine. He looked quite wild. "They've been taken away," he said. "They will be put in one of those terrible concentration camps. I kept on hoping. I thought they might have escaped. But I hear today from my brother that it is true. We do not even know where they are. The S.S. came for them in the middle of the night, and that is the last we have heard. It is probably the last we will ever hear."

I could only whisper, "Oh Mr. Goldschmidt!" and make an ineffectual kind of gesture.

126

"They have never done anyone any harm. My father is seventy-two and my mother is sixty-five. She is badly crippled with arthritis. They could never survive such conditions. They will probably be taken to the gas-chamber."

I was silenced through sheer horror. I no longer heard the sounds indoors, nor did I see the garden. I thought of what my father had said, heard again Zoltan talking of the inevitability of war. The beauty of the garden shimmered into rubble and dust; the sweet smell of the roses turned to putrefaction. Yet despite everything I found myself thinking, Why do they all have to talk like this? Why does he have to tell me such things? It's not fair, I am young, life is gorgeous, and everyone talks of death and beastliness and horror—

I was shocked by my own egotism, then became aware that Mr. Goldschmidt was talking again.

"I think I will kill myself," he said quite calmly. "After all," he went on in the same conversational tone, "I am a Jew, the Germans will come here, I won't have a chance. There is no point in postponement. It would be a kind of sentimentality."

Then I grew angry with him. I forgot that he was our guest, that I was much younger than he was. I shouted at him. Miss Jessamy was still playing, now entirely by herself, and my words came out against a background of juddering cello solo.

"You have no right to talk like this!" I told him. I think he was staring at me, his mouth open, but I paid no attention. I was fighting for my own survival as much as his. "First of all, you don't know that the Germans will come here. Why should they? Even if there is a war, and nobody knows for certain, it doesn't mean they'll win it. Of course they won't win it. They didn't win the last one, did they?"

You little chauvinist. I knew what the word meant now. I had looked it up last night. But I pushed that memory away, and ignored the disdainful noise that Mr. Goldschmidt made. I thought suddenly that I was being not only rude but tactless: no doubt he was brought up in the Germany we defeated. However, I was too committed to stop, so I went on, a little less boldly, "It would be terribly silly to kill yourself. You're doing a wonderful job after all. I know your news is appalling, but can't you work double time and try to make yourself forget it?"

This was a fine way for a young girl to speak to a man who had just learnt of his parents' probable death and who was planning his own, but I was too frightened to care. I could only think that if Mr. Goldschmidt were back in the Ethnographical Department, surrounded by the artifacts that were half his life to him, he might recover his courage. I said then, my voice beginning to trail away, "Haven't you got a girl-friend, Mr. Goldschmidt?"

He said in dazed tones, "Why do you ask me that? You are a very strange young lady."

"I thought — I thought she might perhaps help you."

He stared at me. The music, if it could so be called, had stopped altogether, but neither of us noticed. He said, sounding much more his old self, "Women have such trivial minds. It is the end of the world, and all you do is ask me stupid questions."

"It is not the end of the world!"

"It is at least the end of our world."

My father's voice came out to us: "Mr. Goldschmidt!"

He might have been standing there for some time. I do not know how much he heard of our conversation. We both swung round guiltily, like children caught out in some misdeed.

Mr. Goldschmidt said, "Yes, Mr. Katona?"

"My wife finds this piece too difficult. We are all waiting for you to come back to the piano."

Mr. Goldschmidt answered with an effort, "I am really not in the mood today."

"Don't be ridiculous, Mr. Goldschmidt!" Then my father said more gently, "You are not usually so temperamental."

Mr. Goldschmidt hesitated, then gave my father a rather shamefaced smile. Without another word he went back into the drawing-room. Presently I heard them starting the Schubert again. It seemed to be going better. Mr. Goldschmidt was playing with perfect efficiency. But I remained there on the verandah because somehow I could not bear to be inside, and I cried a little because I was afraid, because even the love I felt for Zoltan could

128

not rid me of the terror of the war to come.

I suppose I was there for a long time. It was growing chilly and I shivered, but still I did not go in. When someone came up behind me, I said without turning my head, "Why is everyone talking of war? The world hasn't changed since yesterday. I want it to go on exactly as it is. I like it. I don't want to hear of horrors and camps and murders. I'd like to have another party tonight, with everyone dressed up and a gorgeous dinner, and people being charming and kissing your hand. I don't see why everyone has to be so gloomy and depressing. We are all the same people. We—"

Then I realised whom I was speaking to, and broke off with a gasp.

Miss Jessamy said in a thin, harsh voice, "I have come to warn you, Victoria."

I said furiously, "Oh, go away, Miss Jessamy. Please go away." Then unable to stop myself, I added like a grizzly child, "I suppose you've told my father."

She looked at me, then glanced behind her as if to make sure the French window was closed. She said, "No, I haven't told him. I'm beginning to think I should have done." Then she said like some Victorian governess, "You are a very foolish girl. You had no right to make a clandestine arrangement with Mr. Halasz. You obviously know that yourself, or you wouldn't be so afraid I'd tell your father. I'm surprised at you."

I said as composedly as I could, though my breathing was badly out of control, "I don't see that this is any of your business."

"It is my business. Very much so."

"Why?"

She looked me over very carefully. I could see her face well enough in the light from the drawing-room, and I realised through my anger and confusion that I had always under-estimated her. It was as if I had never seen her before. The plain, good-natured if slightly malicious woman who played the cello rather badly, had disappeared, had never existed. She was much older than I had believed her to be and — odd but small detail — she dyed her hair. With the light shining upon it, the brassy strands were plainly visible.

She seemed to be pausing as if to consider her words.

She said at last, "What you are doing is extremely dangerous."

"Miss Jessamy, I am seventeen. I'm not a baby."

She made a contemptuous noise. "Seventeen! Do you know how old Mr. Halasz is?"

"Of course I do. He told me. And I still can't see—"

"Do you know who he is?"

"Yes. Yes, yes, yes!"

"I see you know absolutely nothing," said Miss Jessamy. She no longer sounded angry, only rather sad. "I really don't begin to understand you, Victoria. Not only is what you're doing dangerous, but it's something that would upset your poor father terribly. You should have a little more sense. You don't want to end up like Mr. Gyori, do you?"

I exclaimed, "Oh, this is absurd!"

"No. It's not absurd."

"Well, what is all this danger?"

"That," said Miss Jessamy who, to my relief, seemed about to go back into the drawing-room, "I cannot tell you, but you have never until now struck me as a stupid girl, and you must know that all this business is a political one, and what with the murder and the war coming—"

I do not know what made me so silly, only everybody seemed to be set on telling me off, and I suppose I wanted to show that I was not as ignorant as they all seemed to think.

I said in an airy kind of fashion, "I suppose you are referring to the Nazi clans."

The moment the words were out of my mouth, I knew how stupid I had been. I suddenly remembered that I had half considered Miss Jessamy as the murderer. I suppose I had never taken this too seriously, but women did murder — there had been one in the paper recently — and for all I knew she might have a gun tucked away in her cello-case. It would at least make a good hiding-place. And now I had shown her that I knew more than I should: perhaps she realised that I suspected her. I was terrified, and backed towards the railing, which was idiotic of me, for if she chose to give me a push I would fall on to the stony path beneath.

She came right up to me. I clutched on to the railing. I wanted to call my father who, as I could dimly see, was discussing something with Mr. Goldschmidt. Their backs were turned. I suppose they thought I was having a nice little gossip with Miss Jessamy and did not want to interrupt me. But I could not get a sound out, so I simply stared up into her face and thought, quite irrelevantly, how Zoltan would despise me.

She made no attempt to touch me. She only said in a crisp voice that carried conviction, "I don't know how you know about such things. But I'm going to give you a fair warning, Victoria. If you ever make another appointment with Mr. Halasz, I shall tell your father immediately."

I whispered, "You're a horrid, tale-telling old maid."

"I am, aren't I?" said Miss Jessamy quite cheerfully. She sounded like her old self again. "But I mean what I say, you know. I'll keep quiet this time, though I'm not sure if I'm doing you a service, but for everyone's sake you'd better not let it happen again."

I did not answer this, but I thought, You won't know, I'll see to that. Perhaps she read this in my face, for she added, "Don't imagine I won't know. If you do, you're even sillier than I thought. And I'm sorry to say this again, but really I'm surprised at you. I never thought you could behave so badly. And so stupidly."

With this, as coup-de-grâce, she went back into the drawing-room, where I was compelled to follow her, for my mother called out, "Victoria, what on earth are you doing? You'll catch your death of cold. You haven't even got a cardigan on. Come in at once."

It is strange how a scolding — I had to admit it was deserved — reduces one, cuts one down to small child status. Nobody could know what had happened, but I was very much aware of that crushed feeling one has when small, when one knows one has been naughty and one's parents are cross. I did not at that moment feel anything like seventeen. I had behaved with the utmost foolishness, and if Miss Jessamy were a spy or a murderess — it was a safe bet that she was one or the other — I would probably be marked down as the next victim.

I looked sideways at her as she chatted with my mother. She was plainly preparing to go. Her cello was packed into its case, and she was putting her hat on, a little felt affair that she pulled down right over her ears. She

131

did not look like a murderess nor did she look like a spy. She appeared to be simply a dull, ordinary little woman with a job in the Civil Service, who played the cello in her spare time. My mother was telling her how our parrot now speaks Attilian, and this seemed to amuse her very much. When she turned to say goodbye to me, there was no indication on her face that we had talked about anything but the music or the roses in the garden.

Mr. Goldschmidt had already left. The memory of my conversation with him afforded me little pleasure either. It had not been my day for distinguishing myself. I could only hope that he really did have a nice girl-friend who would make him a cosy supper with a bottle of wine, and hold his hand afterwards. Perhaps his department in the Museum would take his mind off his terrible troubles. It seemed unbearable that such things could happen to a nice, ordinary man.

We tidied up the drawing-room then went into supper. Sunday supper is always a dreary meal. Mary and Maggie have the evening off, so it is always something cold. This evening it was cold mutton and salad, and we all looked at it without enthusiasm. The cheese and biscuits did not add much to the occasion.

My father carved the mutton in silence. There was some caper sauce, which redeemed it a little. But we all felt that it had in no way been a successful afternoon: my father no doubt brooded on the musical massacre, and I thought of Mr. Goldschmidt's troubles and my own stupid behaviour with Miss Jessamy. We sat there like all the other families in the street, swallowing down dull, cold food, and feeling chilly because my mother would never light the gas fire until the winter came. My great-grandmother stared down at us. I wished suddenly that our house was more modern. The big, gilt-framed por-trait — it was painted by someone quite famous — the enormous Victorian sideboard polished by Maggie until it could have served as a mirror, and the set of dining-room chairs which had come to us through three genera-tions, depressed me. I thought of Lorna's suburban home, with its bright, modern furniture, the gay coloured rugs one skidded on, and the pink frilly cushions and shades her mother loved. My mother, who had once been there, said it was rather common, and my father would have been lost in all the frillery, but at least it was human, friendly and warm.

I said, thinking that cold mutton was really very nasty, and wishing I had had the energy to make some hot potatoes as I occasionally did, "When are we going to have our next party?"

I do not really know why I said this. I had no particular wish for another party and, with everything that had happened, it would have been ominously haunted. Only as we sat there, the three of us, all silent, all chewing away at our mutton, I saw again the table as it had been, with the best glass and crockery, the candles flickering and the long, lace-embroidered linen cloth. Opposite me would have been Count Asztalos in his immaculate evening dress, and beside me Zoltan with whom I had fallen in love. But the magnificent moment was gone. It would never return. It was different now, still exciting but furtive and dangerous, with Miss Jessamy lurking behind doors. And I knew, as the words passed my lips, that I did not want the next party. I wanted the first one over again, over and over and over again, stopping always at the moment when Mr. Gyori was shot. I wanted us all sitting there, with the pretty dresses and the starched shirt fronts, a brief halcyon pause before the war came and people were murdered and the lights went out.

My father did not immediately answer me. Already searching for a cigarette in the silver initialled case that had been a wedding present, he simply said, "Does anyone want some more mutton?"

My mother said with a shudder, "No, thank you. It was tough. I really must get Mary to speak to the butcher. Why are you talking about the next party. Victoria? I don't think we've got over the last one."

"I don't think we'll have many more," said my father.

Both my mother and I stared at him. She must secretly have been delighted, but she at once drew her face down into a look of the most intense disappointment.

My father went on, "Count Asztalos has been recalled."

I said, "Oh no! He's so nice. And his wife's so pretty."

My father said with his grim little smile, "You will have to find someone else to kiss your hand, Victoria. I don't think it's much in Mr. Palotas's line."

My mother, who likes Mr. Palotas as little as my father does, said in surprise, "Is he to be the new Minister?"

"He already is. Prepared no doubt for the German invasion."

"Oh really, Mikki," said my mother, "you're always croaking." She must have had a great deal more of it than I did. As she spoke she dropped half her cigarette ash into her glass of water. We never drank wine on a Sunday evening. It would have cheered up the meal enormously, but for some reason supper was regarded as a kind of penance.

"He is giving a little celebratory party next Friday. We are not invited."

"Why not?" I asked, surprised. We were always invited to the Legation parties.

"Oh, I fancy our politics do not agree. His views after all have always been consistently fascist." He ignored my mother's grimace. I think she felt compelled to make it as if the very word "fascist" signified depression and gloom.

I said, "Nothing will happen to Count Asztalos, will it?"

"I don't know. Who knows anything these days? He will no doubt retire to his ancestral castle, where life will go on much the same as it has done for the past five or six hundred years. He is still hoping for the return of the Hapsburgs. I pointed out to him once that the family has been doomed through the centuries with, I believe, three murders, several mis-marriages and at least one suicide, but he simply said that anything was preferable to the Communists. I understand his father was murdered by Bela Kun, but except in this one matter he is not a politically minded man. When the Nazis come to power, we hope they will not trouble him, except to take his money, and I do not suppose he will put up any opposition. He has never been pro-German, so it is possible that it might be tricky for him. He kisses a pretty hand, Victoria, but he has been out of date for several generations. Charm, presence and good breeding no longer matter. This, as they always say, is the age of the common man. Palotas will do remarkably well."

My mother, who detests this kind of talk, was jangling away throughout the oration, but I could not stop myself from saying, "Does this mean that the whole Legation staff will now be altered?"

My father looked at me. I prayed that he could not read my thoughts. He said, "There will be changes, yes. Many changes. But I daresay they will not all take place at once. It would be too much like your game of general post, and it might attract the wrong kind of attention. What was Mr. Goldschmidt saying to you, Victoria?"

"I am going into the sitting-room," said my mother. "I hope you're not going on talking politics, Mikki, it really is so boring."

"I was merely asking Victoria about Mr. Goldschmidt who, I may say, played quite abominably this afternoon." He added, "He really should have more self-control. He is after all not a boy. I myself find music extraordinarily soothing and relaxing."

I could have pointed out that however soothing music might be, it was not always improved by my father's shouts of tumpty-tum. But it was plain that he was in one of his disapproving moods, and this disapproval seemed about to be turned on me. We waited until my mother was gone, still jangling away and banging doors, and presently she decided to pour her woes out to her friend, for we heard her shouting on the phone. She always shouts when she phones. If I am at the receiving end I hold the receiver as far away as I can.

"Well?" my father said, eyeing me, "what was it all about? From what I heard, he seemed to be prophesying the end of the world. Don't crumble your bread, Victoria. It's a messy habit and means more work for Maggie."

"He's terribly unhappy, Daddy."

"Well, we're all unhappy. We just have to keep it to ourselves. What's making him so unhappy?"

I thought my father was being singularly unsympathetic. After all, to lose both your parents in such a hideous fashion is surely enough to drive anyone to despair. I said a little crossly, "I thought he had already told you. They've taken his parents away to a concentration camp. He thinks they're probably dead. They're very old, and his mother is an invalid. You can't blame him for feeling awful. I think it's enough to make one commit suicide. He talked of doing it too. I do hope he doesn't."

135

"We all have our troubles," said my father very wearily. I could see now how unhappy he was himself. Heaven knows what was happening to us all: poor little Mr. Gyori, when he got himself shot, seemed to have changed everything. Sunday supper was never our best meal, but usually my father, who did not bother much about food, was rather jolly, and afterwards we used to sit down to cut-throat bridge. This was fun: cut-throat was a remarkably appropriate name, for my mother was very good at cards, cheated like mad, and grew frenzied if anyone revoked or called on a poor hand. As neither my father nor I really took it seriously, she always ended by winning the game and losing her temper.

"There is no point," she would cry, "in playing if you don't do it properly," and then there would be a dreary post-mortem to which neither of us paid the least attention.

"Why don't you join a bridge club?" my father once asked her, but she tossed her head, answering, "And be surrounded by a crowd of ghastly old women? No, thank you!"

It seemed that tonight there would be no bridge. I really wanted to go upstairs and brood and dream, but I did not like to leave my father alone when he looked so desperate, so I said, a little timidly, "You're not ill, are you, Daddy? Is the book not going well?"

He repeated, "The book?" It was as if he did not know what I was talking about. When my mother, having finished her call, came back to wander over to the sideboard, saying, "I think I could do with a wee sherry," he did not even acknowledge her presence, only remained silent until she went away again, with a brimming glass that slopped over as she moved.

Then he smiled at me, patted my hand, and said quite cheerfully, "The book is good and stuck, Victoria, and likely to remain so. I suppose for the first time I can call myself free. Once I believed I would never rid myself of the shackles, but now they've just dropped off. I admit that freedom is a little disconcerting, but I daresay I shall get used to it."

I had no idea what he was talking about. He noticed my puzzled face and laughed. It was the most dismal laughter I had ever heard. "Africa, baby," he said, "Africa!"

"Daddy, I simply don't understand you."

"You're being very stupid tonight, my child. It's simply that I have returned to civilisation. I don't know about Africa any more. It's in the past. Gone. Finished. Kaput. It's just as well. One should never go back. Now I find I've almost forgotten what it's like. It will certainly have changed, and in another ten years it will be completely unrecognisable. But why should I brood about it when I live in such a beautiful world? It is only a continent, something thrown up in the Ice Age. Lakes and forests and mountains — Nothing interesting. Nothing at all."

His desolation communicated itself to me. I had no Africa to retreat to, only my hopes and dreams, but they too made up for me a little fortress, a fortress to which, later in the evening, I would happily retreat, away from wars and Miss Jessamy and my uneasy desires and fears. And my father, throughout my life with him, had always retreated to his beloved country, surrounded by his books, by the little statues, by the memories of a time when he had been happy and fulfilled. To have lost this, to be marooned in a world he hated, was so terrible to me that I wanted to cry.

I said, "Why? Why has this happened? You said something like this before. I didn't think you really meant it."

He sighed. "Yes, I meant it. I don't know why it's happened, baby. Perhaps reality is too strong. There is so much happening around us, and it's pushed me out into the cold. It might be our murder. Our own, personal little murder."

"Have they found out who did it?"

"I should imagine so. It wasn't very subtle. But of course there is no proof. We are dealing with a clever person, to whom murder is as much part of life as – as cold mutton. No, baby, it is not your beloved Count Asztalos. Have you perhaps fallen a little in love with him?"

I blushed to the line of my hair. My father had obviously sensed my state of emotion. I could only be thankful that he had fixed on the wrong man. It would amuse him to think of my having a *schwarm* for this charmer of fifty, who was safely married to a very pretty

137

wife and now miles away in Dunavar. There was no danger, no possibility of my becoming too involved: it was simply the kind of thing that happened to all teenage daughters, it was good for my emotional development and could do me no harm whatsoever.

He looked now much more cheerful. He said in a kindly, amused way, nodding his head, "I thought so. Your old father is not so blind as you seem to imagine. After all, I was once young too. I could see you were up in the stars."

I was thinking, Oh Zoltan, Zoltan — God, I hope Miss Jessamy falls down dead before she says anything.

He went on, "He is of course very charming. A little old for you, baby, almost the same age as your father. He is married too, which is a slight disadvantage. But I can see how the old-world Attilian courtesy would attract you. I think there was a press photo of him when he left the Legation. If I haven't thrown it away, I'll cut it out for you, and you can put it under your pillow and dream about him."

I could see myself stuck with a portrait of Count Asztalos, no doubt framed on my dressing-table. I liked him very much, but I had no wish to gaze at him every time I did my hair. I did not know what to say. I looked down, still scarlet, and this of course confirmed my father in his fantasy.

When I did speak, he was startled and disconcerted.

"What do you think of Miss Jessamy, Daddy?"

"Miss Jessamy? Good God, Victoria, what an extraordinary question."

"But I really want to know." Then I blurted out, "It wasn't she who did the murder, was it?"

He stared at me, then began to laugh. I had the impression that he was relieved. He said derisively, "Miss Jessamy! The only thing Miss Jessamy could murder would be a Mendelssohn trio. What on earth put such an idea in your head?"

I said weakly, "She's rather a strange person."

Once again I was sure he knew more about Miss Jessamy than he chose to admit. But he just said, "Oh, she's an old maid who has never found herself a man. She is so unattractive, poor soul. She's completely harmless. She wouldn't kill a fly. Whatever made you think

138

she killed Gyori? I daresay the police have their suspicions, but certainly she's not on their list."

I said, "I don't know. I just wondered." And really, it did seem rather silly, only I had seen a side of Miss Jessamy that my father did not know, that I could only pray he would never know.

I said, "It's just part of the pattern since the murder. I don't know where I am any longer. And now you say you can't think of Africa any more. I don't believe it's possible. Does this mean you won't finish the book?"

"I'll finish it." He spoke flatly. "It won't be the same, but I'll finish it." Then he slapped his hand down on the table. "What about our game of bridge? I feel in the mood, somehow I think I shall beat the pair of you. Go and ask your mother to set out the cards."

We played our game of cut-throat for over an hour. My mother played with her usual feverish concentration, peering sideways at our cards whenever she had the opportunity, and rating me ferociously for calling no trumps when I had an insufficient hand. And of course she won, she was bound to win. My father, for all he had declared himself in the mood, was still away in some unhappy place of his own, and as for myself, I was still too disturbed by everything to do much more than follow suit. It was as well we did not play for money. We would always have been broke.

My mother hurled her last savage words at us as she rose to go upstairs. She shot the cards together like a Mississippi gambler. "I think you're both fools," she said. "I never thought I'd have so stupid a daughter. If you can't concentrate, Victoria, you shouldn't play at all. And you're no better, Mikki. I'm going to bed. I'm fed up with the pair of you."

We grinned at each other as she left, slamming the door.

"I don't think somehow," my father said, "we're very popular."

I simply said, "Oh dear."

"But it would have been much worse if we had won."

Then we laughed, and he kissed me, ruffling my hair.

He said, "Go to bed, baby. It's late, and head girls mustn't arrive all sleepy in the morning. Go to bed, and dream of Count Asztalos."

139

Chapter 6

I DREAMED VERY strangely, and not of Count Asztalos, though from time to time he strayed through my mind. He at least was not the murderer. It was hard to imagine him gunning someone down. If he killed at all, it would be in a romantic duel with flashing swords. When I was very young I loved *The Three Musketeers.* I could see Count Asztalos as a musketeer. But I also dreamed of Miss Jessamy, and when I woke up, rather earlier than usual, brooded on her, still not quite convinced that she was innocent. She was certainly not the old maid my father called her, and she was certainly not harmless either. I wondered if I could ask Zoltan about her. But then I had no idea when I would hear from him again, and the thought of this upset me so much that I could not lie in bed any longer, waiting for Maggie and the hot water.

I dressed, then paced up and down my room. He had sounded very determined, he had even said he was falling in love with me, but I wondered if this perhaps was not simply an exaggeration of the celebrated Attilian charm. In any case it would be very difficult for him to communicate with me. My mother almost always answered the phone, and she also scrutinised the mail whenever she had the opportunity. I think she would have opened letters if it had been possible. She is quite devoid of the normal scruples. The only solution seemed to be the romantic old oak tree, where we could leave little notes for each other, to be read later in privacy. However, as there was no oak tree nearer than Hyde Park, this was not very helpful, and what with this and Miss Jessamy and a bad night, I became very depressed, and more and more convinced I would never see Zoltan again.

In this of course I completely underestimated him. Even on so brief an acquaintance I might have known that he was by temperament a pirate and a Don Juan who would like nothing better than climbing up a balcony and sliding into his beloved's room in the middle of the night: small details such as an over public telephone and tapped mail would not only not deter him but would positively spur him on.

But there was no balcony either, and after breakfast I set off for school, feeling morose and a little let down by the transition of drama to everyday routine.

Our parrot babbled away at me as I left. He now, as my mother had remarked, seldom spoke anything but Attilian. I wished I could understand him. For once the children who usually hung around him, had deserted him. Perhaps Attilian bored them. As he had no audience he now talked and screeched non-stop. He even burst into song as I came down the last step.

"Beastly bird!" I called down to him, and he at once snuffled disgustingly. "One day," I told him, "I'll pull your tail feathers out," and this provoked a fresh flood of Attilian which, coming from that wicked beak, sounded like swear-words.

I bought a paper to read in the 31 bus. The *News Chronicle* was always at home for me to look at, but usually I just glanced at the headlines and perhaps read the film reviews. However, today I felt I ought to study the news more thoroughly, so I stopped at a news-stand and selected a rather lurid paper, of the kind that my father would never permit at home.

I do not know why I chose this paper. I sometimes think that the accidental things we do are not accidental at all, but certainly it was odd that I should pick on this particular rag.

There were great black headlines across the front page. NAZI NEST said the first one and, HAS THE WAR ALREADY STARTED? the second. I am sure the *News Chronicle* would never have been so lurid. Of course I read the article through. It was all about the Attilian clan, though the nationality was not directly mentioned, and it referred to a big meeting that was to take place at King's Cross on Sunday night. All the people coming were fascist supporters, and I suppose in a way it was very *Boy's Own*, if for the wrong boys: the paper obviously did not take it too seriously but was just cashing in on a provocative story. In the old days I would not have taken it seriously either. I doubt if it would even have interested me: I would have been far more likely to read the book page or take a look at the newest fashions.

Now it interested me very much indeed; it reminded me of that sad little corpse in my father's study, with the red splash on the shirt-front. It was at this moment that I made up my mind to go and see what it was all about: I was weary of all these sinister half-truths and wanted to find out for myself. I knew that I must tell no one, not even Lorna. My father would be utterly horrified; he might even lock me in my room. Miss Jessamy — but then I really could not live my life according to Miss Jessamy's standards. As for Zoltan, he too would certainly forbid me to go: he had more reason than most to know that such meetings were not a game, and it would probably shock him to think of a young girl there without an escort.

I was frightened but I was also excited. I had never done anything like this in my life. Indeed, I was so engrossed in the article that I sailed past my bus-stop and arrived at school ten minutes late.

Lorna, who is invaluable in such crises, was waiting for me. She did her best to cover up, sneaking my beret from me, and sliding me into hall where prayers were in progress. She whispered in my ear, "You're a fine head girl, I must say," and bestowed on me such a meaningful smile that I was quite startled. But of course I assumed she was referring to my late arrival. I grimaced at her, then took my place at the back of the hall. Next term I would have to stand in front, behind Miss Carter and the staff; sometimes I would have to lead the prayers, and at prizegivings would be playing hostess to the wealthy ladies who sat on the Committee.

Now, however, I could only hope that no one had noticed my arrival. We were in the middle of a hymn. I know all the hymns by heart; we always sing the same ones. I sang:

Oh God, our help in ages past,
Our hope for years to come—

142

then saw that someone had noticed. It was Miss Hudson. Miss Hudson notices everything, and she does not like me because I am bad at maths: it is the one subject that always lets me down in exams. She is in any case a very angry woman, and we all think she bullies the life out of Miss Thomas, who is a gentle person and absorbed in the history she teaches.

She waited until prayers were over, then shot out at me as I was leaving the hall.

"You're disgracefully late," she said. "I suppose you think you're privileged. I should have thought you would wish to set a better example, especially as I understand you will be head girl next term."

Lorna, just behind me, kicked me gently on the ankle. I suppose I should have been glad that she did not kick Miss Hudson. She is quite capable of it. Lorna has a violent temper and, when she is in the mood, simply does not care what happens. Once, when she was younger, she was nearly expelled for speaking her mind in a theatrical fashion quite alien to the Upper Fourth.

I was upset enough to answer back. This is always a mistake, especially with people like Miss Hudson. I said, "That's not fair. This is the first time I've ever been late in my life. I simply passed the bus stop. It could happen to anyone."

"I suppose," said Miss Hudson, "you were busy finishing your homework."

At this moment Miss Carter came up. I do not know how much she heard of the conversation, but she simply smiled at me and wished me good morning, and at this Miss Hudson walked away, brooding no doubt on all the nasty things she could say to me at our maths lesson, which came in the second period.

Lorna took my arm and we walked upstairs to the classroom.

She whispered in my ear, "Les old bitch!"

I did not answer this, only shrugged. Then I became aware that Lorna was seething with suppressed excitement: the arm within mine was positively vibrating.

She said nothing until we were seated at our desks, waiting for Miss Mandeville. Then she leaned across and pushed something into my hand. It was a letter, and at the feel of it I blushed scarlet, though I did not know for certain that it was from Zoltan.

Lorna, who had raised her desk lid, said from under it, "I must say! How does he know about me? It's from him, isn't it? It must be. I think it's the most wonderful cheek. When you've finished with him, honey, pass him on to me. He sounds just my type."

We could hear Miss Mandeville coming briskly down the corridor. I hissed back, "Was he there? Did he give it you himself?"

"Oh dear me, no — nothing like that," said Lorna, still rummaging in her desk. "Fine gentlemen don't deliver their own love-letters. He — Good morning, Miss Mandeville."

I cannot pretend that I really concentrated on the lesson, though English has always been my favourite subject. Fortunately it was grammar, so there was nothing much to do but listen, and I am afraid I did not do much of that either. It was at the next lesson with Miss Hudson that I ran into trouble. The subject was algebra at which I am extremely bad, and she made a point of asking me impossible questions and getting me up to the blackboard so that I was pilloried in front of the class. However, by this time I was in such a state of mind that I hardly cared, and at last Miss Hudson gave me up: there is little point in needling someone who does not seem to take in a word you say.

Lorna and I went out of the classroom for our morning break. She said, "Aren't you going to open it?"

"No. I can't." But I looked down at it, I could not take my eyes from it.

"It is from *him*, isn't it?"

"Yes. Oh yes."

"I think you're barmy. Where are you going?"

"I'm going to the lavatory."

For there is little privacy in a school, there is always someone to read over your shoulder, and the lavatory, as innumerable lovelorn ladies have discovered, is the one place where you can be alone. I remember that Cryseyde took Troilus's note to the privy, so it was done even in Chaucer's day.

I said, opening the cloakroom door, "Who gave you this?"

144

"I think it must have been his chauffeur," said Lorna, adoring every minute of this. I know she was fond of me, but it was plain that today I had risen immeasurably in her estimation. "He was hanging round the entrance, waiting for you. He kept on asking for you, and I heard him. I said I was a friend of yours, and could I help. I think he was Attilian too, he had a nice sort of accent. He quite gave me the eye. He said he wasn't sure if he ought to give me the letter, but I told him it was all right, I really was a friend. Then he asked me if my name was Lorna. So you must have mentioned me, honey. When I said it was, he gave me the letter, and then he kissed my hand. It was lovely. Oh go on, do read it! I just can't bear the suspense any longer."

But I did not answer this: I was too choked with emotion. I went into the cloakroom and there, seated unromantically on the lavatory, I opened the letter.

How typical of Zoltan to send a note to my school! I do not think an Englishman would have done this. He would probably have considered it not quite done, whatever that revolting phrase means. To an unscrupulous Attilian — I was already aware how unscrupulous Zoltan was — the fact that it was not done would make it irresistible. It would also provide the perfect cover, and be pretty well foolproof. With a great crowd of girls coming into the school, it would hardly be noticed if one of them received a letter, and apart from Lorna herself, who would see intrigue in a rice pudding, it would not be regarded as anything extraordinary, it would be seen as a hasty note from some outside friend.

It was as before very brief. I think that people who write professionally seldom indulge in long letters, or so a friend of my father's, who is a journalist, once told me. After all, if you are paid so much a thousand words, it seems a pity to do it for free.

I think anyway that Zoltan would be careful not to commit himself.

The note ran as follows:

Dear little Victoria. We will meet this Saturday again. At the same place, by the underground station. And this time we will take care not to meet lady cellists. I have made sure of this. You will come back to my rooms with me. I will have a taxi waiting so no one will see us. *La ci darem la mano!* Zoltan.

And the song was from *Don Giovanni*. I knew it very well. I sometimes sang both parts of the duet, though half should be sung by the wicked Don himself. My father took me to the opera. We never went to the theatre together, for it did not interest him, but opera he loved, and the better musicals like *Lilac Time*. He had no patience with anything modern.

I stayed in the lavatory until the bell went. I read the note over and over again. I had to notice the dictatorial tone. Not "May we meet" or "Can we meet", but simply "We will". And what did he mean when he said he had made sure? But I could not ignore the bell, so I pulled the chain for the sake of verisimilitude, tucked the letter inside my gym tunic — I think this would have amused him — and came back sedately to the classroom. My heightened colour and shining eyes at once betrayed me to Lorna, who could hardly sit still for the excitement of it all. She whispered mockingly, "You have got the trots, haven't you?" but had no time to say much more until the lunch period, when, after a quick meal, we sauntered out into the playground.

We sat down on a bench in the far corner. I handed the note to Lorna without a word. It was a pleasant day. One group was playing netball, some of the younger kids were running races, but most of us were strolling about, arm in arm, as schoolgirls have done through the centuries. There was the vast noise of uninhibited young voices letting off steam, but I was too used to it to hear: I mechanically threw back a ball that landed almost in my lap.

Lorna said at last in an awestruck voice, "He's asking you to his rooms."

"Yes, I know. Is there anything wrong in that?"

She gazed at me out of big blue eyes. I saw then in some detached corner of my mind that Lorna was not really much more sophisticated than I was. She has a vast number of constantly changing boy-friends, and I am sure she flirts with them outrageously, but the studiously voiced implications of passion and wickedness are pure moonshine. Her parents, when they leave her alone, know what they are about. I do not think I really put this into words, but I knew somehow that the professed flirt who has all the boys running in circles around her, is far less in danger than the vicar's daughter who has seldom met anyone but the local curate and who has been brought up to believe that sex is wrong and forbidden.

I am afraid I am the vicar's daughter.

I had to see that Lorna, the daring, the unshockable, the ultra-modern, was secretly appalled. She said at last in a vague, astonished voice, "Honey, I really don't know what to say. Only you hardly know him, do you? How did you meet? You've never told me."

I gave her a vague outline of our meeting. I did not tell her very much. I think I spent most of the time describing our tea in Gunter's.

"Has he kissed you?" demanded Lorna.

"Of course."

"Of course, she says! Does he kiss nicely?" Lorna's self-confidence was returning.

"Yes," I said, then I suddenly laughed.

"I think," said Lorna, "you're a bad girl."

"That's what he says."

"Well, he ought to know. What are you going to wear? You've got to look more sophisticated this time. I have a lovely blue dress, and I'm sure it would fit you to a tee. And this time you must, but simply must, wear one of my bras."

"Oh darling, thank you, but I can't. I'm going as I am."

"Oh no! You're mad."

"I know, but somehow I must. I feel I could almost wear my gym tunic."

"Honey, are you out of your mind?"

"Well, perhaps I won't do that, but at least I want to wear my own clothes. Somehow he's got to see me as I really am. He knows I borrowed that blouse from you. I told him."

"So that's how he knew my name." Then Lorna said quite crossly, "Well, what are you going to wear then? Your mum's got the most frightful taste, if you don't mind me saying so. I mean, she dresses you as if you were still in the Lower Third."

"I know she does. But I expect I'll find something. Lorna—"

The netball landed near us again, and Lorna kicked it away. She is not at all a sporting girl, and has been thrown out of more teams than I can remember. She tends to fall into a dream at vital moments. It is only when we do the school play that she really comes into her own. She looked at me without speaking. There was a wary expression on her face.

I said, "If one's in love — Really in love, I mean. Do you think — What I want to say is, how far should one go?"

Then I went hot and red with embarrassment, for this was something I had never before put into words, not even with Lorna, and it sounded dreadful, so immature, almost comic.

Lorna did not answer for a minute. I think she was as out of her depths as I was. Then she said in a distant voice as she had said before, "I really don't know, honey. I think you've got to make up your own mind about that. I mean, I've never met this gentleman of yours, but he's foreign—"

"Oh, really!"

"Well, my dad once said to me that in their own country they can't get near the girls because they're always chaperoned, so when they come over here, they think we're a piece of cake. Anyway, you say he's much older than you. I think you ought to be careful. Besides, your father would half kill you, from what you tell me about him. He's always very sweet to me, but I gather he can be a bit of a tartar."

"Yes, he can."

The bell went. The noise around us suddenly died. We rose to our feet. Lorna and I looked at each other. Then she put her arm round me and gave me a squeeze. "Do be careful, won't you?" she said, adding more cheerfully, "But if anything happens, you can always depend on me. The parents like you. They think you're ever such a nice girl. Little do they know! Never mind. We'll take you in even if daddy throws you out into the snow."

"I don't really think he'd do that!"

We walked back into the classroom.

Lorna said, "I bet Michael never gave you such problems."

"No."

"Don't you see him any more?"

"No."

"Won't you ever see him again?"

"I honestly don't know."

And indeed I did not know. I had not had a word from him since our quarrel, and he never nowadays came to the school to fetch me. In the inconsistent way of females I quite missed this. It was fun having a handsome young man waiting there for you, and the other girls would giggle and nudge each other, and look at me enviously. I enjoyed the break of going to the little teashop with its flowery ladies, and I liked talking about the coming weekend, discussing what cinema we were going to. But I had not rung him, and he did not ring me. My mother, wildly curious as always, kept on asking me when I was going to see him again; she even told me to stop being silly, he was such a nice boy, I had no business to chuck him like that.

"It's all the fault of Count Asztalos," said my father, overhearing her.

This of course made me blush, and both my parents laughed at me. Count Asztalos, now back in his family castle, would never know that he had been cast as my knight errant. Both my father and my mother were by now entirely convinced that I had lost my heart to him, and any nervous or emotional behaviour on my part was at once attributed to my hopeless love. My father had even found the photo he mentioned, and in one of his erratic fits of humour, placed it on my dressing-table, with a rose, picked from the garden, laid upon it.

Poor Count Asztalos! I do not suppose he even remembered me. But I could not bear to gaze upon his handsome face every moment of the day, so I put the rose in my tooth-mug, and hid the photo in my handkerchief sachet.

Lorna continued to nag at me about what I was to wear. I can only think that when she went out with a boyfriend, she landed the whole household in chaos, but then she had a great many more clothes than I, as well as a far bigger allowance. If she had seen me when I left the house on the Saturday afternoon, I really believe our friendship would have ended for good and all.

I did wear my school clothes after all. I do not quite

know why. It was largely, of course, as Zoltan was the first to see, a gesture of defiance. But it was more than that. It was a kind of assertion of my own individuality. I was saying, All right, I am still a schoolgirl. If as you say you find me attractive, if you love me, you can put up with me, without any trimmings.

It is only fair to say that I took enormous trouble over my appearance, indeed, I cheated, because my white blouse was not the school blouse, my stockings were silk and I wore my best underclothes. But I did put on the school tie, with its green and purple stripes, and on my tunic, above the coloured strips that revealed how many times I had been form captain, I pinned my prefect's badge. My only concessions to the occasion were a touch of perfume, and my hair, which I once again combed forward over my cheek.

I was right to do this. I knew from some purely primitive instinct that I would appeal far more to Zoltan's esoteric taste in this attire than in any of Lorna's proffered clothes. He must have seen a great many ladies in silk and satin, but I would have been willing to bet that never before had he taken out someone in a gym tunic. Besides — this only struck me as I looked at myself in my long mirror — a tunic presumably designed as a decent, modest garment for young girls, actually displays the feminine figure to great advantage, with its pleats and neat waist, and the blouse worn under it.

I spent the rest of the week coping with Lorna. She was not to be easily defeated. She brought in succession three blouses, two dresses and a skirt. I suppose they were lovely and very expensive, but I refused them all. She was upset and angry, especially when, driven to exasperation, I told her she was behaving like a lady in one of those dress-shops where they stand in the doorway and almost solicit your trade.

She wailed at me, "But this black dress is so sophisticated. It's quite plain, honey. I mean, it's not tarty or anything like that."

"No, I couldn't wear that. It's not my style."

"Well, what about the blue one? I tell you what. Wear a blouse and skirt as you did last time. Only try this blouse, the one with the lace. It's the kind of thing foreigners go for like mad. It's so feminine. It's chic."

Lorna and I have never quarrelled but this time we all but came to words. I was after all in a very emotional state, and she hates being thwarted. She was quite chilly when we said goodbye on the Friday, only at the last minute, overcome by the drama of the occasion, she relented enough to give my hand a squeeze and say, "If you can't be good, be careful," adding with genuine feeling, "Oh be careful, honey, won't you?"

"I will. Really I will. Don't worry. And I'll tell you all about it on Monday."

"Can't you ring me before?" Lorna, even when cross, never sulks, and by now she was her old self. "I can't possibly wait till Monday. Ring me Sunday afternoon."

But of course I was going to the meeting on Sunday. It was going to be quite a weekend. I explained to her that the phone was in the hall, and everything could be overheard: she knew this perfectly well, for we had always had this difficulty, and Lorna is extremely indiscreet on the telephone, bursting out with intimate details that would give my mother a fit. We parted with our usual friendliness. I did not admit to her that I was, despite my bold speech, terrified.

On Saturday there was of course not the slightest difficulty. I hardly troubled to lie. I simply said I was going out, and sailed downstairs in my school uniform. If my mother noticed the silk stockings, she said nothing: in any case she would never believe that I was going to a date in such clothes. She only said, "I wish you wouldn't wear those ghastly things at the weekend. Why don't you put on one of the pretty dresses I got you?"

She dislikes uniform of any kind. When I first went to school she made a terrible fuss about buying the regulation clothes. She says it is ridiculous to dress young girls up as if they belong to an orphanage. However, as the clothes she chooses for me are so revolting, I am sometimes thankful that during term time I do not have to wear them.

She watched me as I opened the front door. I believe that despite everything she was a little suspicious. I was secretly shivering with excitement but I managed to look composed and calm. She said, "I hope your father doesn't find out you've got scent on."

Then she wandered back to the sitting-room to get

151

down to one of the innumerable library novels she reads; perhaps later she would practise the piano.

I did not think that Miss Jessamy might be watching out for me. I had far too much on my mind to think of Miss Jessamy at all. I walked to the station and of course I was too early: however, this time I made no pretence, simply waited, standing back against the wall.

Zoltan came punctual to the minute. He was, as he had said, in a taxi. He stepped out. He looked me up and down. There was a brief flicker of astonishment in his eyes. But he simply kissed me on the cheek and said, "Come. We will not give your cello lady any opportunity," then handed me into the waiting cab.

We did not speak for a while. He could not take his eyes off me. I think he was genuinely disconcerted. It must have seemed incredible to a man of his age, looks and kind, who knew perfectly well that I was in love with him, that I had not troubled to dress up for him. Then he began to laugh silently, and all this time I sat there, gazing ahead, as if I really were a little girl being taken out by uncle for a weekend treat. Only when I saw him laughing — he did not make a sound — I found my composure cracking and the tears coming to my eyes. But I still kept my eyes on the driver's window, and then Zoltan leaned forward and touched the badges on my tunic: he did this so delicately and naturally that it seemed like idle curiosity, only of course it was nothing of the kind, it was an intimate caress as I very well knew.

He said, "What are these ribbons you are wearing? I did not know you had been decorated. What is this service you have performed for so many governments?"

I replied, "They are captains' badges. The purple one is for the Lower Fourth, the green for the Upper Fourth, and the yellow for the Fifth. The badge is a prefect's badge."

"You keep order?"

"I do my best. Next term I shall be head girl, and there will be a little bronze shield."

Then at last I looked at him, and the tears fell on to his still moving hand. He made an impatient sound and, putting his arms round me, kissed me. He said, "I have never kissed a head girl before. It is a little like embracing a nun. Do you think I shall be excommunicated?"

We both began to laugh, like silly children, and the cabby, absorbed by all this in his driving mirror, nearly ran a passer-by down.

"I think," Zoltan said, "you will be an actress. You have an extraordinary sense of occasion." He stared at me again, then once more stretching out his hand, pulled my tie loose. "But this I do not like. This I will not tolerate. The ribbons, yes, they are pretty colours. The badge amuses me. It makes me feel important. But a tie, no. I do not kiss ladies with ties. It is too masculine, and you are so very feminine. I can perhaps embrace a nun, though so far I have not tried, but I will not kiss a boy. It is not my inclination."

I said after a while, "What did you do about Miss Jessamy?"

"Oh!—" He gave me a half-smile. It was an impudent smile. "I do not like being spied on. I made an appointment for her. She will by now be a long way away."

I said, bewildered, "Then you know where she lives?"

"I know where she lives. I know what she does too."

"What does she do?"

But this he would not answer, and I was left to wonder confusedly what kind of appointment he could possibly have made that would bring Miss Jessamy out on a Saturday afternoon on what was apparently a long journey.

He lived in Hampstead, in a shabby tall house that was plainly all furnished apartments. I think it was not far from the Bradleys. It would have been interesting if Mrs. Bradley had walked by when I got out of the cab, but I doubt if I would so much as have noticed her, for by now I was in such a state that I hardly knew what I was doing, or where I was going.

We came up three flights of stairs. Zoltan saw that I was trembling. He said, "Are you frightened of me? I did not think prefects were ever frightened. Or is it because you are going to my flat? I think English girls do not go alone to gentlemen's flats."

I thought it was probable that Attilian girls did not do this either, but I only said, "My father would kill me."

"But your father will never know. He won't know, will he?"

"I hope not. I'll never tell him. You've made me such a liar."

"Were you not a liar before?" He was unlocking his door. There was a small landing and what looked like a coal bunker. There was a pot of flowers on it. It needed watering and was nearly dead. "One of my girl-friends gave it me," Zoltan said. He opened the door. He said, "She is a liar too. All women are liars. Even head girls."

We went in. It was a two-roomed flat, and the rooms led into each other. There was a minute kitchen leading off the hall that looked as if it were hardly used, and what was presumably the bathroom at the side. The sitting-room was quite big, but sparsely furnished: there was a settee and one armchair. There were no ornaments or photographs, but a great many books, and stacks of old newspapers in one corner. In the other corner was a small table with a typewriter and a hardbacked chair. It was entirely a man's room. It was not very clean. It did not look very occupied. If Zoltan had a great many girl-friends, none of them troubled to look after him.

I sat primly down on the settee, not because I wanted to be prim but because I was frightened and ill-at-ease. My knees were close together and my hands tightly clasped. It was only then that I remembered I had left my school tie in the taxi. It did not seem to matter. The only thing that mattered was that I was alone with Zoltan, that I was enchanted, terrified, appalled, and felt as if I had walked into an electric storm.

He looked at me. He probably understood me very well. He went over to a cupboard, took out a bottle and two glasses, then poured me out something that looked like water. I took a grateful swallow of it, then choked into coughing. I had no idea what it was, but it certainly was not water, it was very strong and caught at my throat.

He said reflectively, "It should be champagne, shouldn't it? I forgot. This is gin. I think perhaps I shouldn't give you that, but I have nothing else except half a bottle of wine, and it's probably gone sour. Have you never drunk gin before?"

I shook my head. Gin was something we never had in the house. My father did not approve of spirits, and the only drink we offered guests was sherry, with, on state occasions, brandy after the meal. Gin, if I had considered it at all, would have seemed to me a working-class drink, the kind of thing that men drank in pubs. But it calmed my trembling, though I knew from the warmth that instantly flooded through me that I must be careful and not drink too much of it. I had never been drunk in my life. Lorna once told me that she had drunk too much wine and been dreadfully ill — "Never again, honey, never again!" — and this was an additional warning. In any case my father, like a good Attilian, had once delivered me an oration on the perils of drink. In this, as so often, he was entirely sensible, and I always remembered it. I do not think for one moment that Zoltan wanted to make me drunk, though a tipsy schoolgirl might have amused him, but I was firmly resolved to stay dead-sober and, after the one gulp, put my glass down.

He seemed as ill-at-ease as myself. I was aware of a kind of kaleidoscope in my mind, a confusion of colours and pictures, all disturbing. He kept on looking at me as if he wanted to sit beside me on the settee, then moved away with a jerk. I suppose if I had known more about everything, I could have said something to bring him to my side, but I had no idea what to say, only thought again how handsome he was. I began to wish he would keep still: every time he made a half-move towards me, I caught my breath and began shaking again.

He said at last, "I will make some tea." It sounded like a declaration of war, and he laughed rather loudly as he said it. "I expect you don't think Attilians can make tea. But I am very good, and I even have some cakes for you. They are not so good as those we had in Gunter's, but I daresay you will enjoy them."

He went into the kitchen. I longed to follow him but did not dare. I heard him whistling through his teeth as he filled the kettle, and presently he reappeared with a tray which he dumped down beside me, then, after a palpable hesitation, he settled himself beside me too.

We drank weak tea which had been made with water off the boil, and I tried to eat one of the cakes. It was not very nice, and the cream was not real cream. Mary would have taken one look at it and thrown it away. I could only choke down a couple of mouthfuls, but I crumbled it up so that it looked as if I had eaten most of it.

I do not remember much of what we talked about during the next quarter of an hour, but I do know that as conversation it was quite dreadful. We did not actually discuss the weather: if we had done so it would have provided a comparatively intellectual note. I told Zoltan that our parrot now spoke nothing but Attilian. I asked about Count Asztalos. He, for so talkative a man, said practically nothing, only he never took his eyes off me and his tea went cold in the cup.

Then suddenly he jumped to his feet. He was wearing a black sweater with red and green stripes round the throat and wrists. It was hand-made. I wondered if one of his girl-friends had knitted it for him and, because I was by now as disorientated as if I were running a fever, said so before I could stop myself. I said, "That's a nice sweater. Did one of your girl-friends knit it for you?"

I think this remark, prompted so plainly by emotion and jealousy, shot him back to normal. It was at least something he could cope with. He came back to me and crouched at my feet, and presently he took my hands in his, smoothing the backs of them with his thumb. He looked at me gravely in silence, but the light grey eyes were bright with something that I knew without knowledge, my body answered for me, my mind no longer mattered. I could hear the words he still could not bring himself to say, and knew how I would answer.

My father had done his best. He was more Victorian than most. Lorna said he always astonished her by his condemnation of make-up and perfume, it was so old-fashioned and he did not seem to her an old-fashioned man. Why he was so fanatically strict, I do not know: in many ways he was a cynical yet tolerant man. I can only guess that his marriage had left him unhappy and deprived, yet he had never, to the best of my knowledge, found anyone else. Perhaps his own frustration had turned him fiercely against any kind of sensual self-indulgence. He was after all an attractive man, and not very old: some of the students who came to see him were female and pretty. One I knew was in love with him. I recognised this the moment I saw them together, and I think my mother did too, for she was so rude to her and said afterwards that she found her a most disagreeable girl. I do not really know my father's reactions, but I believe that if he had discovered any weakness in himself, he would never have seen the girl again.

He had always warned me from the very beginning that he would tolerate no bad behaviour from me. The other night had been more violent than most, but this had happened many times before. The widowed doctor issued a variety of vague, undefined warnings, but my father defined his preaching only too clearly. I could not in my heart believe that he would throw me out, but I was not quite sure, I was never quite sure. The very love that he felt so deeply for me would turn into the most savage of weapons. It would be himself he was punishing. I think I would become for him a kind of blasphemy, and the thought of what he would say or do if this happened, terrified me so that I was nearly physically sick.

And now, even with the fear consuming me, I knew quite simply that I would do whatever Zoltan wanted. I no longer cared. It was as if I could not help myself, it was beyond reason. If he had at that moment said, "Come—" and led me to that connecting door, I knew I would follow him blindly, without so much as a murmur of protest.

He did not say it. He understood of course, and I imagine that the adoration of this young girl in her gym tunic, with the school badges on her breast, touched and amused him. I suspect that there were barriers of which I knew nothing, but I thought then that the main obstacle was my own appalling, boring innocence, and I longed passionately to break it down, without the faintest idea of how to do it.

He broke it down for me, smashed it without effort. He sighed, as if he really were bored — I think he must have been, I think frightened virgins must be the most tiresome people — then he said, "I am going back to Attilia."

I felt as if the world had crashed about me. Whatever I had expected it was not this. I made no pretence of concealing my feelings. I turned on him a horrified, shocked face, then I began to cry, sobbing, "Oh no, no, you can't — You don't mean it. You can't go. I won't let you."

He said calmly, "Don't be silly, little Victoria. Why don't you let me finish what I have to say? I want you to come with me. Are you going to come with me?"

The world was revolving again. Outside the world were the widowed doctor and my father, mouthing puppets who no longer had anything to do with me. I said simply, "Yes."

He said, "I can't marry you until we reach Dunavar."

"It doesn't matter."

His eyes moved to the prefect's badge. I knew he was looking at it. He could not stop himself. He began to laugh, and in that laughter in which I joined, the feeling of being in a nightmare vanished. I knew I was simply doing what I had to do. For that moment I was no longer afraid.

He sat down beside me again and took me in his arms. "I see," he said, "that I know nothing about English schools. Your educational system seems to be very advanced." Then more gravely, "You are seventeen. You are much too young for me. And you listen to me saying that we will have to travel unmarried. You should be afraid. Why aren't you afraid? Go on. Say it again in that prim little voice. I want to hear you. *It doesn't matter.* Say it!"

"It doesn't matter."

"And what will Daddy say?"

"Oh, it doesn't matter either."

"Good God! I have no right to do this—"

I was not going to tolerate this melodrama. I had by now recovered myself and was no longer crying. I said, "You don't mean that, you know. You really think you have every right. You are just trying to show me that you have a conscience."

"Do you often talk like that?" he said.

"Oh yes. My mother says I'm showing off. But I can't help it. It's the way I am."

He said almost savagely, "It's the way I am too. Do you really mean that you'll come with me?"

"Of course I mean it."

He said again, "Good God!" and muttered something in Attilian. He once more rose to his feet and moved back as if he did not want to be too near me. He said, sounding almost dazed, "Do you really know what you are saying?" Then before I could answer, probably in a priggish, pompous manner, he went on quite sharply, "All right. I'll make you happy. It will be a good place for

158

you, Attilia, and you'll be away from the war, it won't touch you. We'll let the rest of the world go to hell. I don't care. You won't care. The bombs will fall, but not on us. Why do you look at me like that? Don't you want to be happy? If you stay here, you'll be killed. I suppose I could make this a sop to my conscience, but you don't seem to believe I have a conscience, and the truth is I want you, and I'm going to have you."

I did not answer him, yet his words knocked me back into a kind of sobriety. I did not mind the fact that we could not marry until we arrived in Dunavar. I did not mind that I was breaking every rule and precept by which I had regulated my life. I did not at that moment even consider how appalled and hurt my parents would be. But I could not accept this ruthless ignoring of the rest of the world. If there must be a war — and it seemed inevitable — I hated the thought of running away and so coolly leaving my father and mother, Mary and Maggie, all my friends, to be killed by enemy bombs while I apparently lived in comfort and safety.

And I would have liked him to say he loved me. To say he wanted me and was going to have me was not enough. I did not expect violent romantic protestations, perhaps he was not that kind of man, but the simple phrase "I love you" would not have cost him much and it would have meant the whole world to me.

He did not say it. I think it did not enter his head to do so. And when I at last spoke I too was unromantic: indeed, the words were so prosaic and matter-of-fact that they brought the angry colour into his cheeks.

I said, "Who will we be fighting against?"

It must have seemed a very odd question in the circumstances. He exclaimed, "I'm telling you you're coming away with me, and all you can do is to ask me something so silly and unimportant."

"But it is important. I truly want to know. It matters. Please tell me. I suppose it's the Germans again. It's Hitler. Will Attilia be safe from Hitler? After all, it's awfully near."

He did not answer this at all. He no longer looked loving. He looked almost considering as if he did not quite know what to say. And it was at this point that I nearly told him about the meeting tomorrow and asked him if he would be there, only something stopped me, and then, in my usual idiotic fashion I began to cry: it was all too much, I did not know how to take it any more.

The tears were my best weapon, though they did not fall for that reason. He at once became tender again. He sat beside me, caressed me and kissed me: I lay back in his arms and all thoughts of the outside world left me, nothing seemed to matter except the love that was nearly breaking me in pieces. I could not contemplate a life without Zoltan, and it seemed impossible that in a little while I must take up my ordinary life again.

His next words brought that ordinary life only too near.

He said, "I'm afraid you must now go home. I'm sorry but I have an article to do. Besides, it would not be wise for you to be here any longer. If you stay with me now, it will be for good, and you cannot live here, this is no place for you."

"I don't mind," I said into the sweater that his girl-friend had knitted.

He hesitated, then said more briskly, "But I do. This is a horrible flat. Do you imagine I have no better plans for you? Besides—" He hesitated again, then he said, "You must know that what we plan to do is against the law."

"Why? I don't understand." And it was true that I did not, because this kind of situation had never so far come within my knowledge.

He looked at me in astonishment. I think that at that moment it began to dawn on him that I really was a schoolgirl, that he was taking on more than he realised. He said quite angrily, "But you must know—" He checked himself. He said more quietly, "You are only seventeen. You are, as they say, below the age of consent. I am not allowed to live with you in this country. Your father would put the police on me, and I would end up in prison."

"Oh no!"

"Oh yes. Of course. I imagine he wouldn't even hesitate. I don't blame him. I would do the same if my beautiful young daughter had been seduced by a wicked foreigner. That is why you must come away with me, why we cannot be together until we leave this country, or

160

get married. You will of course have to have a passport."

I said, thankful that at last I could help him, "Oh but I do have a passport."

I think that at this point my innocence, which was simply ignorance, really exasperated him. I saw his face tighten up. He gave an irritated sigh. He said carefully like someone trying not to lose his temper, "You cannot use your own passport. You will need another. It can be arranged. For Christ's sake, Victoria, if you took your own passport you would be stopped at Dover and I would be instantly arrested. But once across the Channel everything will be all right. I have friends who will help. You can leave it all to me." Then he said more gently, "It will not be long, my darling; a month perhaps—"

"A month!"

The word came out of me in a gasp. A month! For the first time I was really afraid, afraid in my bones. Somehow this had all seemed something that would happen in the misty future, with Zoltan and myself meeting secretly at weekends, and school still there, and my home. It had never entered my head that it could happen so soon. In one month I would be away from home for ever, in the company of a man whom I hardly knew, in an alien country which for all it was half mine I had never visited.

I stammered, "But that's so soon. I thought—"

He said icily, "So you don't really want to come with me. You are just playing a little game."

"Oh no, no—" I was nearly in tears again. "That's not fair. Of course I'm not. And I do want to come with you, more than anything in the whole world."

"I suppose I must accept that," he said.

"But I mean it, honestly I do!"

He looked at me steadily. There was not much love in that gaze, and for that moment I was not sure of my own love either: I think he knew this. He said, with a faint smile, "We are almost quarrelling. We are like a married couple. But you must go now. We'll talk about this again. I will put you in a taxi—"

"I can't come home in a taxi. They'll think I've gone mad."

"You can get down at the corner of the road, silly girl. I would come with you," said Zoltan, "but I cannot,

161

and in any case it would be unwise. Your cello lady might be hanging around." Then he said very gently what I had been longing to hear, "I love you, Victoria. It will be all right. I promise you it will be all right. How could it be anything else with me to look after you?" Then he said abruptly, "Are you afraid of me?"

"I think I am. A little."

"Well, we'll have to do something about that, won't we?" He was as he spoke edging me out of the room. I was sure he expected another visitor. I could not help wondering if it were a woman. But I did not protest, and we came down the stairs, out into the street. A taxi came by almost immediately. Zoltan kissed me goodbye. He kissed me on the cheek. The cabby must have thought that he was saying goodbye to his little daughter. Only as we drove off, I looked back to have one final glimpse of him, and saw Mr. Palotas just turning the corner.

So it was not a woman after all. It astonished me, and disturbed me a little too, but did not make much impact. I had after all a great many more important things on my mind. It was quite natural that the two men should be friends: we disliked Mr. Palotas, but that was no reason for Zoltan to share our prejudices. Only it seemed a little unusual for the Attilian Minister to call on one of his journalists: one would have expected the meeting to take place at the Legation. However, I could understand now why I had to go. It would never have done for Mr. Palotas to find Mr. Katona's young daughter in Zoltan's rooms: I do not know if he would have informed my father, but he would have been perfectly entitled to do so.

I huddled in the taxi. I suppose I should have felt happy, but I did not, I was simply afraid. I am a terrible coward. I wondered dimly if I would have enough money to pay the taxi, but found that Zoltan had already paid him.

When we reached the end of our road, I asked the driver to put me down.

He said, "What school do you go to, miss?"

I know he meant to be friendly, but somehow the question seemed a little obscene. I do not know what I answered, but I am sure I gave him a wild, scared look. He probably thought I was not allowed to speak to strange men.

Once home I went straight to my room. My father was working. I could hear the sound of his typewriter. My mother was probably lying down with her wee glass of sherry, for there was no sign of her.

Maggie, bringing something up to the dining-room, called after me, "Miss Victoria, what have you done with your tie?"

I blushed guiltily at once, and she paused on the landing to stare up at me. I saw what I was sure was suspicion on her face. Maggie though simple in some ways is far more perceptive about such things than my parents. She has a primitive understanding of physical matters, she sensed that something was wrong, and that to her would certainly mean a man. She has never shared my parents' innocence about the young. I gather that her sisters are not allowed to get away with anything. She told me once how Jeannie, who must be about my age, went out with a boy and did not come back until very late.

"I gave her a good hiding," Maggie told me, with the curious satisfaction that comes upon people who make this kind of remark. "She'll not do it again, I can tell you. I'm not putting up with that kind of carry-on."

I was very cross with her over this and told her she was a horrid bully. But though of course she has not the least authority over me, I found myself retreating from her stern gaze: I positively stumbled over my words, as I told her that I had taken my tie off and left it on a park bench.

She exclaimed, "Miss Victoria, you didn't! Madam will be ever so cross."

I said angrily, "I've got another one." Then because it really was too much to be rated by the parlour-maid when I had just taken the decision to elope, I snapped at her, "Anyway it's nothing to do with you, Maggie. Stop nagging at me. I'm not one of your little sisters."

And with this I stormed upstairs, leaving Maggie muttering, "You'd have an awful sore backside if you was."

It was not very dignified, but perhaps it was in keeping with the rest of the day.

I spent the afternoon wandering about my room, playing records and trying to calm myself, but after dinner I settled down to my homework, which I always did in the dining-room, as the table was large and took all my papers. I found it terribly difficult to concentrate. I kept on meeting my great-grandmother's gaze, and each time I looked at her, she seemed to become more cynical and disapproving. It is one of those portraits like the Laughing Cavalier that follow you round the room, and I could not dodge those bright, pouched eyes.

After an hour I was forced to abandon my history essay altogether. I love history as much as I do English, and usually this is my favourite homework, especially as Miss Thomas encourages us to express our personal views and does not simply concentrate on dates and kings and queens. But I found I could no longer consider the causes of the French Revolution, for I was planning so violent a personal revolution of my own, it knocked everything else out of my mind.

It was frightening how the glamour of it was fading away. Somehow with Zoltan not there, without his kisses to sustain me, I could only see that I was taking the most appalling risk, that I was possibly behaving like a gull and a fool. There was scarcely a tatter of romance to cling on to. I had to realise that I would be in the power of a man I did not know at all, in a country that, for all it was my father's, was to me foreign, that I was after all very young and I would have no one to turn to if things went wrong. Suppose, said the rational part of my mind — I had not realised it was so strong but it was there — suppose you find you are no longer in love. Suppose his love-making — a process that the widowed doctor never dwelt on — repelled you.

There would not be one friend to help me, no one like Lorna to take me in. And I would never be able to go back home.

I would never be able to go back home.

The words tolled at me like a funeral bell. I thought of my parents with an unexpectedly passionate love. They were after all good and affectionate parents. I suppose I have never been much in tune with my mother, and she does buy me dreadful clothes, but she has always in her way looked after me, and she does something that many parents do not do: she leaves me alone. Even Lorna's parents like to look in when she has friends to tea: my mother, I suspect, is glad to have me off her hands, and

164

never so much as opens the door. I sometimes think that she carries this lack of interest too far: I am pretty sure that she never reads my school reports, though she carries them round with her for days after they arrive.

As for my father, I think until this moment I had not realised how much I loved him. He is a difficult man, he sometimes frightens me with his puritanic views, he is strangely inconsistent in giving me cigarettes and forbidding the use of lipstick, but the thought of a life without him, even at his most impossible, is unbearable, and the thought too of the pain and shock I will cause him, almost breaks my heart.

How can I leave them in such a fashion?

And the words ring in my mind: I will never see my home and my parents again.

Chapter 7

I PASSED THE night as the lovelorn are supposed to do. I tossed and turned, I banged my pillow, I sent half the bedclothes to the floor. Maggie was very cross with me afterwards. The knowledge that I was going to the meeting the next day did not help. I came down to breakfast so pale and puffy-eyed that even my mother noticed.

"What's the matter?" she demanded. "Is it your usual?"

"No, Mummy, it isn't. There's nothing wrong. I've just a bit of a headache."

"What you need," said my mother predictably, "is an early night. I don't like you going out so much in term-time. It's bad for your work and bad for your health. You seem to forget that you're still at school."

My father, who was reading his paper, peered at me over the top of it. He obviously and correctly assumed from my silence that I was ignoring this. "You're always gadding about," he said. "What is it this time?"

"I'm going to the pictures," I said. It was a perfectly normal thing to do on a Sunday evening, and I had already looked up the film guide to see what was on at the local. It was *A Yank at Oxford* with Robert Taylor. I did not say I was going with anyone: my parents would take this for granted. It was another thing in their favour: they seldom interrogated me.

"Well, I think it would be much better for you to go to bed early," said my mother. She added irrelevantly, "The Bradleys are coming to tea."

I said in surprise and relief, "What about Mr. Goldschmidt and Miss Jessamy?"

"Oh," said my father, folding the paper so hard that it almost snapped, "I think it's time we all had a rest. After last Sunday I feel I couldn't possibly stand the pair of them — Mr. Goldschmidt brooding away in that adolescent fashion, and Miss Jessamy apparently unable to read music. I really think," he added to my mother, "that we should find ourselves two more competent musicians. After all, both of them are supposed to be trained, and Mr. Goldschmidt was at the Academy of Music." Then, to my astonishment, he suddenly declaimed, "Ah! Mr. Goldschmidt!" and he looked at my mother, and both of them began to laugh.

I thought they had gone mad, but they looked so delighted with themselves, and my mother was tossing her head in a meaning kind of way, darting mischievous glances at me, that I had to say, "What's all this about Mr. Goldschmidt?"

"Do you hear that, Helen?" said my father. "What's all this about Mr. Goldschmidt?" and really, this was so tiresome that I nearly walked out of the dining-room. When they both get into this teasing mood, I cannot bear them, but of course by now I was so filled with curiosity that I had to know what it was all about.

"First Count Asztalos," said my father, "and now Mr. Goldschmidt. I think we have a siren for a daughter."

"Daddy, for goodness' sake!—"

"Mr. Goldschmidt," said my father with the utmost gravity, "wishes to take you out."

"What!"

"Yes. To the *Missa Solemnis* at the Albert Hall in two weeks' time. He felt, however, as he is considerably older than you are, and you are very young, that he should ask my permission. He delivered a note by hand. It came this afternoon while you were out. I see no reason," said my father, his eyes glinting, "why I should withhold that permission. I am sure you would enjoy the concert, and I cannot believe that Mr. Goldschmidt would in any way behave indecorously."

I could only stare at him, my mouth falling open. The thought of going to the *Missa Solemnis* with Mr. Goldschmidt was so extraordinary that I could hardly believe it.

"I agree," said my father, obviously deriving the utmost amusement from the situation, "that it is unusual in these days to ask a parent's permission to take a young lady out. If he was offering marriage, of course — But perhaps that will come later."

"Daddy, really!"

"But then he is a German. The Germans are very correct. Even if they kick your teeth in, they click their heels before doing so."

I said nothing. I saw that Mr. Goldschmidt had after all taken my advice. I had asked him if he had a girl-friend who could comfort and help him. He seemed to have decided that I would fit the role. I really could not see myself holding Mr. Goldschmidt's hand and saying, There there, but I found it equally hard to imagine myself sitting beside him in the Albert Hall listening to Beethoven. I wondered in a perilous way if he would take me out afterwards to tea at Gunter's.

"I presume," said my father, "you will go."

"Of course she will go," said my mother.

"Well," I said, "you seem to have made up my mind for me."

"You don't sound very enthusiastic," said my father.

I looked at him expressively, and he grinned. He said, "He's not a bad chap. I agree there's nothing very romantic about him, and he's not as good-looking as Count Asztalos, but I am sure he will prove a most considerate escort. And after all you will get a beautiful concert for free."

I said, "Yes, Daddy," and sighed.

"Then I may accept on your behalf? Or perhaps you would care to write him a little note yourself. I suggest it should be on the lines of 'Miss Katona thanks Mr. Goldschmidt for his kind invitation' — Or, to be more personal, Victoria thanks — Now what is his first name? I fancy he doesn't have one."

I threw my napkin ring at him. He fielded it neatly enough. He and my mother were laughing like anything. They really have a most childish sense of humour. Then we dropped the subject of poor Mr. Goldschmidt, my father opened his newspaper again, and my mother wandered off to prepare Mary and Maggie for the tea-party.

Only my father called after me as I left the dining-room. "Baby! I've just remembered Mr. Goldschmidt's first name."

"Oh?"

"It's Siegfried." He looked delightedly at my face. "Well, it's very fashionable in Germany these days. You may count yourself lucky that I didn't call you Brunhilde."

I think sometimes my parents are retarded.

Mrs. Bradley came with Dorothy, the eldest girl. She is my own age and quite nice though dull: she considers that boy-friends and falling in love are awfully sloppy. The expression is hers. She belongs to the Guides and is always trying to persuade me to join. When I was younger, I considered this quite seriously, but the uniform put me off and I did not feel I could endure the woollen stockings. She also has a tendency to laugh loudly at me when I am being serious, and tells me I am a scream.

But everything went well enough, and Mrs. Bradley and my mother discussed the murder once again; with occasional strayings to the subject of servants. Dorothy and I gossiped on the verandah. It all seemed extraordinarily remote. Dorothy was describing some camp-fire singsong — "You'd have enjoyed that, Victoria, you're so jolly good at music," — and I, in an odd contrapuntal way, was silently saying, I am going to run off with a man who is much older than myself, in a month's time I shall no longer be here, you will never see me again and you will never want to see me again, because you will regard me as a fallen woman.

I wonder what she would have said. I think she would have thought I was joking, though even as a joke it would have seemed in pretty poor taste. I of course said nothing. I listened to her. She has a great friend called Winnie, which is a silly name, and Winnie apparently is going to be a nun: I do not think Dorothy entirely approves. She fixed me earnestly with the myopic eyes she has inherited from her mother, and I nodded and smiled. I only hope I nodded and smiled in the right places, for towards the end of the afternoon I was not hearing one word she said. I looked at that amiable, pink-cheeked face, I listened to the sound of her voice, and I noticed that the blue frock she was wearing was considerably worse than my own. And I was in no way laughing at her or thinking her silly. I was envying her for being so sane, so settled, so sensible. Dorothy will never run away with anyone. If she marries, and I expect she will, as she is quite attractive in a wholesome way, she will choose some nice man whom her parents approve of, she will have two or three children and settle into a decent, respectable middle-age.

Perhaps after all she will not. Perhaps she will shed the Girl Guides and go on the loose, fall for a married man or something impossible. You never know with people. All this talk of singsongs may be camouflage. I too till now have been quite sensible, choosing for my boy-friend someone whom my parents like, I do well at school, I am going to be head girl.

"Mummy says you're going to be head girl," Dorothy says, coming neatly in on my thoughts. "I think that's simply marvellous. I bet you're pleased."

Yes, Dorothy, I'm pleased, but you see, I shall never be head girl, I shall be sleeping with my new husband in Dunavar, you'll never want to speak again to someone like me who runs away from home and upsets everyone.

"Yes, of course I'm pleased. Dorothy—"

They were about to go. I could see Mrs. Bradley gathering up her things. She is the sort of person who has a vast amount to gather up: gloves, handbag, several parcels, her spectacles, and a string bag to put them all in. She usually leaves something behind. She was talking busily as she gathered. She and my mother were on their own: my father is bored by her and shows it quite shamelessly: he had long ago retreated to his study, ignoring the jangling faces my mother made at him.

"What is it, old thing?" asks Dorothy. I know she is fond of me, but I do wish she would not call me old thing.

I want to say, What am I to do? Help me. I can't go through with this, yet I can't bear the thought of never seeing him again. Oh Dorothy, leave your camp-fire, forget about Winnie, and tell me what to do.

I said in a gasp, "Have you ever been in love?"

She broke into a great peal of laughter. I think this was largely nerves, because I doubt if anyone in the Bradley household ever asks such a question, but it had a salutary effect on me. I was almost in my desperation on the point of pouring everything out. If I had done so, I cannot imagine what would have happened. But she must have regretted that laughter, she was a good-natured girl, for she instantly became grave again, saying in a deep whisper, "Oh Victoria, have you really found Mr. Right?"

Mr. Right! Zoltan! I wanted to say, I'm afraid it's Mr. Wrong, but fortunately she went on talking.

"Is he a nice chap?" she asked. "When can I meet him?"

"Dorothy!" called Mrs. Bradley, tapping on the French window. "Get your things, on, dearie. We must be going." She added to my mother, "One should never outstay one's welcome. That's what Jim always says. Don't you agree?"

"Of course," said my mother, who probably was not listening, and was simply thankful that everyone was going.

Dorothy said, "Oh bother!" then, "Just tell me his name. I won't breathe a word. Guide's honour."

I said in a fit of insanity, "Siegfried!" and this completely finished her, for she gaped at me and began to giggle. However, her mother was calling her again, so we all said goodbye with the ritual kisses, and I came to the front-door and waved as they trotted off home. Dorothy whispered to me just before she went, "Give me a ring," and I nodded and smiled.

"Such a dreary woman," said my mother when I came back into the drawing-room. "I really don't like women at all. They just talk." She did not explain what she meant by this, but then I think she leads two lives, one of which is full of sinister subterranean tunnels. She turned to gaze at me. "You look much better. Now if you only had an early night—"

"Mummy, I told you, I'm going to the pictures."

"I think sometimes," said my mother, turning into one of her tunnels, "you are very silly."

But I ignored this and simply went upstairs to collect my coat. My father heard me and came to the top of the stairs. I did not want to see him at that moment, and looked up guiltily.

He said, "Mr. Goldschmidt is not as old as you might think."

I was completely fed up with the subject of Mr. Goldschmidt, and wished my father would submerge his mis-guided sense of humour, but this reminded me that I had not yet acknowledged his invitation. I said crossly, "Does it matter?"

"Of course it matters," said my father. "He is twenty-nine. I expect you thought he was much older."

I suppose I had thought so, not that I had really bothered to consider the matter. Mr. Goldschmidt is the kind of man who might be any age: he will probably look just the same in ten years' time. But I only said, "Goodbye, Daddy, I'm off now," and ran down the stairs before he could think of more biographical details.

When I arrived at the station, to get to King's Cross on the Piccadilly line, I toyed with the idea of ringing Lorna, just to put heart in myself. She would certainly be going out with her latest boy-friend, but I might just have caught her while she was making-up her face. It would have been comforting to hear her voice, for I was filled with presentiment, though I had no idea why. But, though I hesitated for a few minutes outside the call-box, I never put the call through. Lorna is understanding and easy: she possesses few of the ordinary inhibitions. But she is, as I had just discovered, at heart a conventional girl. She adores secret love-affairs, pointed bras and frilly blouses: she loves being used as a go-between and would lie her-self to death for her friends. But she would not approve at all of my going to a fascist meeting, because she would think it dirty, dangerous and stupid, and the idea of my eloping, unmarried, to a foreign country with a comparative stranger, would horrify her. She has very much what the eighteenth century called a bottom of good sense. She would never give me away, but she would bring all of her considerable powers of persuasion to bear on me to make me change my mind.

And she would of course be utterly and completely right.

So I did not ring her, and half an hour later I arrived at the meeting which had already started.

It was in no way impressive. It really was dirty, danger-ous and stupid. To begin with the hall was in a very nasty part of King's Cross, which is not a quarter of London that I know well. It was in a little side street full of small hotels, all of which looked very uninviting;

the people I passed seemed tough and rough, and there was a pub at the corner from which two men emerged very drunk and lurching towards me. I was thankful to get into the hall, but inside it was not much better.

I began to wish I had not come. Indeed, I could not think why I had, except that as always I was driven by curiosity, and wanted to know about everything remotely connected with Zoltan and Attilia.

There were people on the platform behind a long table. They were all dressed like our parrot, just as Mr. Gyori had described them. Polly, incidentally, though out in the area as usual, had remained silent as I went out. He sat there in a huddle and did not even snuffle at me. I had to think of him as I looked around me. All these men wore grey tunics and trousers, braided with scarlet, and the trousers were all tucked into what I could only think of as jack-boots. There were no swastika armlets, but everyone looked both military and fascist, and made me feel a little cold as I sat at the back of the hall. On the wall behind them was the symbol of the Attilian Life Society, the golden doe. I could not help studying its profile. Mr. Gyori had been quite right: it definitely had a Jewish nose. The Society had obviously not yet got down to choosing something more appropriate.

I had never been to a political meeting before. When we had elections I never really bothered much about them except to hope that Labour would get in. My father, being stateless, had of course no vote, and neither had I, being seventeen. Maggie did not vote at all — "Havers!" she said, shrugging her shoulders — and Mary was staunchly Conservative. I never even looked at the leaflets that fell through our letter-box, and I simply glanced at the results in the paper, though my father followed it all with a passionate absorption.

I did not find it very interesting. I looked around me nervously, terrified lest Miss Jessamy was there, or even Zoltan who, as an Attilian journalist, might well be covering the proceedings. But there was, thank goodness, no sign of either of them, though for one horrifying moment I thought I saw someone remarkably like Miss Jessamy near the platform. But when I looked again, very intently, whoever it was had gone. There are after all a great many Miss Jessamys in the world, and I

173

could not see why she should come to such a meeting, however politically involved she might be.

And, I told myself, to restore my flagging courage, I was not doing anything wrong, merely being rather silly. If she had seen me yesterday, going to Zoltan's rooms, it would have been very different, especially as she had threatened to tell my father. But plainly my father had not heard from her, so Zoltan's subterfuge had worked.

None of this really comforted me or removed my feeling of unease. I found it all very stupid and wished again heartily that I had not come. I would have gone away at this point, and perhaps really taken myself to a cinema, but by now the hall had filled up, people were pushing and shouting, and in one corner not far away from me there seemed to be some kind of scuffle. I was in the middle of a row, and to get to the door I should have had to push my way past what seemed to be a very angry crowd. There were some police there, and I thought of going up to them, but somehow they did not look as if they would be helpful: they made no attempt to interfere in the scuffle, and I saw one of them nudge his comrade, and then they both laughed.

At this point leaflets were being handed round, and one was shoved at me. I took it. It seemed to be a song, and I could recognise that it was in German. The name "Horst Wessel" was in the right-hand corner, but it meant nothing to me, I had never heard of it before.

I could not even hear much of the speeches, for half the audience seemed determined to shout the speakers down. What I did hear was childish, abusive and ugly, like a squalling baby yelling defiance at the world. There was considerable talk of Jews, and each time the word was mentioned there was a violent outcry in the hall, some cheering and some hissing, and soon several fights broke out, so that the police, still watching in a bored kind of way, were at last stirred to action. It seemed to me that they were on the side of the Society. A number of protesters were thrown out, and one was carried struggling past me, his kicking feet bruising my leg. I saw that he had a black eye, and blood was running down his cheek.

By this time I was terrified. I would have been relieved to see Miss Jessamy. Once I tried to get up, thinking that perhaps I could push my way out, but when I tried to do so, a violent fight broke out in the row directly behind me, and I did not dare, only sank down again, wishing that I had had more sense than to come to something quite unsuitable for a young girl on her own.

By this time the noise was so tremendous that I could not hear one word of what anyone was saying. The main speaker, who was plainly an Attilian — I recognised his accent — suddenly broke into a chant of "Sieg heil, Sieg heil", like Hitler in the news-reels, and at this the whole audience began to sing, one half chanting something German, perhaps the song on my leaflet, and the other the "Red Flag", which I recognised, because Michael had once chanted it at me in derision.

This was too much for me to take. The fighting, which had been spasmodic, now broke out in earnest, with the police, from what I could see of them, doing remarkably little to prevent it. I could not imagine how I would fight my way out, but if I stayed I would probably be knocked down, like the woman three rows ahead, who received someone's fist full in her face and disappeared under the seats, probably to be trampled on. I was by now hysterical with panic, but I jumped up and began to push my way past, my eyes fixed on the entrance which seemed a hundred miles away and which was beginning to shimmer in my gaze.

When a hand came beneath my elbow, I thought it was someone attacking me and kicked out at him. Immediately the person picked me up under his arm as if I were a baby, and the next minute we were out in the street where, dizzy with shock and fright, I disgraced myself finally by sitting down on the pavement, my knees buckled beneath me, In the distance I could still hear the singing and a sudden crash as if a chair had been hurled to the floor.

I looked up into Zoltan's face.

He was staring at me with such a look of fury that I nearly passed out altogether. He made no attempt to pick me up. I said weakly, "What is that song they are singing? The German one—"

It was utterly absurd to ask him such a trivial question at this moment, especially as he was plainly so angry with me, but he snapped, "The Horst Wessel song. What the devil are you doing here? You bloody little fool! I suppose you are spying on me. Get up! Don't pretend you can't. Get up at once and answer me."

Nobody had ever spoken to me like this in my life. The tears of shock and resentment and reaction were pouring down my face. I did not answer his question, only wailed, "I can't get up."

"Then you'll just have to stay there. You don't imagine I'm going to help you, do you?"

But he must have seen that I was on the verge of fainting, for he put his hands under my armpits and lugged me inelegantly to my feet. Then, ignoring the startled looks of passers-by, he began to shake me so that my beret, already pushed over one eye, flew into the gutter and my hair streamed about my face.

I sobbed, "How dare you? Stop it. Stop it at once!"

Then he released me so violently that I was hurtled against the wall. He said in a bitter, savage voice, "You were spying on me."

"I wasn't! Of course I wasn't."

"Of course you were. Do you take me for a fool? If you weren't, what the hell were you doing there?"

"Don't swear at me like that! I was curious. Why shouldn't I be? I read about it in the paper, and you told me about the Attilian Life Society—"

"It wasn't I who told you about the Attilian Life Society." His face was cold and still with anger. The light grey eyes were like pebbles, and it was as if rage had dissolved the flesh on his bones for the aquiline nose and square chin jutted forth; the mouth was set in a long, thin line. He looked so murderous that I began to shake again. The thought came dimly into my befogged mind that I would be lunatic to entrust myself to such a person. There seemed neither help nor pity here for someone who would be vulnerable, lost and alone. And then it was as if my foreboding somehow communicated itself to him, for the fury was wiped off his face as if it had never existed, and suddenly he was again the man I knew and loved.

He began to laugh, though it was a brittle laugh without much humour. He stooped down and picked up my beret, setting it back on my head, and smoothing the tangled hair away from my cheeks

He said, "I shall never know where I am with you. It seems to me you'll always get yourself into trouble. Why do you worry yourself about the Attilian Life Society? It's nothing to do with you. I remember now you men‑tioned it in Gunter's."

I said faintly, "Of course it's something to do with me. I'm half Attilian. I ought to know about these things."

He said dryly, "Don't be too sure. You should remem‑ber what happened to Mr. Gyori. You are too inquisitive, Victoria. Is there not some nursery tale of a lady who was inquisitive and had her head chopped off? You must learn not to stick your little nose into what doesn't con‑cern you. This kind of meeting is no place for young English ladies. You might have been badly hurt, or even killed. I just couldn't believe my eyes when I saw you there."

I said, suddenly on the defensive, "And what were you doing there?"

He raised his head sharply. For a second the anger returned. Then he shrugged, and once again laughed.

"I see," he said, "we shall have a fine life together. It will be, Zoltan, what have you been doing? Zoltan, where have you been? Zoltan, be a good boy. I'm not a good boy, Victoria. I'll never be a good boy. But you must learn to be a good girl and not interfere. I do not like people who interfere. However, I will forgive you this time because I love you, and now we will kiss and make up, and then you must go home for I am busy. I have no time today for young English ladies fresh from school who ought to be doing their exercises."

It was to strike me afterwards that he had not answered my question, but I was only shaking with relief that he was no longer angry with me. I came into his arms, hold‑ing up my face, ignoring the curious stares around us.

He kissed me briefly, then his hold tightened, and the kisses became more satisfactory. At last he released me. He tweaked my beret into place again, and did up my coat buttons.

"There is a button gone," he said. Then, "I will get another note delivered to you. I must see you again. I think we may have to go sooner than I planned."

I suppose I should have rejoiced. Instead, the cold fear tightened my stomach, and again I was aware of a strange presentiment. I did not answer, and he said in a harsh voice, "What's the matter? Have you changed your mind?"

"No, of course not."

But he was not quite sure: he must have heard the frightened defiance in my voice. He looked at me warily, and I added in a kind of desperation, "I do love you so much."

"Do you? And so you should," he said, "for I am a very lovable man. And you are a very naughty little girl. You know that, don't you?"

"Yes, Zoltan," I said.

He said, banging one fist down on the other in exasperation, "I cannot think why you came here. You must never, never do anything like that again. You are to promise. Promise, Victoria. Say after me: I will never do anything like this again."

"I will never do anything like this again. But," I said, speaking as I might have done at home, for I was always encouraged to say what I chose, "I don't see why it upset you so much. I know it was a bit silly and dangerous too, but I wasn't to know that it would end in a free fight. I thought it was just an ordinary political meeting. After all, one should take an interest in politics. And you go on so about the war that's coming, and these people are all obviously pro-German, they were saying dreadful things about the Jews, and all that 'Sieg heil' stuff — It's the kind of thing we should all know about. If there really is a war, they'll be very dangerous. They'll probably be interned. They'll certainly have to be put out of the way."

He did not answer any of this immediately. I saw his chest rising and falling as if he were struggling to restrain himself. He said at last in a tight voice, "I had no idea you were so interested in politics. Your views are very naïve. Anyway, politics are not for women."

I exclaimed, "Oh nonsense! You sound like Hitler."

He snapped at me, "Don't talk to me like that. It's not nonsense at all. In Attilia we like our women to be feminine. You are far too young to understand any of this. You should leave such matters to people who know about them. Now I want you to forget all about this meeting, and next time we meet we will not mention it again, we will talk of pleasant things like our journey and our life together. You will go home now, and we will see each other very soon. By the way, this friend of yours, this Lorna — Is she to be trusted?"

"But of course! She's my best friend."

"Best friend!" He heaved a great sigh then said, "I would not like to count the number of people who have been betrayed by their best friends. You are not to trust her too much. You certainly must not tell her of our plans. Will you please promise me not to say one word?"

I said I would, then he gave me a little push, and turned away. He suddenly ran back to push a pound note into my hand.

"For your taxi," he said, then disappeared round the corner.

The meeting seemed to be over. People were streaming out of the hall. I suppose the police had broken it up, but fights were still going on in the crowd. I saw several men being bundled into police vans. One of them was dragged along, his feet trailing behind him. An ambulance drew up, and two men went into the hall with a stretcher. It was more than I could take. I began to feel dizzy again, so I thankfully hailed a passing taxi, giving him my address.

I forgot to get down at the corner of my road, but I thought no one saw me. Nonetheless I was cautious enough not to go in immediately. My parents might hear the sound of the taxi and would then certainly ask me awkward questions. Until all this happened I had never taken a taxi except when coming back from a party: it had frankly never entered my head to do so. I walked round the block several times until I felt I had calmed down. I still felt ill and distraught. Zoltan had been so angry, and I had never seen him angry before. And the whole thing had been so beastly, so violent and horrible. I could not forget the sight of that man with the trailing legs: I am sure he was unconscious.

I came in at last, meaning to go straight up to my room. I met Maggie in the hall. I thought she would comment on my untidiness, especially the missing button — she is remarkably observant in such things — but instead of scolding me she gave me a frantic look, whispered, "Oh, Miss Victoria!" and flung her hand to her mouth.

"What's the matter, Maggie?"

But she only said again, "Miss Victoria!" burst into noisy sobbing, and rushed away down the kitchen stairs.

I could not understand this at all. I had never seen Maggie in such a state. Mary is always upset, over people being late, the butcher delivering the wrong joint, or the milk going off, but Maggie, though she scolds me, is usually cheerful, singing little Scots songs about her work, rather off-key.

However, I was too exhausted to pursue the matter, and went on up the stairs to my room.

I came in. My father was standing by the mantelpiece, with a look on his face such as I had never seen. They say your heart sinks into your boots. I have always thought that a ridiculous phrase; but when I saw his expression of cold, accusing fury, I knew exactly what the words meant. I thought in my swimming, aghast mind, It's that Miss Jessamy, she was there, I knew I saw her. Then I knew it was even worse. Zoltan's ruse had not worked at all. He would never believe any woman to be as clever as himself, but Miss Jessamy would not be as easily taken in as he imagined. She knew about the visit and she must have told my father: he would dislike my going to the meeting but it would not arouse in him this murderous rage.

He did not say a word. He came up to me as I stood there, staring at him. I think I must have gone white because I felt somehow as if the blood had left my body. He slapped me across the head, first on one side and then on the other. Then he spoke. "You whore!" he said then, as if he could not control himself, hit me again and again.

I made no attempt to dodge the blows. I swayed from side to side beneath them, my beret falling to the floor. I did not cry or make one sound of protest. My reaction was not so much of fear as of outraged anger. My parents never really hit me when I was a child. I do not think that up till now my father had so much as raised a hand to me. My mother, when I was small, delivered the odd slap from time to time, when exasperated beyond endurance, but believed far more in the dictum, "Mummy is upset," or, "You are making Mummy very unhappy." As this signified as little as the slap, it never meant much

180

to me: I was in any case a fairly obedient child who usually did as she was told, if only because it made life easier.

I heard my mother's little shriek from the doorway. My father instantly stopped. He put his hand to his forehead. He looked as if he were on the verge of collapse. If he had done so I would not have put out a finger to help him. My head was roaring with pain, as much from shock as the actual blows, but I still remained standing, I was not going to let him see me defeated.

My mother came into the room. She looked aghast, her mouth fallen open. She whispered, "Mikki, what are you doing? Oh Mikki, how could you!"

He answered in an exhausted voice, "Helen, please go away."

"I will do nothing of the kind! If you think I'm going to stand here and let you knock Victoria about in that frightful way—"

He said, "I've finished."

"I should hope you have—"

"Helen. Please. I won't touch her again. I give you my word. But we must be alone. Please go away."

My mother looked helplessly at the pair of us. If I had burst into tears or called her name, she would at once have run to protect me. But our united silence defeated her. Her head turned wildly from one to the other of us. I could see that she had no idea what to do, and certainly nothing like this had ever happened in our home before. She went away at last. I am certain that she rushed to help herself to a glass of sherry, and it would not be a wee one. I could not blame her. In as far as I was capable of coherent thought I could have swallowed a bottleful myself.

My father said at last in this new harsh voice, "Sit down, please. Do you want a glass of water?"

I did not answer him. I gave him a look of savage contempt. I hated him, hated him for the humiliation he had inflicted on me, hated him for the destruction of my happiness, hated him for the beastliness in which he had submerged my love, my feeling for Zoltan. But I obeyed him insofar that I sat down on the bed. I would have preferred to remain standing, but I could not do so, I felt too weak. I wanted to lie down, to rest my aching head

181

on the pillow, but this I managed not to do. I simply sat there, very upright, staring at my father.

He said, "I know all about it."

I would have been wiser to remain silent. But the words came out before I could stop them. "I suppose Miss Jessamy told you."

"She only did her duty," said my father. Then he burst into passionate speech, so violent that the spittle flew from the corner of his lips. "What have you done to me? You've lied and deceived me, you've traded on the freedom I've always permitted you. You went out with him when you said you were going to Lorna's. You've just met him again at that infamous fascist meeting. And you went to his rooms alone — I don't understand you. I see I've never understood you. You're not my daughter any more. And he is such a bad, wicked man. I cannot believe you know how bad he is."

I still did not answer, though at long last, what with the blows and the fright and the guilt and the anger, I could no longer contain my tears. I could have killed myself for crying, but they trickled down my cheeks on to the hands tightly clasped in my lap.

My father, from sheer force of habit, half took his handkerchief out of his pocket, then with a kind of angry grimace, shoved it back again. He said, "Have you slept with him?" As I did not answer, he half-raised his hand again, then said almost in a whisper, "For Christ's sake, answer me. I've got to know. You must see that." Then in a roar, "Have you slept with him?"

I shook my head.

"But no doubt you are planning to do so?"

This I would not answer, I was beginning to feel utterly unreal. This was a nightmare. This could not be happening to me.

My father said almost unbelievingly, "Don't you know what kind of man he is? He is a traitor and a spy. He is a womaniser. He will never stay with any one woman once he's got what he wants out of her. He certainly doesn't love you."

Then I did answer. I said, "I don't believe you."

"How many times have you seen him alone?"

"You've just told me. Three times."

I had never before used such a tone to him. He

blinked but only said, as if to himself, "And every time you lied — To go to his rooms like that—"

I thought dazedly that Miss Jessamy had an extraordinarily efficient spy system. But I still sat there with poker back, and never took my eyes off my father.

He said again, "I don't understand. How am I to believe that my daughter could behave like this, behave like a whore? I have no doubt that you let him make love to you, even if you didn't actually sleep with him Will you answer me, you bitch? If you don't—"

I did answer him. The words that came from my lips were those of a stranger-enemy. I said, "Why should I answer you? It's none of your business."

"You talk to me like that, your own father!"

It was all straight from a Victorian melodrama, but it was real, not a play, and we both meant what we said. I said, "You're no longer my father. I hate you. I don't care if I lie to you or deceive you. I love Zoltan. I'm going to marry him. I don't mind who he is or what you say he is. After what you've done, it doesn't matter to me if I never see you again. You're horrible. You don't love me. If you really loved me, I'd have told you what was happening. But you've got this thing about behaving badly, as you put it, you think all women are really whores, you go on and on about lipstick and perfume and silly things like that, and now you're astonished and shocked that I actually fall in love with someone and don't tell you about it. Of course I lied. You left me no alternative. You would just have forbidden me to see him. I'll tell you this, Daddy—"

Daddy. The affectionate pet-name. It came naturally from my lips. I had always called him Daddy. Now it sounded dirty and obscene.

I said more weakly, "I'll tell you this. I'm seventeen. I know it's not very old, but it does mean I'm no longer a child. And in future I'm going to do what I please. You can't stop me, you know. I suppose I'm what they call a minor, but what can you really do? You can hit me. You can starve me. But in the end I'll just go my own way. Why should you worry? You can go back to Africa. That's all you really care about."

It was intolerably cruel of me, but then I had taken more than I could be expected to endure, and I was so

183

afraid, so miserable, so faint with pain and humiliation: the worst of it all was the conviction that, despite my defiant words, this was the end.

He did not answer any of this. He was white to the lips. He walked towards the door. He said, "You will stay in your room until I give you permission to come down. I want your word that you will do as I say."

I said, "I'm not giving you my word. I shall do as I please."

I thought he would hit me again. But he did not. He shut the door behind him, and I heard the key turning in the lock. I did not take this seriously. First, my mother would never permit it, secondly, I had of course to go to the bathroom, and thirdly I had to be fed, even if it was only bread and water. But it was a frightening sound, and then I forgot my dignity and became a little girl again: I put my head down on the pillow and cried and cried until my eyes were swollen and sore and my headache unendurable.

I did not hear the door opening. But I smelt the smell of food, then I heard Maggie's voice saying, "Oh Miss Victoria, you'll just make yourself ill. Here's a nice bit of supper for you. You'll feel ever so much better when you've eaten something, and Mary's put some sherry on the tray, she says she's sure you need it."

At that moment I dimly realised that Maggie was not the dragon-sister she pretended to be. All this talk of hidings and carry-ons was simply moonshine. The naughty Jeannie probably received a slap and a hug and a sweetie. I suppose I should have been given bread and water, but here there was chicken and vegetables, followed by one of Mary's extra-special cream sweets. I suspect that the dinner my parents had downstairs was not nearly so grand. As I looked at it, beautifully set out, with the little glass of sherry at the side, I began to cry again. Maggie at once took me in her arms as if I were her smallest sister, Kirsty, and rocked me to and fro, saying, "There, there," in such a tender voice that I at once began to feel better. Presently I drank my sherry and even ate some of the supper, while Maggie, tut-tutting, wetted a flannel in the wash-basin, and began gently to dab at my swollen face.

She did not reproach me, nor did she ask what had

happened. Of course she knew all about it. The kitchen always knows all about everything. My parents undoubtedly had a screaming row after Miss Jessamy had gone, and Mary and Maggie would be hovering on the top stair, with the door a little ajar. My mother might even have told them, she always tells everyone everything, from the postman to the girl behind the counter in the shop.

Only as Maggie left, carefully covering the tray with a clean napkin — it looked as if my father had insisted on bread and water, after all — she said suddenly, "Poor Polly's dead."

"What!"

Maggie sniffed a little. I think she and Mary were really fond of our parrot and, though I could not pretend to love the beastly bird, he was after all part of my home, and I was quite upset.

"We found him dead in his cage," said Maggie. "Mary came into the area to take him in for the night. He was lying on his back with his poor little legs in the air. Mr. Katona thinks he was poisoned."

"But who on earth would want to kill him? He never did anyone any harm."

"I don't know," said Maggie, in a flat, despairing voice. "I just don't know what's happening to any of us. I think we're all quite daft. Now you go to sleep, Miss Victoria. You'll feel better in the morning. Mr. Katona is a dear, kind man, and he'll soon get over it, especially after a good night's sleep."

"Yes, I expect he will."

But I won't get over it, I'll never get over it—

"Good night, Maggie darling. Thank you for being so nice, and please thank Mary too." And then because I was so battered by emotion and everything else that I had lost all control, "I do love you both so much. You won't ever leave us, will you?"

I might have known this would be too much for Maggie. She wailed, "Oh, Miss Victoria!" and broke into howling sobs. I heard her crying all the way down the stairs. Our neighbours must by now be thinking our home a madhouse.

I lay in bed for a long time. I no longer wanted to cry. I knew now what I had to do, but I must wait till my parents went to bed. My mother came in about an hour later. Goodness knows what happened between her and my father. I heard her take the key out of the lock. I knew she would not let me be locked in. I pretended to be asleep. I saw through my half-closed lids that she was peering down at me. Once she touched my cheek. My mother is in some ways a violent person who loves drama, but she must have been horrified by my father's display of temper. She stood beside me for quite a time, then went out, meaning no doubt not to make a sound, but in her jangling way knocking against the bedside table and slamming the door.

I do not know how long I lay there. I did not look at my watch. I heard my parents coming up to bed. They did not seem to be speaking to each other, there was a deathly silence. I heard them go to the bathroom. I heard the water running. Then they shut their door, and there was the click of the light-switch.

I crept out of bed. I felt very ill and shaky, but so remote that it did not seem to matter. I dressed again, in a blouse and skirt, then packed a small suitcase. I hardly knew what I was putting in it, but I took a change of underclothes, a sweater, some handkerchiefs and my toilet things. The effort of all this made me feel dizzy, so I sat down on the bed again and smoked a cigarette. When I looked at my watch, it was three in the morning. I still loitered. This was after all my home where I had been born, this was my own little room, I had lived here all my life. It was unbearable to leave it, never, never, to come back.

But it seemed to me that I had no choice. Before I left, I opened my dressing-table drawer and took out the pearl choker that I had never returned. I had after all no money in the world except a couple of pounds from my allowance, and a little change from the money Zoltan gave me for the taxi. I had never in my life pawned anything, but I was sure the choker was worth a great deal. It was, of course, stealing. I knew that. My mother had forgotten all about it — only my mother could forget something like a pearl choker — but nonetheless it belonged to her as it had belonged to her grandmother before her. However, I did not hesitate. I pushed it down to the bottom of my handbag, then with my case in one hand and my shoes in the other, I stole down the stairs.

It was now nearly half past four.

I had never seen my home at such an hour. Sometimes at Christmas, when I went to parties, I would come back about two o'clock, but that would be the very latest. I did not dare to put the light on, but the street lamp outside the front door shone through the glass panelling so that everything was visible with a kind of ghostly effect. I gazed at everything as if it were for the last time, it probably was for the last time. Even the things I did not much care for seemed beautiful. The Holbein prints on the staircase wall. The odd pieces of bric-à-brac that Maggie grumbled at, and which normally I did not notice. The grandfather clock in the hall that I always knocked with my satchel when I was in a hurry. The valuable and badly-worn Turkish carpet that stretched from the front-door to the kitchen stairs—

But I dared not wait, and there was no point in being sentimental. I shut the door with great care, and stepped out into the street, pausing on the bottom step to put my shoes on again. My parents' room faced the street. I did not look up at it. I made my way to the main road, was lucky enough to find a night taxi, and directed the driver to King's Cross, where yesterday I had noticed so many hotels.

Zoltan had told me to come to him if anything happened, even if it were in the middle of the night. It could hardly be said that I had behaved with much common sense during the past few days, but somehow I knew with a deep, unshakable knowledge that first, he would not be pleased if I took him at his word, and secondly, for my own sake, this was something I must not do.

It would be like people you meet on holiday who say, "You must ring us when you are back, and come to dinner." You never do. If you did, you would probably be greeted with an aghast silence as they frantically try to remember who you are.

But of course it was more than that. I had now made up my mind to go to Attilia with Zoltan, for it seemed to me that I no longer had any choice. As, however, I was under age, both my father and the police would instantly go to the Hampstead flat, now that I had run away from home. Zoltan, as I instinctively knew, could not afford trouble of that kind, or indeed of any kind: he was already in it, and in every conceivable way.

No. I would write to him from the hotel, and in the meantime I must find myself a room for the night. I paid off the taxi, and walked down the little side street that led into the hall where the Attilian Life Society held its meetings.

It was an ugly street, and they were bad little hotels. I do not know much about these things, and the only hotels I knew were where we spent our holidays: they were clean and friendly, with the proprietor coming out to greet us. But these were horrid and unwelcoming, with something furtive about them. However, they were open, even at five in the morning, and as each one looked as nasty as the next, I simply chose the first, which was called the Nelson Hotel, came in rather uneasily and, dumping my case on the floor, asked the night porter if I could have a room.

He stared at me in a kind of derisive surprise. I suppose I did not look like the usual type of customer. His eyes moved over my bruised face, and he plainly did an addition sum. He said, "What's all this, then? Run away from home, have you?"

Naturally I flushed scarlet, especially as he added, still eyeing my face, "What's the matter? Dad got a bit rough with you? What you been doing?"

I managed to answer haughtily, "I simply want a room. For about a week."

He looked behind me as if expecting me to be followed. He frowned a little. He plainly thought I spelt trouble. He said surlily, "Can you pay?"

"Of course I can pay!"

"We'll want a night in advance."

I opened my handbag in silence. I could see the choker gleaming at the bottom of it, and hastily shoved it down. The sum was very small, only a few shillings, and I paid him, instantly closing the bag so that he could not see the contents.

He picked up my case and beckoned me to follow him up the stairs. When we reached the landing, he stopped. He said not unkindly, "If I was you miss, I'd go home. I expect they've got over it by now. They'll welcome you with open arms."

"Will you show me my room, please?"

He grimaced and shrugged. I think he was quite a decent sort of man who felt this was not the right place for me. But I was too tired to appreciate this and, when he at last opened the door of my room and told me if I wanted breakfast it was served between seven thirty and nine, I collapsed on the bed, thinking of nothing but sleep.

I did not sleep much after all. The room was horrid, very small and grubby, with no furniture except a bed, wardrobe and chair. The lavatory, which was down the corridor, was even nastier and it smelt. The bathroom, into which I peered, had the kind of old-fashioned bath that is like a tank, and the last occupant had left a greasy tidemark. Even the sheets on my bed were dubious, but by this time I was too exhausted to care. I cried a little into the grimy pillow, and wished with all my heart that yesterday could be erased, that I were back home in my own lovely bed, from which I would go down to breakfast at eight o'clock to eat bacon and egg, and smile at my father behind his paper.

I had after all been spoilt, and one never knows how spoilt one is until it is all over. We did not keep a particularly luxurious home, but Maggie saw to it that it was scrupulously clean: the sheets were always spotless, the bath and lavatory white, and our meals were lovely and served on time.

However, it was my decision, and I got up early, looking dismally at my face which showed the bruises only too clearly. I wished I had some powder to cover them. I combed my hair into a droop so as to hide what I could, and went downstairs to eat a breakfast that was enormous and surprisingly good, then sat for a while in the dingy lounge, and wrote to Zoltan.

I told him what had happened. After all, he had to know. I said my father had found out everything, was furious with me and had beaten me. I had been locked up in my room on bread and water, which was not strictly speaking true, but which sounded impressive. He would probably think I climbed out of the window. I said I was very unhappy, which was certainly true, and please,

189

would he come to see me as soon as possible.

Then I went out to post the letter, and stopped at the nearest pawnbroker, which I recognised by the sign of the three balls outside.

I had never been to a pawnbroker in my life. The old man behind the counter eyed me with bitter suspicion. I suppose that he, like the porter, thought I was too young. He turned the choker over and over in his hands, then put one of the pearls between his teeth and bit it.

He said, "Where did you get this from, miss?"

I answered with as much dignity as I could, "It's mine. Are you insinuating that I've stolen it?"

"I don't handle stolen goods."

"This isn't stolen goods."

He looked me up and down, no doubt pricing my clothes and general appearance. The things my mother buys me are dreadful, but they are always good quality, so I suppose they passed his inspection. But he still did not like it. He kept on glancing at me and grumbling beneath his breath as he examined the choker, holding it up to the light, then running his grimy fingers over it. I thought my great-grandmother would have had a fit.

He said at last, "Twenty pounds."

I do not know much about the value of things, but one thing I was certain of: the choker was worth a great deal more than that. But I did not hesitate. Twenty pounds seemed to me a lot of money, I needed it badly, and I was sure the old man would not raise his price. I said that I agreed, took the money and the pawn ticket, then went out of the shop.

I heard him still muttering as I closed the door.

I wandered about for a little, for I felt I could not bear to sit in my dingy room. I bought myself a sixpenny paperback to read, had a cup of coffee, and at last came back, to find Miss Jessamy waiting for me.

We looked at each other across the hall. She was dowdier than I had ever seen her. She wore a suit that looked as if she had slept in it, and one of the little felt hats that she always pulls down right over her forehead. Her shoes needed soling. Her handbag had one strap broken. But her face, the face I had seen so many times bent over her cello, was old and implacable, and the

190

furious words that surged up in me, were instantly checked.

For once she did not smile. She was always a smiling woman, wearing that rather silly, half-malicious grin that seemed to mock one. Now she looked grim and sad. She said, "I have to talk to you, Victoria. I gather you've booked a room here. We'll go upstairs."

I could not begin to imagine how she knew all this, but one thing was certain: I did not want her to see my room. It was such a frightful place, I could not bear her to know where my foolishness had led me. I said, "There is a lounge here—"

"No. Don't be silly. You've been silly enough already. What I have to say is entirely private. You wouldn't thank me if anyone overheard."

Short of making a scene, there was nothing I could do. I led the way in a silent rage, and we went up the stairs. Once in the room Miss Jessamy locked the door. Then I could stand it no longer and burst into hysterical speech.

I cried out, "I don't know what you have against me, but you have done your best to ruin my life. You're the most horrible woman I've ever met. You've been spying on me — I suppose that's what you are. A spy."

"You could call it that," said Miss Jessamy. She was sitting on the one hard-backed chair. She looked at me with that same infuriatingly calm air, yet as she looked she must have noticed the bruise on my cheek that not even the carefully combed hair could hide, and for a second an expression of what seemed like horror and pity flickered across her face. The fact that she was apparently sorry for me made it all worse than ever, and I burst out again.

"Why have you done this? Anyone would think I'm a criminal or something. You really seem out to destroy me. All right, Miss Jessamy. I gather you know all about my affairs anyway, so it doesn't matter any longer what I say. I've fallen in love with Zoltan. I'm going to marry him."

"Oh no," said Miss Jessamy. "No. That is something you are not going to do."

"Oh course I am." There was triumph in my voice. After all, even Miss Jessamy could not prevent my marrying Zoltan: she might be able to delay it, but only for

191

a while. I said, "I know you'll try to stop me. But you won't. Nothing can stop me. Oh, I know I'm under age, but I can't be locked up for ever, I'll run away, to — to Gretna Green if necessary. You've spied on me, you've broken my relationship with my father, you've persecuted me, but this is something even you can't do. You're a horrid, interfering old maid. I suppose you've never loved anyone but yourself. I don't think any man would look twice at you. You're just — just taking your repressions out on me. But you won't stop me from marrying Zoltan, I can tell you that—"

"I won't need to," said Miss Jessamy. She had accepted my childish, unmannerly railing as if it were nothing more than a spatter of rain against the window. Her next words fell into a vast silence. "He's got one wife already."

I said at last in a choked voice, "What do you mean?"

"He is married Victoria. He has two children. I think they are aged twelve and seven. His wife is a devout Catholic. She will never divorce him. So unless he murders her, which I suppose is quite possible, there is absolutely no question of you marrying him. I don't suppose," said Miss Jessamy, "you believe me, but you will find out soon enough, and it is perfectly true."

I did believe her. I had no choice. There was something about that quiet, remorseless voice that could not be a lie. I hated Miss Jessamy, but I knew she was not lying.

I did not say anything more. The shock was too great. I only stared at her with loathing and terror, for I knew there was worse to come, and the horror of it was that I realised it would not entirely astonish me.

"I had to tell you," said Miss Jessamy. She swung round on the chair to face me, sitting there on the bed. Her knees straddled as if she were playing the cello. Perhaps cellists always sit with their knees apart. She said, "I know you think I'm enjoying all this, but I assure you I'm not. I may be everything you say, but I do know a great many things that you don't know, and when you hear about them, you might begin to understand a little why I've been following you around, and why I had no choice but to tell your father. You really are a silly girl, Victoria. I know Halasz is handsome and charming, but doesn't it seem just a little strange that a man of his age should fall for a schoolgirl like that, and after one meeting too? I know you're very pretty, but you're not the only pretty girl in the world."

I said in a voice that seemed to come from afar off, "He loves me."

"I should imagine," said Miss Jessamy, "that he's the kind of man who never loves anyone." She gave me a look, and a curious smile twisted her mouth. "You're wishing me to drop down dead, aren't you?"

"Yes," I said.

"So no doubt is Halasz." She never seemed to call him by his first name, it was as if she were speaking of a stranger. "I cannot believe he loves you. I think he wants you safely away. You know too much, and of course your father, with his knowledge of the members of the Attilian Life Society, has always been a menace to him. He once attended a meeting—"

"He told me."

"Did he? Did he also tell you that though the people there were masked, he still recognised some of them? I don't suppose he did. He wouldn't want to frighten you. I think myself you should have been frightened a long time ago. Halasz knows this. He was looking for incriminating papers in the study — He murdered Ferencz Gyori, of course."

"That's not true! How can you say such a dreadful thing?"

She completely ignored this. She went on as if I had not spoken. "You were the last person to talk to poor Ferencz, before he went up to the study. I suppose he heard something. Also you had that long chat together in the area. He was a clever man, but he could be so silly at times — I understand that the parrot is dead. I am not really surprised. Nobody knew what he might suddenly say—"

"You're not telling me that Zoltan—"

"Victoria. I know you're very angry with me, but I want you to be quiet and listen. I've taken a great deal of trouble over you, and one day you might even thank me."

I could not see myself ever thanking Miss Jessamy, but now I had the sense to be silent. I lit myself a cigarette with a badly shaking hand. I could not believe this was

193

really happening, but then after last night anything was possible.

She went on, "Your father knows he murdered Gyori too. If—" For the first time she looked ill-at-ease, and her eyes moved away from me. "If he was harsh with you, you must try to understand—"

I said frantically, "I don't think that's any of your business."

"No. Perhaps it isn't. But the rest is very much my business. Your father knows too much about Halasz, and Halasz wants to get his own back as well as removing someone who is dangerous to him. Of course your father is on our side, and as anxious to see the clan destroyed as anyone here. But there is not yet any proof of the kind we can use. Though you nearly did for yourself by going to that meeting yesterday — What got into you? I just could not believe my eyes. I thought you had a little more sense. Halasz must have been appalled. I think you are lucky to be still alive."

I said in a whisper, "I don't believe a word of this. He would never harm me."

Miss Jessamy said sternly, "How can you say that? He wouldn't harm you—! What sort of man would ask a young schoolgirl of seventeen to elope with him, to go to a foreign country that is already half in the hands of the Nazis, knowing perfectly well that he can't marry you and, even if he could, with not the slightest intention of doing so. And then dump you in an enemy country in the middle of a war, with not a soul to help you or protect you — When I saw the pair of you drive up to his flat, I really," said Miss Jessamy, looking a little like the public hangman, "nearly washed my hands of you." She met my gaze, then heaved an exasperated sigh.

I said weakly, "How did you see us?"

"You don't imagine, I hope," said Miss Jessamy briskly, "that that stupid note took me in for one second? People like Halasz always think all women are idiots. And most of them admittedly are." Then she said, in a tone that was almost bewildered, "You say he loves you. Well, if that's love, it's something I personally could do without. He may of course want you. It's not the same thing. He probably likes your looks, and I suppose he finds your innocence charming. I myself find it terrifying,

194

but then we look on things from different angles. He is a dangerous, bad man, Victoria, and how you can see anything in someone so phoney I just do not know. He is a murderer many times over, and if your father is still alive it's simply that he's so badly in trouble he daren't risk anything more. I'll tell you this. Once he's away with you in tow, he'll make quite sure your father's days are numbered. Down to one, I would guess. The Society has plenty of gunmen to do a little job like that, and Halasz will be safely out of the country. He'd love to murder me too, I daresay, but though I've no doubt you'd be delighted, I shall do my best to avoid it. But I think your father would not have a chance. He's not a man who is any good at self-preservation. He'll walk into his death without knowing what has happened to him."

I cried out childishly, "Oh, this is not true, it's not true—"

Miss Jessamy rose to her feet. She certainly was the plainest woman, but at that moment she was entirely impressive, and I moved a little back on the bed as she came towards me.

She said, "You have just written to Halasz."

"Are you opening my letters now?"

"There is surely no need to do that. When a young girl leaves home after a violent quarrel — Yes, Victoria. Your father did tell me. I promised I would find you. I suggested he did not go to the police unless everything else failed. But knowing all this, I saw you post your letter, and of course I knew it was to Halasz. Who else would you write to in the circumstances? It is to him, isn't it? Answer me, please. It's important that I should know."

"Yes!"

"Telling him no doubt how badly your father treated you, that you'll go away with him any time, and will he come as soon as possible—"

I suppose this was not particularly clever, for what else could I have written, but I was beginning to feel as if Miss Jessamy was permanently looking over my shoulder. I said wearily, "Yes. Yes, yes."

"Well, at least you didn't go to his rooms. Not that he's there any longer. It was only a pied-à-terre. People like Halasz seldom live anywhere for long, it isn't safe.

But don't worry. He'll get your letter all right. And he'll come. I imagine he'll be here first thing tomorrow morning. He will no doubt put his arms round you, comfort you and tell you you will soon be safely in Dunavar. And that will be that. From that moment," said Miss Jessamy, "the Katona family will virtually no longer exist. Daddy will soon be dead, and little daughter will be exiled in Nazi Attilia, with no chance of getting out again, even if she's alive to do so. Are you going to let all this happen, Victoria? It's up to you, you know."

I said helplessly, "What on earth can I do? Even if it's true, what can I do?"

"That is what I am here to tell you."

Then Miss Jessamy fell silent, and we sat there for a while listening to the distant traffic in the Euston Road.

I longed for her to go. I did not want to hear what she was going to say. But I had no choice, and so I sat there, feeling oddly insignificant, a plain, silly little girl who had got herself into one hell of a mess, and apparently everyone else around her.

"Halasz," remarked Miss Jessamy — every time she referred to him in this way somehow disassociated him from the Zoltan I knew — "will of course be at his most charming. He has always been charming. It is one of his greatest assets."

I said with a childish rudeness that I immediately longed to unsay, "That's something no one could accuse you of."

She looked at me. I felt at once like a naughty schoolgirl who would be sent to the head. I wondered dimly if she had ever been a schoolmistress. She said dryly, "It would be no asset to me. In my profession it is better to be entirely ordinary. It doesn't matter anyway. Now if I may please continue. His purpose will be not to charm you or console you, but to fix a meeting place for the journey. He won't dare to collect you here. He won't dare to collect you anywhere. He knows perfectly well that we are after him, for spying and treason and murder. I have no idea where he lives at the moment—"

I said bitterly, "Surely you could easily find out."

"Oh, I daresay I could," said Miss Jessamy. "It's my profession after all. I suppose you consider it a nasty profession. But I happen to do it very well, and it is something I have to do. But I am not particularly interested in where he is sleeping, or whom he is sleeping with. I have far more important things to do, and after all, he is by no means the only person involved. He is a very dangerous man, Victoria. You have selected an odd person to fall in love with. He is far more dangerous than Palotas who really is a tool — a powerful one — but still a Nazi tool."

"You got on very well at our party."

She gave me a sudden smile. "That astonished you, didn't it? But why not? Palotas and I know each other. I have even had a drive in the Legation Rolls. He knows perfectly well who I am. There is no reason why we should not meet socially, even though one day we will cut each other's throats. He is rather a silly man. He will come to a bad end. He is the kind of person the Nazis make use of and will eventually discard. Never mind him. I am not concerned with him. I am not concerned with that stupid meeting of yours either—"

"You were there!"

She said quietly, "I was keeping an eye on you."

I whispered furiously, "If that's what you call it—"

"I have my responsibilities," said Miss Jessamy, "and your father, though impossible to play music with, has been very good to me. I daresay he chose to give you the impression he knows nothing about me, but that is not true. I didn't come to your household just by chance, you know. Anyway, never mind that meeting. It really is not important, just sound and fury to hoodwink the press. The real thing is underground, waiting for when the war comes. There are thousands of people involved, and some of the names might surprise you. But I don't suppose you are remotely interested, you are only taken up with your adolescent emotions. Now let's come back to Halasz. He will, as I said, arrange a meeting. And there he will have your false passport with him. That is precisely what we are waiting for. We want a silly pretext to arrest him, to avoid a grand international scandal that at the moment would be extremely dangerous. Abducting a minor, forgery — what more could we ask for? Now, I am going to leave you a phone number. You will ring and tell me where the meeting place is—"

I said in a gasp, "Do you really imagine I will?"

"I see," said Miss Jessamy, "it's no use appealing to your patriotism, though I'm surprised that even you would sell us out to the Nazis, but I cannot believe you would murder your own father."

I said nothing to this for a moment. What was there to say? Only at last I stammered, "If — if I do, if the police get him, what will they do to him?"

"Oh, we shall intern him. There is after all no proof of murder. We shall intern him as a spy, as an enemy alien." Miss Jessamy added with a tight-lipped smile, "He will be quite comfortable. Much more comfortable than you would be in Dunavar. I know. I was interned once myself."

"What do you mean?"

"In the last war. I am German," said Miss Jessamy. "Jewish. Jessamy is not my real name."

I said sullenly, "You have no accent."

"I have a good ear. I may not play the cello very well, but I have an excellent ear. I have perfect pitch. It is a great help."

She became silent again, and we sat there, occasionally shooting glances at each other like enemies.

I said at last, "I shan't do any of this, you know. I don't believe one word of what you're saying. I think you're the enemy. I think you're just lying to me."

She said nothing.

"I want to go away with him more than I've ever wanted anything in my life. You won't believe me, of course, but I do love him. I don't suppose you know what love is."

Miss Jessamy still remained silent.

I said desperately, "I shall warn him when he comes here. I shall tell him everything you've said. Do you imagine I could let him be sent to prison, whatever he's done?"

Miss Jessamy asked with apparent irrelevancy, "Have you ever been to Attilia?"

"No. I'm longing to see it. After all, it's half my country. It will be almost like going home."

"Will it? Alone there, with a man you're not married to, and a man who will have precious little patience with a silly, frightened girl. You'll find yourself looked on as an enemy. Attilia doesn't care much for

England at the moment, and shortly the two countries will be at war. Palotas, when he returns, will be in power as Hitler's henchman, and he would be one of the first to throw you into prison. By that time Halasz will probably be glad to be rid of you. I should think his appetite for little girls is rather brief."

"You have no right to say these things!"

"Oh," said Miss Jessamy, jumping to her feet, "I've no patience with you. I suppose we'll have to stop you somehow, but it certainly won't be for your sake, you'll deserve everything you get. And of course your father will die. But I don't suppose that bothers you, you are too selfish. As far as I'm concerned you can go to Attilia with your murderer-lover, and die there. I'm not going to waste any more time on you. But here is the phone number. If you change your mind, ring me. It will be an answering phone. You simply give us the meeting-place, date and time. You won't save him, you know. You'll simply save us all a lot of trouble. You'll save yourself a lot of trouble too. We want to make an easy arrest. But he won't get away with it, whatever you do. He's too dangerous. We can't afford to let him go."

And with this she unlocked the door and went out into the corridor. She moved very quietly. I did not hear her footsteps at all.

Chapter 8

I DO NOT know how I managed to survive the rest of that lonely, frightening day. I could not think properly. I longed with passion for the friendly and familiar. I wanted to go home. I wanted to ring Lorna. I thought with a tearful craving of school, my friends, the classes I enjoyed, the little walk to the bus-stop with Michael to accompany me, and give me coffee in the flowery ladies' tea-shop.

But mostly I thought of my parents and home.

I went down to the dining-room that evening, not because I was hungry, but because it would fill in the time: perhaps I might meet someone to talk to. There was no one to talk to, and the food was uneatable. Probably breakfast was the only meal that really mattered. The dining-room itself was a long, large room, rather like a public lavatory, with tiled walls and mirrors that reflected one at disconcerting angles. There were a couple of bored, elderly waitresses, and three other customers. They were all middle-aged men. They looked like commercial travellers. I suppose they were. I cannot think of anyone else who would stay at such an hotel. One of them winked at me, and I gazed stonily down at the tablecloth. The other two did not seem to notice my existence.

As for the dinner, it started off with something called Brown Windsor soup, which was like a treacly glue, went on to cottage pie with blackened potatoes and cabbage floating in water, and ended with tinned fruit salad and custard. It cost three and six. I left almost all of it: my waitress gave me a very old-fashioned look. I could not help thinking of Mary's gorgeous cottage pie. We did not have it very often, but sometimes she made it specially

200

for me, with fresh meat and herbs and onions and crisply browned potato on top. It was lovely, and I always finished it to the last crumb.

I thought I might go to a cinema. There was one almost opposite in the Euston Road. But I did not care much for the film they were showing, and I was so desperately tired that I lacked the energy to cross the road.

So I went upstairs again to my nasty little room, meaning to read my paperback. But I did not do so: I curled up on the bed, which was badly made, and came back to thinking of my father and home.

I think I had an especially happy childhood. In some ways, as Lorna always informs me, it was very restricted. I was not allowed to go about alone until I was twelve, and only then after a long, involved, fierce campaign. Perhaps this was because of my year's illness, though nowadays I am very strong and hardly ever ill with worse than a cold. My parents for the most part left me alone though this is something Lorna would never understand, I flourished on the privacy that gave me time to read and write and think and dream. I might not be able always to dash about with my friends, my clothes, of course, were pretty awful and, when I went to a party, I had to be fetched, but somehow I never really minded, for it seemed to me I had privileges that my friends did not share. I might be chaperoned and not allowed a key until I was fourteen, but from the age of ten I always came down to dinner with my parents, even when we had guests, and I loved these little parties which for the most part were quite informal and full of interesting conversation.

My mother, of course, detested these as much as the Attilian parties, but then I think the trouble with my mother is that she has never really known what she wanted. If we had never entertained she would have declared herself bored to death, but the entertaining we did do, was not of the kind she liked, as it was she who had to make all the arrangements. No doubt my great-grandmother with her lion parties, acted as hostess to politicians and poets, actors and scientists, with young Helen basking in reflected glory: it would all be catered for by a legion of servants. After that an Attilian Minister was small beer, and the African dinners we had meant nothing to her.

They meant a great deal to me. I sat there and listened. I seldom spoke a word. But I took it all in: the Belgian missionaries who spoke in a language I did not understand — my father is a wonderful linguist, speaking French, German and Italian, apart from at least twenty African dialects — the anthropologists and the occasional black student. I loved them all, especially one very black young man who was a chieftain's son studying sociology and revolution at L.S.E.: he had a most glorious laugh, a kind of roaring falsetto, and every time he laughed I used to laugh myself in the sheer joy of it. He must have liked the little ten-year-old daughter who so appreciated his jokes, for he always brought me a present of some kind, usually far too young for me but which I greatly treasured.

I still have upstairs in my cupboard a little black doll in native costume, some wooden animals and a long necklace made of nuts and coffee beans.

And I think of this, I think of the happy times, and I am so miserable that I want to die: I am no longer a young girl in love who is about to join her lover in Dunavar.

The paperback — it is a Dorothy L. Sayers — lies unopened on the bed. I fell in love with Peter Wimsey a long time ago, but now I cannot endure him. He is too academic, too clever, too facetious, there is no feeling in him, and I simply do not care if he marries that horrid Harriet or not. I am finding that, extraordinary as it may seem, I no longer bear my father any grudge. He had no right to hit me, I think one never has the right to hit people, and I am no longer a child, I am grown up. He had no right either to forbid me to use lipstick, to call me whore because I wore perfume like all my friends in the Sixth, to supervise my life for me. But at this moment I see him as a lost man as I am a lost girl. We have both left the place where we were happy and fulfilled. I do not know if I will ever return, but he cannot return, it is one of the laws of life. There is no going back into the past. He has to live here, and he lives with the wrong woman, there is hardly any communication between them except when they quarrel. And nowadays they quarrel less and less: a few screams, a few harsh words, and it is all over: they retreat again to opposite ends of the world.

I believe I am his only link with the present world. He loves me. I know he loves me. I know I love him. I know too, deep in my heart, that he would give everything he has to wipe out that hideous evening. It was yesterday. My God, yesterday! He is not really a violent man, only a bitterly unhappy one: to see his idolised young daughter behaving like any other girl is too much for him to take, it is unendurable.

There are worse things you can do to people than hit them.

Oh, how I want to go home! I begin to cry. I must stop crying. It is a childish habit, it does no good, it makes one look so ugly. But I cannot stop. I long so passionately to get up this very moment, settle my bill and climb into a taxi in the Euston Road. The thought of giving the driver my address, of uttering the actual words, makes me sick with grief and longing. To get out of the taxi, open the door, see my parents rushing out to greet me, have Maggie crying all over me and Mary tearing about the kitchen to make some special, wonderful meal—

And to be back in my own room. To put the *Wiegenlied* on the turntable—

But it is now half past ten, and I am not home, I cannot go home, I have to see Zoltan. I am hemmed in by four dingy walls with a spider's web in the right-hand corner. There is no comfort, warmth or beauty around me. I can hear the lavatory flushing in the corridor, and the heavy, unsteady steps of someone who is probably drunk, coming back to his room. I jump up from the bed and make sure the door is locked.

What sort of man would ask a young schoolgirl of seventeen to elope with him?

But that is only Miss Jessamy who is an old maid. She has probably made it all up. He cannot be married, he could never be so wicked, so cruel to me. He does love me, he said so, I can feel it, I can see it, I know it.

Can I? Do I? How strange that Zoltan, my love, for whom I am about to break my life in two, is at this moment as nebulous as Peter Wimsey, is something within a paperback thriller, a cardboard man whose features I can no longer discern.

And I sleep at last, to dream not of Zoltan but of little black dolls somehow confused with my father's rude statues, of beautifully-cooked cottage pie, and a parrot in a cage, lying on his back.

This last jerks me awake with a scream. Probably, as is the way of dreams, it was just a whimper, but it still rings in my ears as I open my eyes. I see by my watch that it is eight o'clock.

Zoltan will soon be here.

He came. He came just after ten o'clock. I had had my breakfast which I could barely choke down, though I drank three cups of tea, and I was waiting for him in the lounge: I sat by the entrance so that I could see him coming.

I knew almost to the moment when he would arrive. There was still between us a strange, tenuous bond, like the thin thread of the spider's web in my room. As I sat there in the armchair, the air stale from yesterday's cigarettes, looking at yesterday's evening paper that some-one had left there, the tug came unmistakably.

I got up quite calmly and went into the hall.

He looked a little ill at ease. He stared at me. He did not move towards me. Only as I came up to him, saying, "Hallo, Zoltan," he briefly closed his eyes, said, "For God's sake!" then, "Where can we talk?"

"I have a room upstairs."

"Then we'll go. Where is it?"

"On the first floor."

We went up the stairs. The porter's eyes followed us, accompanied by a cynical smile. I suppose he must have seen a great many women taking friends to their rooms. He was probably saying to himself, "She's just like all the rest, they start young these days."

Zoltan did not exclaim at my room. But then I think he hardly saw it. He was not a man much concerned with material things, especially in the way of comfort. His own flat had after all been little better. He was probably used to cheap hotel rooms and found this nothing out of the ordinary, though the bed was not yet made, and I had forgotten to remove a pair of stockings hanging on the towel rail.

He held out his arms to me, and I came into them. Only, as he enfolded me and began to kiss me, I was aware not of love but of a vast disturbance: it was so agonising that I stiffened within his hands.

He said sharply, "What's the matter?"

But I only said, "I'm glad you've come at last."

This appeased him. We sat on the bed together, and he idly picked up the paperback that I had thrown down on the pillow, and flicked over the pages. He said, "I didn't know you read such things."

"You don't really know me at all."

"Oh," he said, putting his arm round me again, "of course I know you. I have always known you. I can read you like a book, Victoria. Do you imagine you will ever have any secrets from me?"

The remark jarred me. Perhaps I knew that nobody, nobody in the world, can ever read another person like a book. Perhaps it was the proprietory tone. But I think it was because there was so much that he must never read, and I moved a little away from him, causing him to exclaim, "There is something the matter. You seem quite different. What is it? Tell me. You must tell me. After all, I'm going to be your husband."

He should not have said that. He should not — Once it would have made me feel so happy. But now the words hit me as my father had hit me, and I felt suddenly the pain and shock of his hand cracking against the side of my head. It made me wince, and I said with a gasp, "A great deal has happened, Zoltan. I told you in my letter. I have run away from home. I think my father will never forgive me."

For the first time he seemed to take in the bruises on my cheeks. He stared at me, then suddenly, to my amazement, laughed. When he laughed, his face looked sneering and cruel. He said, "He did give you a thrashing, didn't he? I would never have thought him capable of it."

Then he saw the outraged, horrified look on my face. His own changed at once, and so did his voice. He said, "How dared he? The bastard — To ill-treat you like that. I am only thankful you are away from him."

I did not believe him. I could only see that my suffering amused him. But I said wearily, looking away from him, "It doesn't really matter."

He half-smiled. "Your favourite phrase — I will always associate it with you. It doesn't matter!" The smile

205

vanished. "But of course it matters. I only wish I'd known. Do you imagine I'll ever permit anyone to touch you?"

I said, "It's over and done with. He didn't really mean it."

"What the devil do you mean?"

"He loves me very much."

"A fine way to show it! I can promise you one thing, little Victoria. We shall perhaps quarrel, for we are violent people, like all Attilians, but whatever you say or do, I'll never beat you when we're married."

I felt that blow again. But I managed to smile. I said, "You never know what will happen. You might lose your temper with me as you did after that meeting. I thought you were going to hit me then."

He said, his voice irritated, "Well, you'd no right to go there, no right at all. It was damned silly. You might have been killed." Then, that mobile voice changing again, "But why are we wasting time talking like this? Let's forget about everything. I have wonderful news for you. We are going to Dunavar tomorrow."

He said this calmly and amusedly as if it were the most natural thing in the world. I could only stare at him, aware of the shocked sickness inside me and, as I did so, he laughed, produced from his pocket a little camera of a kind that I had never seen, and suddenly snapped it at me twice.

"There!" he said. "For your passport. For Mrs. Halasz to be. You look like a scared rabbit with your mouth open, but never mind, it will serve. It'll probably make it more unrecognisable, which will be a good thing."

Mrs. Halasz to be. I wonder what she is like, Mrs. Halasz. Perhaps she is waiting desperately for him. Perhaps she prays he will never come back. I said in a brittle voice that did not sound like my own, "I didn't know you were going to snap me. You might have given me some warning. You say tomorrow — How can I go tomorrow? I — I have no clothes—"

He liked this. This fitted in the pattern he had made of me. "Oh women," he said. "They always think of clothes. Don't worry your little head about such things. I'll see to your clothes as a good husband should, and they won't be the kind your Mummy buys for you. But you don't

206

seem excited. I thought you would be so pleased. Why are you not pleased?"

"Zoltan—"

"Well?"

His voice was uncompromising, but I was learning, learning in a horrid, mean, deceitful sort of way. I put my hand on his, and he turned it to entwine the fingers. I said, "Couldn't we put it off for just a few days? Tomorrow is so soon."

"You have changed your mind!"

"Oh no, no, truly. I don't think so. But—"

"Never mind the buts." He rose to his feet and stepped over to the window. "Look," he said in a harsh voice, "we have no choice. I didn't mean to frighten you, but I see I have to tell you. I've got to leave this country immediately. If I stay, I shall be killed. The people you saw at that meeting are after me. They intend to murder me."

"Like Mr. Gyori?"

His face changed. Suddenly it looked bleak, savage and ugly. He said in a soft, angry voice, "Yes, Victoria. Like Mr. Gyori. In any case, even if we could postpone things for a couple of days, what would happen to you? You've run away from home. You can't possibly go back. God knows what your father would do to you. You wouldn't be safe with him. He's obviously quite mad. But he'll be looking for you, my darling. I'm amazed the police haven't been round already — You haven't seen anyone, have you?"

"No."

And I looked at him as I said this. My gaze met his with perfect calm.

"Well they'll probably come any moment now. Your English police are remarkably inefficient, but surely they've traced you by now. Our only hope is to go immediately. I have taken a great risk in coming here, and I daren't do so again. There is fortunately a back entrance to the hotel. I'm afraid it must be tomorrow. I don't want to rush you, but do you really mind? We shall be together at last. Don't you want to be with me, darling? I love you so much, and you say you love me."

I said, "When will we be married?"

I suppose it was a little dashing that after such protestations of love I should persist in talking of mundane things like clothes and marriage. He looked for a moment disconcerted and angry. He was breathing quickly. He said, "What a conventional little soul you are!"

"We are getting married, aren't we?"

"Of course we are!" He was trying, rather unsuccessfully, to control his exasperation. "How many times do I have to tell you? It's not very flattering to me that you doubt me like this. We'll be married the moment we're across the Channel. I give you my word. There will be a priest waiting to perform the ceremony."

I said, "Are you a Catholic, Zoltan?"

He did not like this either. I saw his mouth tighten. But he managed to laugh. He said, "Well, I wouldn't describe myself as devout. Would you prefer another kind of ceremony?"

"Oh no, it doesn't matter. It doesn't matter."

"You'll say that the day you die! Well, at least you now believe I'm making an honest woman of you. You do believe me, don't you?"

"Yes," I said, "I believe you."

He said, with what seemed unmistakably to me relief, "I must go. And so must you. You should not stay here a moment longer than you have to. We leave tomorrow morning, but tonight you'll be staying with these friends of mine. This is the address. Put it away carefully. If anything goes wrong, you must destroy this piece of paper. Don't just tear it up. Burn it. But nothing will go wrong, I'm sure of that. Follow me as soon as you can, and for God's sake dodge any police you see. Have you got enough money?"

"I've plenty, thank you. Zoltan—"

"Oh, what is it now?" Then he must have realised that this angry voice was hardly reassuring to a young girl preparing to take the biggest step in her life. He came back to me and took me in his arms. I could feel his heart pounding against my breast. There seemed to me no love in him, only a fierce determination to get his own way. He whispered, his mouth on mine, "Sweetheart, I'm sorry. But I'm so afraid to lose you, you are so young and so lovely — And so silly, my darling, so hell-bent on trouble. First Gyori, and then the meeting — What am I to do with you?"

"I couldn't help talking to Mr. Gyori." Then I said, "You shot him, didn't you?"

He had not expected this. But I suppose the calm tone of my question reassured him. He said flatly, "Yes. He was a Nazi spy. When I found him in your father's study, I knew I had no choice. I saw him come upstairs and I followed him. I knew he was dangerous. Your parrot was talking in the Attilian Gyori taught him, and when I heard this, I knew Gyori was out for mischief. I never meant to tell you. You are too young to hear such things. But I think there should be no secrets between husband and wife."

I did not answer this. I could not answer this. I let him kiss me, and his lips seemed cold and hard, as cold and hard as my own heart.

He said after a while, "I can't stay any longer. You'll come quickly, won't you?"

"I must say goodbye to my parents."

"What! Are you out of your mind?"

"Oh, I won't go round. But I must at least write them a letter. It won't take long. Don't be too angry with my father."

"Do you expect me not to be? I'll never forgive him, never. I don't understand why you even want to write. But there is no time to do it here. If you must, write from my friends' house. I'll see that the letter is posted."

I said very earnestly, my hand clutching his, "Zoltan, you won't harm my father, will you?"

He moved back from me. He was smiling. "You're a sentimental little thing, aren't you?" he said. "You're a softie, you know. He beats you up, and you still love him, you are frightened that I'll hurt him. I won't hurt him. He's not worth the trouble. I don't think I could trust myself alone with him, but that doesn't matter now, I'm never likely to see him again."

I said, almost frantically, "But you do give me your word that no harm will come to him?"

He was still smiling. He had laughed at my bruises. Now he spoke as if they shocked him. His light grey eyes were fixed on mine. They were as bright and clear as water: there was as little feeling. I looked at him, my eyes moving to take in every detail. I felt he was not

209

really there at all. I was expending my love and grief on a handsome shadow.

He said, "You would not expect me to harm my dear father-in-law. Of course I give you my word. I wouldn't touch him with — how do you say it? — a barge-pole. He can live to a hundred for all I care. There! Are you satisfied now? I see that I am saddling myself with a very suspicious wife who will constantly need reassuring."

I still gazed at him. I would never see him again. My eyes were the camera, photographing him upon my mind. But as I looked, I suddenly did not see him at all. I saw instead the white, starched shirt front, and across it was a slowly increasing scarlet stain. It was murder I saw, and in that second the room shimmered round me so that, if Zoltan had not caught at me, I would have fallen back on the bed.

He exclaimed, "What's the matter? Are you ill?"

"No. I'm all right now. I just felt a little dizzy. I didn't sleep much last night, and it's all been such a shock."

"My poor darling!" But the endearment came out like a stone, and his eyes moved to his wrist watch. "I tell you, I must go. I can't bear to leave you like this, but I have no choice. Now you'll wait about half an hour, then come after me. You really have enough money?"

"Yes."

"After today you'll never be alone again. Goodbye, sweetheart. I love you. Say you love me."

He was moving towards the door. He was receding, misting in my vision.

"Goodbye, Zoltan. I love you."

"I love you too."

Goodbye, Zoltan.

To wait for a while in this ugly room. To put things back into my case. No tears. Almost no feeling. Only an emptiness as if I too am not there, as if I too am a shadow, an insubstantial being without a body, without a heart.

I love you.

"I'd like my bill, please. And — and may I use your phone?"

I take a taxi. Nowadays I seem always to be taking

taxis. But I do not have the strength to cope with buses or trains. I use the stolen money to pay for it.

The house still stands. There is no reason why it should not do so, only I never thought to see it again, I would not be astonished to find instead a great gap. But it is there. It is half past eleven in the morning. Only there is no parrot cage in the area. Polly learnt Attilian too well. I do not suppose he could have done the least harm, but if you are a spy in an enemy country you cannot afford to take the least risk. I think poison must have been dropped in his seeds. It seems strange not to hear him snuffling at me.

I can see Mary and Maggie through the kitchen window. I can smell the lunch that is being prepared.

But Maggie has quick hearing. She hears my footsteps as I go up to the door, a little heavily because I am so exhausted. She flings open the back door and sees the taxi disappearing round the corner. She gives a great shriek. "Miss Victoria! Oh Mary, she's back, she's back!"

"Hallo, Maggie."

"Miss Victoria!"

I think they are both crying. They stand in the area, gawping up at me. I am too tired to talk. I open the door. My parents have heard Maggie's scream. They must have been in the sitting-room. The fact that they are together at this hour shows what they must be feeling. They both come out. We look at each other.

I say, "Hallo."

It is not much in the circumstances, but there seems nothing else to say. My mother rushes up to me, hugging me, but my father simply stands there and stares. I can see that he looks terribly ill, he seems to have aged by a hundred years.

I say again, "Hallo, Daddy."

He says, "I'm sorry."

"It doesn't matter."

Your favourite phrase I will always associate it with you.

Then I say, "You don't mind if I go straight to my room, do you? I'm so tired. I'm so tired."

I make no attempt to apologise or explain. I know I have behaved badly. But I can't think about that. I only know that I am home, I am back where I belong, I love my parents dearly, I did not mean to hurt them, but I am hurt too, I am so tired that I want to sleep my life away.

I walk up the stairs with the Holbein prints on the wall. The grandfather clock ticks away. Mary and Maggie have come up from the kitchen. Mary, who is usually so abrupt, says in a tentative voice, "I'll send some lunch up to your room, Miss Victoria."

I am too exhausted even to say thank you, but I smile at her. I think she is wonderful, I love her too. Maggie is still crying. My parents still stand there like statues. In the morning it will be all right. I shall probably go back to school.

And Zoltan will be waiting for me.

The police will come for him. He will hate me so much, and I still love him. He would never have married me, and I still love him. He would have murdered my father, and I still love him.

It doesn't matter.

I came down to breakfast in the morning as I always did, in my school uniform, but my mother suggests that I stay away one more day, and I still feel so tired that I agree with her. I see her eyeing my bruised face. The marks are disappearing, but I think she feels this is something the school should not see. I do not really mind, but decide to go to the British Museum. I feel I must get out, and I have never acknowledged Mr. Goldschmidt's invitation. I cannot really see myself sitting beside him at the *Missa Solemnis*, but somehow he represents sanity and everyday life.

I believed I would never sleep again, but I fell asleep in my lovely clean bed as soon as my head touched the pillow. I did not even undress, and the nicely laid tray brought up by Maggie remained untouched. I slept without dreaming until the small hours of the next morning. Someone — Maggie, I should imagine — undressed me, and there was another tray by my bedside, with milk and sandwiches. The sandwiches were wrapped in a nice, white cloth, and there was a saucer over the glass. I seem now to notice these things with sheer delight. I ate a sandwich, then I felt hungry and finished them all. After that I fell asleep again until Maggie brought in my can of hot water.

212

We ate our breakfast. My father read his paper. My mother jangled away. It was a normal day except that somehow I felt I was not there at all.

My father put his paper down and said, "Don't be too angry with me, baby. I was misled. I know I shouldn't have done it. Whatever you did, I had no right. Do you think you will be able to forgive me? I know it will take time, but I don't think I could bear it if you hated me."

I said, astonishing myself as much as him, "I really don't mind any more. That's true. And of course I don't hate you. I couldn't. After all, I did behave badly. I told you terrible lies. Only nothing like this has ever happened to me before. I didn't quite know what I was doing." Then I said, "How is the book going?"

He shook his head without answering, raised his hands. Then he smiled at me, and I smiled back.

I knew somehow that in the whole of our life together we would never mention the matter again.

I set off for the Museum. I still felt unreal. I felt almost as if Zoltan, furious and unforgiving, were walking beside me. I supposed he was in prison, and I had sent him there. I had no idea of what internment was like. Miss Jessamy appeared to have been quite comfortable, but perhaps she was simply trying to appease me. There must be bars. All prisons had bars, and internment was after all surely a kind of prison. He would be sitting there, alone, and oh how he must hate me. Perhaps he was planning to get me murdered too. Certainly he would never forgive me as long as he lived, and I could not blame him, I would never forgive anyone either who deceived me, lied to me, and handed me over to the police.

What with my exhaustion, all that had happened, and my horror at myself, I nearly passed the Museum and had to retrace my steps.

But when I came inside and up the stairs to the Ethnographical Department, I felt calmer. There is something about the atmosphere of such a place, with its antiquities, its priceless contents, its air of academic calm, that gives one the appropriate feeling of timelessness. I cannot pretend that I felt happy, but somehow, gazing at calm Egyptian faces, the detached beauty of Greek gods, and magnificent pottery, I no longer wanted to cry and rail at myself.

I saw Mr. Goldschmidt dealing with something in packing cases. He was so absorbed that he did not see me until I came up to him. I said hallo, and he raised his head to stare at me as if I were the last person he expected to see.

I said, "I'm so sorry I never wrote to thank you for your invitation. It was very rude of me. I thought I would just look in to say I'd love to come. I hope I'm not disturbing you."

He still stared, and his eyes moved over my face, where the bruises still showed. I always thought of him as a correct, calm kind of man with no particular emotion, except for that one occasion on our verandah, and the circumstances then were so awful that no one could behave in a normal fashion. But up till then I had regarded him as rather dull, handsome in his own way, but apparently with no fire or spirit. If I thought of him at all, I pictured him sitting at the piano with a weary, slightly disdainful expression on his face as my father waved his bow about and roared, "Tumpty-*tum*, Mr. Goldschmidt!"

But at this moment he looked neither weary nor disdainful, and I realised with a shock that sent the colour into my cheeks that he knew what had happened. I suppose my mother told him. I don't know how she managed to do so, but perhaps he rang, and she poured the whole story out to him. I saw his dark eyes fix themselves on the bruises, and for a second his face was convulsed with such passionate rage that I could hardly recognise him. There was certainly no amusement there. It passed instantly but, when he answered me, his voice still quivered.

He half put out his hand then at once withdrew it. I saw that the case he was unpacking contained some little statues like the ones in my father's study. He said, "Of course you're not disturbing me. You could never disturb me."

This was not like Mr. Goldschmidt either, and I began to feel that our musical afternoons were numbered. It was really not possible that Miss Jessamy would turn up again, and it looked now as if any criticism levelled at Mr. Goldschmidt would bring my father's bow crashing

214

about his own head. A new warm feeling of liking for Mr. Goldschmidt flooded through me, and I smiled at him, saying, "I really am looking forward to the concert."

And I was too, which was extraordinary. I half turned to go, for he looked so busy, but he began to walk with me to the door, saying, "I hope you will enjoy it." Then he said in a voice I had never heard from him, "I hope too, Miss Katona, you will always look upon me as a friend. I do not forget how you put courage into me. You made me feel ashamed of myself. I saw at last that I was a coward, that there is always hope. You saved my life. If I had not talked to you, I believe I would have killed myself. I can never thank you enough. I think you are a wonderful girl, and I would be proud to feel you are my friend. If ever you need help, whatever the circumstances, you will please come to me."

Zoltan had said much the same thing, and I think in my heart I never believed it. I did believe Mr. Goldschmidt. For the first time it struck me that the name Siegfried was not so funny after all. I could not quite see myself using it, but perhaps that would come in time.

He repeated as I held out my hand to him, "You are not to hesitate, Miss Katona. I mean what I say."

I said, "I know you do." And then I said, "Thank you," and the ridiculous tears flooded my eyes. I retreated hastily before they could fall. I hoped he had not noticed, but I am quite sure he did.

I glanced back rather mistily as I came to the staircase. He was still standing there, watching me, with one of the little rude statues in his hand. I suppose he was so used to them that they meant nothing more to him than any other carving, but he had always seemed to me such a prim kind of man, and the incongruity of it made me want to laugh, though the tears were already trickling down my cheeks.

I hoped I would soon stop being so emotional. I seemed to be in the state where anything and everything made me cry. Perhaps I would be better when I was back at school. I thought of school almost with longing: it was as if I craved the ordinary, the normal, the routine. To have a nice, sane English lesson, to discuss the French Revolution, even to have words with Miss Hud-

215

son about the *Pons Asinorum* theorem, which I never could bring myself to understand. And to stroll about the playground, arm-in-arm with Lorna, talking the sort of things that girls talk, planning to see Laurence Olivier in his latest performance.

But I knew I could not tell her the whole story of Zoltan. Zoltan was not girls' talk. Zoltan bore no resemblance to our silly flirts, the boy-friends who moved in and out of our lives, our quarrels, our reconciliations. Zoltan was for me linked with murder and death: one could not giggle at death, it was not a subject that Lorna and I ever mentioned.

I came home about five o'clock. I bought myself a sandwich and ate it in Russell Square, where the leaves were falling and a soft autumn wind blew my hair about my face. I liked the melancholy of it and, as it was not really cold, sat there for a while watching the children playing, the nannies gossiping there, the old people sitting alone on the benches.

My parents were arguing when I came in, and my mother as usual was shouting, so that neither of them heard me close the door. There was nothing out of the ordinary in this, and I had my foot on the bottom stair on my way up to my room, when my mother's words caught my ear, and I stopped dead.

They were in the sitting-room. The door must have been left open.

My mother said, "She is not to be told."

My father answered angrily, "Of course she must be told."

"I absolutely forbid it, Mikki. Yes, I mean it. She's obviously had an awful time, I've never seen her look so ill, and she's being surprisingly sensible about it all and not creating any carry-on. If she hears about this, I can't imagine what will happen. She might have a nervous breakdown, or something. There's no reason why she should find out. She's going to school tomorrow and will have other things to think about. Besides, she never bothers to read the paper."

"She's no longer a child," said my father. But I could hear the hesitation in his voice. He said, "It's only fair that she should be told. If she finds out, she'll never forgive us."

"She won't find out!"

"You simply can't be sure of that, Helen. People always find out things they shouldn't."

"Well, I don't care. I just won't have it." This was very unusual in my mother who, though she was always arguing, seldom asserted herself against my father's wishes. She added in a triumphant shout, "If you tell her, I'll leave you. I mean it. After the way you've treated her—"

Then I heard a great crash. I have no idea what it was. It was probably my mother knocking half the furniture over. I went on upstairs. I felt sick and faint, and the feeling of foreboding that had never left me entirely, half paralysed me so that it was difficult to move. It did not need any intelligence to see that this concerned Zoltan. Perhaps he had escaped from prison. Perhaps — But I knew it was not that. I knew it was something far worse. However, I dared not pick up the paper while my parents were there, so I continued on my way up, very slowly as if I were old and sick.

My mother came out of the sitting-room. She called after me in a jolly fashion that confirmed my worst premonitions, "Did you have a good day, dear?"

"Yes, thank you, Mummy."

"And how was Mr. Goldschmidt?"

"He seemed very well."

"He's quite a nice man, really," said my mother. "Rather cold, I always think. Still it's better than playing the cello badly."

I hardly took in this typical *non sequitur*. I think my mother simply misses out all linking sentences, which is why she often sounds so crazy.

I waited for a while in my room. It seemed to me an eternity, and I felt very ill. When I heard my father go into his study and my mother into her bedroom to change for dinner, I came quietly downstairs again.

I found that the paper had been removed. My father was not taking any risks, and this made me shiver as if I had a fever. But I did not think he would actually tear it up, and I know where the old newspapers are kept to light the fires in the morning, so I crept down the back stairs to the cupboard behind the larder.

I could hear Mary and Maggie talking in the kitchen.

I was careful to make as little noise as possible. I found the paper easily enough: it was on top of the pile. I folded it up and came upstairs again, into the dining-room, which was laid for dinner, with my great-grandmother staring down at me.

I found the paragraph at last. It was very small. The heading was: "Attilian journalist killed in hit-and-run." I was not shocked, or perhaps I was beyond shock. I knew. I had known all along. I read it through, holding the paper in a steady hand. I saw that Mr. Zoltan Halasz, who was attached to the Attilian Legation, was knocked down yesterday evening by a motorist who did not stop. The police, so it said, were looking for a red car. The paragraph concluded by saying that it was believed that Mr. Halasz had affiliations with a secret society, the headquarters of which had just been discovered. Many arrests had been made—

It was very cold in the dining-room. I wanted to light the gas fire, but I had no energy to move. I put the paper in the sideboard cupboard. Maggie would find it when she cleared away, and take it down again. I do not quite know what I was thinking, except that Miss Jessamy had lied from beginning to end. It was all a monumental hoax to get the address out of me, and to push me out of the way. I should have had the sense to know it. There had never been the smallest question of internment. He was too dangerous. And now, thanks to me, they had the address of the clan's headquarters, and Zoltan was dead.

It was not his death they wanted. They could have killed him any time. Our police are not so inefficient as he imagined. It was the address that was important.

And Zoltan was dead. I had murdered him.

Mrs. Halasz would wait for a long time in Dunavar. Perhaps she did not really care. It must be difficult to have a murderer for a husband. It would have been even worse to have a murderer with one, who was not a husband.

Neither of us would have him now. He was dead.

It didn't matter any more.

I thought of a confusion of things. I sat down at the dining-table. We were having fish. I saw the knives and forks. *I was not quite happy about the Sunlight soap.*

218

Such a short time ago. Such an eternity ago. The pictures snapped before my eyes like lantern slides. Click-click. A kiss beneath the table. Click-click. A stained shirt front with a small neat hole in it. Click-click. A plate of little sandwiches and cream cakes. Click-click. A laughing face. *He did give you a thrashing, didn't he?*

I love you. Click-click.

And Miss Jessamy lying and lying and lying. Playing me like a fish. Filling me up with every kind of fabrication, all moonshine, carefully piled on to make a stupid schoolgirl do as she wanted. I wanted to kill her. I wanted to batter her, beat her, shoot her—

And Zoltan was dead. Click-click.

Then at last the tears came, the sobs welled up in my throat. I buried my head on my outstretched arms, and the young, uneasy voice came dimly to my ears: "I say, what's the matter? Can I do anything? Oh Victoria, don't cry. I've never seen you cry before."

Michael must have come in without my even hearing the door bell. He stood in the doorway, patently embarrassed, with no idea what to do. We had parted pretty miserably, and it is true we had never seriously quarrelled before, but to come here on what was plainly a planned reconciliation and find your girl-friend crying her eyes out on the dining-room table must have been disconcerting.

I said, "I'm sorry," blew my nose and mopped at my eyes. It was a little while before I could see him properly. When my vision at last cleared it seemed to me that I was looking at a little boy.

I had never realised how young Michael was. He was, it is true, a year older than me, which is not very much, but he was sophisticated in his own way, he was intelligent, he talked well, and he always dressed beautifully. One never saw Michael in an old jersey or uncreased trousers. Now he simply looked to me a handsome little boy, wearing a blue polo-necked sweater and grey slacks, shoes immaculately cleaned, hair brushed back over a charming pink and white face. I liked him, I had always liked him, but it was as if I had moved a light-year away: there were only a few yards between us and they might as well have been a mile.

He came up to me and patted me on the shoulder. He could not have known anything of what had happened, but I think that he too felt I had somehow moved out of his orbit, for he looked uneasy, and his voice when he spoke to me, cracked a little.

He said, "What's the matter, old thing? Do tell me. Has — has someone said something horrible to you? Who is it? I'll deal with him for you. I don't like people making you cry."

I noticed the "him". Michael might be young but he was not by any means unaware: he must have known that when one finds a young woman in desperate tears, the odds are the cause is a man. But he was the last person in the world I could confide in, so I simply said, "It's nothing, really. No one's been horrible. I've just had a bit of a shock, but it will pass, it doesn't matter."

He said quite gaily, "You always say things don't matter." He must have seen my face change. He said, "Shouldn't I have said that? There really is something wrong, isn't there?"

"Oh," I said, beginning at last to pull myself together, "it's all right. I think I'm just a bit tired. It's nice to see you again, Mike. I'm sorry I was so beastly."

At this he came up to me and gave me a tentative kiss. Then he took my hand, holding it in both of his. It was charming, it was warm and friendly, but it was not the same as it had been, and I think at that moment he knew it never would be again.

We looked at each other. We looked with affection, and I was truly pleased that we were no longer enemies, but we both knew that whatever there had been between us was gone for ever.

He moved away from me. He said, "What about a flick to celebrate? On Saturday. I know your mother doesn't like you going out in the week."

"I'd love that." And I said again, to reassure myself, "It's nice to see you. I've missed you."

"I've missed you too. I meant to come round before. But you know how it is. And I wasn't quite sure if you wanted to see me. I did ring Sunday evening, but you were out."

"Yes, I was out."

Another silence. It was dreadful, but really we had nothing to say to each other.

"Well," he said at last, "I expect you'll be having

dinner. I'll — I'll look in at school tomorrow. We could have a coffee together."

"That'd be nice."

"So long then. You're not going to cry any more, are you?"

"Oh no. That's over and done with."

"Good-oh. Well — Goodbye, Victoria."

"Goodbye, Michael."

He hesitated, then kissed me again. He waved his hand. He walked out of the dining-room. I heard the front door close behind him.

I came out into the hall. My mother was there. I could see she was very pleased. She has always liked Michael. He is the kind of boy-friend she thinks I ought to have. A nice English boy. That is what she once called him. Perhaps marriage to an Attilian has jaundiced her.

"Such a nice boy," she said.

"Yes, he is."

"I knew it wasn't anything serious. They always come back."

They don't always come back, Mummy, only the ones one does not want. "Yes, I suppose they do."

"You've made it up, haven't you?"

"Yes."

"A little tiff sometimes clears the air."

"Yes."

She peers at me. "Have you been crying?"

"No. I've a bit of a headache."

"Well, you'll be back at school tomorrow and everything will be all right."

But she is not sure. Perhaps she is thinking of that newspaper paragraph. She begins to jangle as always when disturbed, and for some unknown reason this reminds me of the confession I have to make.

"Mummy—"

"You ought to get ready for dinner, dear. You needn't change as you're not feeling very well, but you must do something to your hair, it looks like the wrath of God."

"Yes. Mummy, you must listen to me. I'm a thief."

"Are you?" said my mother, not really listening. "How nice." Then it dawned on her that my remark was a little odd. She asked in mild surprise, "What have you stolen?"

"I took your pearl choker. I pawned it. I've got the ticket. They gave me twenty pounds."

This really did impinge on her. My mother is fanatically interested in money, and one of Michael's many assets is that his family is extremely well off. She gave a shriek of fury. "Twenty pounds! But that's daylight robbery!"

"Mummy, I don't think you've understood what I've been saying. I took your choker and pawned it. I thought I needed the money. I stole it. It was stealing. And I haven't enough to reclaim it. I need another five pounds. You can deduct it from my next allowance. I'm terribly sorry. I'll go tomorrow on my way back from school."

"You will do nothing of the kind!" My mother's voice is bristling with indignation. "I will go myself, first thing tomorrow morning. Oh, I won't half give them a piece of my mind! You just give me that ticket. Twenty pounds — Twenty pounds! I've never heard anything so outrageous in my life. Wait till I tell your father. He'll have a fit."

My father will not have a fit, for he knows nothing about the value of money, but I bet the old pawnbroker will. He won't know what has hit him. He will never have seen anything like my mother in a state of righteous fury, especially when she feels she has been diddled. I watch her rushing up the stairs, jangling like mad, waving the pawn ticket in the air. I never thought I would laugh again, but this is too much for me, it is so incongruous, so absurd. I sit down on the bottom step and I laugh and laugh quite hysterically, until Maggie, bringing up the cheese and biscuits to set out on the table, stops and stares at me.

"Miss Victoria," she says in her normal scolding voice, "what on earth is the matter with you? Anyone would think you're tipsy."

"No. I wish I were. Oh Maggie, I'm so unhappy. I think it's the end of the world."

"Havers!" says Maggie, then looks at me more closely. She knows perfectly well that my puffy eyes are not caused by a headache. She is much more perceptive than my mother. She dumps the tray on the floor, then sits down beside me on the step. She puts her arms round me and begins to rock me to and fro. She smells nice, of

222

Maggie and soap and silver polish. She does not say a word, but I can feel the tenderness coming out of her, and I lean my head against her shoulder, soothed by the rocking.

"Maggie," I say at last, "It is the end of the world. The end of our world. There's going to be a war, Maggie."

She says again, "Havers!"

"No, it's not havers. I wish it were. We'll be fighting the Germans again, and there'll be bombs falling and London will be blown to pieces."

"Nonsense!" says Maggie in a more English style. "We beat the nasty Germans once and we'll do it again."

"But it will still be the end of our world. You won't be in service any more."

"Of course I'll be in service!"

"You won't. You'll go into munitions. Or perhaps you'll join up. You'll become an army girl. How would you like that?"

"I wouldn't like it at all," said Maggie, but I heard the faint doubt in her voice and raised my head to grin at her. I could see she was picturing herself in uniform, with lots of dashing, handsome soldiers at her beck and call. Maggie has a nice figure and a trim waist. She will look good in uniform. I think her milkman had better marry her quickly if he wants her, because once the war comes he will not have a chance. She says, "And what will you do, Miss Victoria?"

"Oh, I shall just be an old maid."

At this she jumps to her feet, letting me go so quickly that I nearly bang my head.

"I'll not listen to that kind of talk," she says quite sharply. "Just because one fellow's let you down doesn't mean there aren't plenty more. You're a bonnie lass, Miss Victoria, when you do your hair properly and don't wear your eyes out with crying. You'll have them after you in droves. Only that boy's no good to you, mind—"

"What do you mean, Maggie?" I'm staring at her.

"He's too young. Oh he's a nice enough kid, but he's just a baby. You need a real man to keep you in order," says Maggie very firmly, "to give you a good skelp when you need it."

"Really, Maggie!"

"So do I," she says, and suddenly beams at me. She

223

really is a very pretty girl, and the man who gets her will be a lucky fellow. I am beginning to feel much better. I get up from the stair, and prepare to go to my bedroom.

"Maggie," I say again.

"Yes, Miss Victoria?" She too is on her feet and is picking up the tray.

"It's not such a bad world really."

"Oh," she says, "I daresay all worlds are very much the same. It's only when they're a long way away that they seem better. But I've got my work to do, even if you haven't. You make yourself look nice now, and Mr. Right will be ringing the bell so hard he'll pull it half off."

"What about Mr. Wrong, Maggie?"

"Huh!" says Maggie. "I'd throw him down the stairs if I was you. And don't you cry any more. Miss Victoria. There's plenty more fish in the sea, and anyway, men aren't worth it. Not with pretty girls like you. When you reckon it up, none of it really matters."

"No. It doesn't matter."

And I go upstairs, to comb my hair for dinner.

SEPTEMBER 1939   THE TIMES

Invasion of Poland.
German Attack across the Frontier.
Warsaw and other cities bombed.

September 4, 1939

"A State of War." The Ultimatum to Berlin.

It is notified that a state of War exists between His Majesty's Government and Germany as from 11 o'clock a.m. today, 3rd September, 1939.

Forthcoming Marriages, THE TIMES, 1939

Mr. S. Goldschmidt and Miss V. Katona

The engagement is announced between Seigfried Goldschmidt and Victoria Katona, daughter of Miklos and Helen Katona of London S.W.10.